"Are you ⟨...⟩ r to keep an e⟨...⟩er?"

Layne asked

"Both," Brant admitted. "I'm not taking the chance that the sniper will come back and take another try at you. I want you safe, Layne."

"You don't really expect my brother to show up here, in a hospital, do you? This place is too public. He won't come."

"You don't expect your brother to stay in hiding once he finds out you'd been shot, Layne."

"And that's what you're counting on, isn't it?" she asked, her voice barely above a whisper.

She clenched her fist. Her glance traveled to the badge pinned to his shirt, then lifted to stare into his eyes. "With all due respect, Mr. Texas Ranger, go to hell!"

He tipped his hat. "I've been there, Layne."

Dear Reader,

It may still be winter outside, but here at Intimate Moments, things couldn't be hotter. Take our American Hero title, for instance: Paula Detmer Riggs's *Firebrand*. Judd Calhoun left his Oregon home—and his first love, Darcy Kerrigan—in disgrace. Now he's back—as the new fire chief—and the heat that sizzled between the two of them is as powerful as ever. But there are still old wounds to heal and new dangers to face. Talk about the flames of passion...!

Rachel Lee is on tap with the third of her Conard County series, *Miss Emmaline and the Archangel*. It seems the town spinster has a darker past than anyone suspects, and now it's catching up to her. With no one to turn to except Gage Dalton, the man they call Hell's Own Archangel, her future looks grim. But there's more to this man than his forbidding looks would indicate—much more—and Miss Emmaline is about to learn just what it means to be a woman in love. Marilyn Pappano's *Memories of Laura* takes place in the quintessential small town—Nowhere, Montana—where a woman without a memory meets a man who's sure he knows her past. And it's not a pretty one. So why does sheriff Buck Logan find himself falling for her all over again? In her second book, *Dixon's Bluff*, Sally Tyler Hayes mixes danger and desire and love for a small girl and comes up with a novel you won't want to miss. Harlequin Historical author Suzanne Barclay enters the contemporary arena with *Man with a Mission*, a suspense-filled and highly romantic tale linking two seemingly mismatched people who actually have one very important thing in common: love. Finally, welcome new author Raine Hollister. In *Exception to the Rule*, heroine Layne Taylor finds herself running afoul of the law when she tries to defend her brother against a murder charge. But with Texas Ranger Brant Wade as her opponent, things soon start to get extremely personal.

As always, enjoy!

Leslie Wainger
Senior Editor and Editorial Coordinator

EXCEPTION TO THE RULE

Raine Hollister

Silhouette®
INTIMATE MOMENTS®

Published by Silhouette Books New York

America's Publisher of Contemporary Romance

SILHOUETTE BOOKS
300 East 42nd St., New York, N.Y. 10017

EXCEPTION TO THE RULE

ISBN: 0-373-07484-0

First Silhouette Books printing March 1993

Printed in the U.S.A.

RAINE HOLLISTER

lives in Houston, Texas, with her husband, daughter and two cats. She's worked for a politician, has been a legal secretary with the City Attorney's office, was editor of the Northwest Houston Chapter of Romance Writers of America newsletter and is a member of Mystery Writers of America.

An award-winning author, she enjoys combining romance and suspense. She recalls that as an only child, there were times when she had no one to talk to but herself. How did she handle that? By developing an active imagination and making up zillions and zillions of stories. She loves animals, music, shopping with her daughter and watching romantic comedies of the forties and fifties.

Chapter 1

In the fading evening light the crudely hand-painted sign read *Juan's Cantina*. Inside, half the populace of the small south-Texas border town was fast coming to life.

Standing just outside the door, Layne Tyler cast a searching glance around the room. A smoky haze rose steadily to the ceiling, settling over the room like a gray shroud. Cigarette butts littered the wooden floor and tables showed wear and tear from stains, knife punctures and cigarette burns. Over the bar several cardboard signs lined the wall, advertising Carta Blanca and Lone Star beer. From the corner, a Mexican polka spun from an old jukebox, competing for attention over the loud din of voices and raucous laughter.

Layne hesitated for a second before crossing the room and settling herself at a small table close to the bar. Several heads turned her way in curious speculation.

She smoothed the skirt of her suit and crossed one leg over the other. Her glance slid to a group of people who were watching her from several tables away. One of the men turned to say something to his companions and they laughed, alerting Layne to the fact that she was probably the source of amusement. She uncrossed her legs.

Every instinct warned her to get up and walk out of here, but Layne Tyler never ran from anything. Besides, Dan's phone call had sounded urgent, and for the second time that night Layne wondered what her brother could have gotten himself into this time. Another gambling debt? As an assistant district attorney she got paid for prosecuting offenders, for heaven's sake. Why hadn't she been able to keep one boy in line? Because, a small voice intruded, that boy was now a man. And he was all the family she had left. She'd been both mother and sister to Dan since the summer she had turned twenty-one, the same age Dan was now. The experience had taught her how important family really was. A stab of pain gripped Layne as she thought of her parents. If only they had lived, maybe things might have turned out differently for her and Dan. Maybe.

"You want something?" A heavily accented voice broke into her thoughts.

The barmaid looked down at Layne from beneath long ebony lashes. A black floral skirt draped her hips seductively and a white peasant blouse hung loosely below her shoulders, exposing a great expanse of dusky skin. A flash of resentment flared in her dark eyes as they swept over Layne's clothing, measuring their worth.

"A cola, please," Layne answered, feeling a twinge of annoyance. She was neither a snob nor an ambitious shrew and she disliked other women making her feel as if she were. The media had once referred to her as "one tough cookie," but Layne preferred to think of herself as conscientious and hardworking.

The woman walked off with a toss of her head, a strong, pungent scent of musk trailing behind her, mingling with the room's odor of sweat, smoke and stale beer. Layne's empty stomach rumbled in protest.

When her soda arrived, Layne lifted the glass to her lips and wondered briefly if it was clean.

Brant Wade leaned against the bar nursing a drink, one shiny boot resting on a brass foot rail. From time to time his glance touched Layne. He watched her now. She looked like a lost kitten in an alley full of tomcats, yet she appeared remarkably unaffected. Her icy reserve annoyed him for some reason. The conservative cut of her suit gave her a distinct look of efficiency, yet her appearance contained contradictions. The hair she had smoothed back into a businesslike bun was a rich auburn. Her green eyes slanted upward at the corners. She appeared cool as a cucumber, yet her lips were full and soft. His eyes lingered on her mouth.

"Hey, hombre." The slightly rotund man sitting next to Brant had unwittingly mistaken the flash of interest in his eyes for desire. *"¿La señorita es muy bella, verdad?"*

"Yeah, a real looker," Brant answered with a bored expression.

"But amigo, look at her. A woman like her would not give a man like me a second glance. But perhaps you will be luckier, eh?" he said with a suggestive smile.

Brant shrugged and glanced away.

The man leaned over and added in a conspiratorial whisper. "As for me, I prefer my women with a little more flesh . . . like Rosita over there."

At that moment, the tall, curvaceous Rosita, the same barmaid who had waited on Layne, walked by the bar and paused, eyeing Brant with more than a passing interest.

Brant returned her scrutiny with cool disinterest. Rosita's eyes spat fire as she tossed her head back and walked on. Smiling, he watched the provocative sway of her hips. Not bad. But at the moment he was more interested in Layne Tyler. So far, she was his best lead. His only lead. And he'd lay odds she was here to meet her brother. A woman like her wouldn't set foot in a dump like this without a damned good reason. Now all he had to do was wait.

But where the hell was that brother of hers? Judging by the lewd glances Layne was getting, he'd bet a month's pay that her composure was going to slip a few notches before too long. Women were trouble. He knew that from experience and he sure as hell didn't feel like fighting his way out of this hole tonight. Not over some fancy skirt like her, anyway.

Layne tapped one long polished nail against the side of her glass and shifted uncomfortably in her chair. She'd been waiting for twenty minutes. What in the world was keeping Dan?

Once again she glanced around the room. She spied a man openly fondling his date and averted her eyes toward the bar. One man in particular caught her attention and she studied his profile, more out of curiosity than any interest. At three or four inches over six feet, he wasn't the type of man one ignored so easily. A cream-colored Stetson sat low on his head, shadowing most of his face. Dark hair brushed his collar and the tan lightweight jacket he wore did little to conceal the muscular width of his shoulders. His skin was dark and she wondered if he was of Mexican descent.

Her gaze slowly returned to his face and their eyes locked. Eyes the color of turquoise impaled her. There was an undertone of challenge in the measuring look he gave her, while the mocking lift of his mouth clearly showed interest.

Layne's stomach did a crazy somersault. She felt a certain fascination—or was it fear? The sensation of being caught in a snare gripped her and she mentally shook the image away, returning his bold look with one of cool indifference.

"Miss Tyler?"

Layne glanced up into the smiling features of another barmaid who leaned over and placed a drink on the table.

"Oh, but I didn't order anything."

"The drink is from Dan."

Layne's eyes widened at the mention of her brother's name and she glanced over her shoulder, expecting him to be standing there.

"He asked me to give you this." She handed Layne a folded piece of paper.

An acute sense of unease settled in the pit of Layne's stomach as she stared at the note. She glanced up to ask the woman where Dan was, but it was too late. The barmaid had moved away from the table and was now lost in the crowd.

Adjusting her eyes to the dim light, Layne studied the piece of paper clutched between her fingers. It took her a moment to focus on the words as confusion mixed with concern.

Laynie, meet me upstairs. Second door on the right. Hurry!

D

A shiver of apprehension settled over Layne like a dark cloud. Grabbing her purse, she slipped the note inside and stood up.

As Layne walked past the bar, her skin tingled with the sensation of being watched. She mentally counted each step as her heels echoed loudly on the wooden floor—it was much easier than counting her uneven heartbeat as it raced wildly out of control.

She wanted to run the rest of the way but resisted the impulse. When she reached the stairs she took a long breath, exhaled and started climbing.

At the top she paused to look down the dimly lit corridor. There were three rooms on the right. She walked to the center one and rapped lightly on the door.

"Laynie?" Dan's muffled voice was unmistakable.

"Yes, Dan, it's me." Her face was drawn into an anxious frown.

The door opened a crack to reveal a nervous and relieved Dan, then swung wider. Just as Layne started forward, she heard the sound of movement behind her.

Her breath caught in half a whisper, half a cry as she was pushed into the room. Shock made her lungs strain to breathe in more air and she winced as strong fingers locked around the soft flesh of her arm.

"Allow me," a man's husky voice drawled as he kicked the door shut behind him.

Dan turned to run, but the sharp-edged steel in the man's voice halted his flight. "Freeze! That's good. Now place your hands on the wall and spread your feet."

Layne jerked her head toward him and a shock of recognition lit her eyes. It was the man she'd been admiring earlier.

He was taller than he'd first appeared and his presence in the room was intimidating. There was masculine strength in his features. He would be stubborn and determined—she could sense it even though she didn't know him.

His jacket hung loosely over his belt and he had pulled it back to whip out a revolver. The gun was aimed at Dan. A prickle of fear shot through her and she swallowed, fighting the urge to collapse against him.

But Layne had never fainted before and she wasn't about to start now. Dangerous or not, he had no right to scare the hell out of her like that. Leaving the momentary fear behind, she threw caution to the wind.

"Let me go!" she demanded, struggling to pull free.

He ignored her, his attention never wavering from Dan.

Layne's temper flared quickly and her voice rose to a louder pitch. "Are you crazy or something? Who are you?"

"Stay still," he warned.

Her gaze shifted to Dan and as she stared at him, a confusing rush of dread whirled inside her. *Oh, Dan,* she thought, *what have you gotten us into now?*

"Dan, does this man have something to do with you?" Frowning, Layne watched as Dan shifted uneasily and shook his head in dismay.

She looked away, more as a ploy to think than anything else. When she raised her eyes toward the man again, a professional mask had settled over her features. "If you've got a beef with us, spit it out. Otherwise, it's late."

"The name's Brant Wade. I'm a Texas Ranger." His voice was deceptively soft, but his eyes, hard and unyielding, were directed at Layne for the first time.

Her eyes widened in surprise, then just as quickly turned stormy. "I suppose I could take your word for it, but I'd rather see some ID." Saccharine sweetness laced each word.

The corners of his sensual mouth lifted in a hint of a smile. "Be my guest," he said, releasing her arm long enough to pull one side of his jacket back so it rested behind his holster. Pinned to his shirt was the famous Ranger badge, stamped with an antique Mexican five-peso silver coin. The coin had a blunt edge, but there was nothing sharper for cutting jurisdictional red tape.

Her confusion mounted. "What do you want with us?"

"Your brother's wanted for questioning."

"What kind of questioning?" Dan shot over his shoulder.

"A man was killed and the man who did it fits your description."

There was a charged silence before Layne cried out, "No! There has to be some mistake." She took a tentative step toward Dan, her eyes glaring at Brant like a tigress protecting her cub.

The pain in her voice pierced Brant's composure. It surprised him that he felt even this small amount of emotion, given his long distrust of women. He wondered why this particular woman should affect him so strongly.

The momentary weakness disturbed him. He had a job to do and regardless of how he felt Brant never stopped to analyze his actions; he always handled a situation in the way that seemed appropriate at the time. Forcing his hardcore veneer to take over, Brant spoke more harshly than he intended. "Hold still, lady, and you—" he pointed to Dan "—stay right where you are."

"I didn't kill anybody." Dan's voice shook with fear as he stared at the wall, then he glanced over his shoulder at Layne. "I swear, Laynie...I didn't do it. I—"

"Wait, Dan!" Layne held up a warning hand. "Don't say anything until I can help you." Her attempt to regain her composure almost floundered.

One dark eyebrow rose slightly. "I told you to stay still, Miss Tyler," Brant commanded, tightening his hold on her arm.

"Take your hand off me," she said between clenched teeth.

He did, then moved to stand behind her.

Layne's relief at being released was short-lived. She felt his hand slip in front of her and gasped as strong, warm fingers traveled impersonally over her body in a frisking motion.

A stranger's hands were roaming over her body with mechanical thoroughness. Layne's eyes widened in disbelief, then narrowed dangerously.

The stiffening of her body should have alerted Brant.

In one swift, rapid motion, Layne pivoted around and swung high. Her open palm connected with his neck in a loud, whacking sound, the force snapping his head to one side.

The unexpected movement caught Brant by surprise. His gun fell to the floor. At the same moment, Dan grabbed a floor lamp, the only lighting in the room, and tore its cord from the wall. Flinging the lamp at Brant, Dan turned and ran toward the window.

"Dammit, woman!" Brant bellowed as he raced through the dark after Dan. Layne, standing in front of him, moved forward at the same time and her slight frame collided with his much larger one. She cried out as the force of the impact sent her body reeling backward.

Instinctively Brant reached out to grab her and they both went down together.

As they hit the floor with a resounding thud, they heard the roar of an engine and the squeal of rubber as a motorcycle tore out of the parking lot.

Brant lay sprawled halfway across Layne's body. He could barely see the outline of her profile in the darkness, but he could feel the warm softness of her body where his hand rested along the curve between her waist and hip. She was so silent, he wondered if he had hurt her.

"You all right?" The husky timbre of his voice vibrated with concern.

He felt her stiffen and touched her shoulder gently. "Are you all right?" he repeated.

"Yes! Get off me!"

Brant disengaged his arms from around her body and moved away. For an instant he'd allowed himself to feel more than concern for her, then silently berated himself. The last thing he wanted or needed was to become involved with Layne Tyler. Right now he had to concentrate on her brother. This woman had already caused him a great deal of inconvenience. Because of her, Dan had escaped. He knew it would do no good to go after Dan now. That motorcycle could race through places Brant's car wouldn't be able to follow.

He stood up abruptly and leaned over. "Give me your hand," he said, his tone harsh.

She slapped his hand aside. "I don't need your help."

Powerful arms tightened around her and as Brant yanked Layne up against his chest they both heard the ripping of material. Layne felt the left sleeve of her jacket tear—her new suit, she thought in disgust. She'd bought it just last week.

Neither one of them moved. Layne waited for an apology. After all, she wasn't used to being hauled up like a sack of flour.

She was destined for disappointment.

"Stay here until I find a light." His voice rang with authority and his superior attitude grated on her nerves.

Damn her suit, she thought. What she bristled at was his rudeness and his arrogance. As for staying where she was, just where did he think she was going to go? One of her shoes had flown off during the fall and she didn't want to stumble around in the dark looking for it.

She stood for a brief moment, feeling wholly bereft, wanting nothing more than to be away from here. But she couldn't weaken now. Dan had always been able to depend on her and right now he needed her, needed her strength.

Suddenly the room was illuminated and Layne blinked in an attempt to adjust her eyes. She watched Brant Wade as he picked up his revolver and slipped it back into its holster. He walked over to the window and looked out, then turned to face her.

By the glow of light she noticed again how the startling aqua shade of his eyes contrasted with the dark tan of his skin. Surrounded by unusually long lashes for a man, his eyes were definitely his most attractive feature. When she'd seen him standing at the bar she had liked the look of him, the masculine strength, the slight cleft in his chin. There were laugh lines around his eyes and she wondered how often he used them.

Too bad he was also rude, obnoxious and domineering. Not her type at all. Her chin lifted defiantly.

"Congratulations," he said as his eyes narrowed thoughtfully. "I underestimated you. That was a neat trick you pulled, taking me off guard so your brother could get away."

She looked shocked. "Wh-what? I haven't the slightest idea what you're talking about!" She didn't like his tone. Not one bit.

"Don't you?" he challenged smoothly. "Didn't you warn him not to say anything until you could help him?"

She was the picture of offended dignity. "Yes, but I meant help him with legal advice. You know my name. If you've done your homework, then you also know that I'm with the D.A.'s office. Why in the world would I want to do something so foolish as to help my brother escape?''

He looked skeptical. "I've never been able to figure out women, period. For instance, I didn't think you'd be dumb enough to hit a law-enforcement officer. That was a stupid thing to do."

A rebellious sparkle lit Layne's green eyes. She made a mental note to add insulting and opinionated to rude, obnoxious and domineering.

"Stupid, am I? And I'd say your manners are as bad as your judgment! If you'd kept your hands to yourself in the first place, none of this would've happened!"

Brant glanced at her in surprise before flashing her a smile. "I assure you I was only doing my job."

Layne colored slightly. "Well, I don't intend to stand here and argue with you. I have more important things to do. Where's my shoe?" she muttered.

A quick scan of the room located the missing shoe, and hobbling over to where it lay Layne leaned over to pick it up. The action afforded Brant a full, clear view of her shapely derriere.

As Layne straightened, she turned to see a speculative gleam in Brant's eyes. Her own gaze faltered under such close scrutiny. She slipped on her shoe, then glanced away to search for her purse. This time when she stooped over to pick it up, Layne made certain she was facing Brant.

She walked to the door and stopped, glancing back over her shoulder. "I can't say it's been a pleasure," she said and reached for the doorknob.

"Just a minute!"

Layne threw him a questioning glance.

"Where do you think *you're* going?"

"Home." Her reply was clipped.

Brant's gaze traveled slowly over her body. Her jacket was torn and the hem of her blouse had escaped from her skirt. The once neatly coiffed chignon had now come loose, causing its silken strands to fall in a softly tangled mass around her shoulders.

Layne followed his glance down to her disheveled appearance and with some modicum of dignity she attempted to tuck in her blouse, then reached up and discarded the rest of her hairpins. There was nothing she could do about the ripped jacket, so she took it off and draped it over one arm. When she glanced up she saw he was smiling at her. And as his smile deepened so did the grooves on each side of his mouth. It was almost as though he enjoyed seeing her this way. He was mocking her.

"Let's go," he said, grabbing her arm.

Wonderful. She couldn't leave here fast enough.

But he wasn't opening the door. Instead he led her to the window. Layne's eyes widened in disbelief.

"What are you doing?" As if she couldn't guess.

"We'd better go out the same way Dan did," he said matter-of-factly.

"And just what's wrong with us going out the same way we came in?"

"Miss Tyler." He placed one hand on his hip and stood in that arrogant stance she disliked so much. "Unless you want to help us fight our way out of here, I suggest you listen. By now, that crowd downstairs ought to be rip-roaring drunk and if you'll excuse my bluntness you look like hell. With your clothes torn, they're going to think you and I had one hell of a party up here and they're liable to want to share in the ... uh ... fun. Do you get my drift?"

"Perfectly." Her face burned.

She stared dismally out the window, then down at her narrow skirt. She shook her head. No way she was going to hike her skirt up to her hips in order to get through that window. Absolutely not!

"There's a fire escape out there, or at least what passes for one. I'll go first, then I'll help you get through." He looked down at her skirt and his voice gentled. "Trust me, okay?"

Trust him! Wasn't that what J. R. Ewing always said before he shafted someone? Who did Brant Wade think he was kidding? Layne knew he blamed her for Dan's escape and he'd probably like nothing better than to get her though that window, only to drop her once they were out on the ledge. Of course, he'd claim it had been an accident.

"Tell you what," she said, "*you* go out the window. *I'm* going out this way." She started toward the door.

"You sure you want to go that way?"

Her reply was a quick shake of her head.

Brant studied the stubborn tilt of her chin, then shrugged. "Suit yourself," he said, following her.

With firm strides, a disheveled and tired Layne made her way through the cantina. She ignored the lustful stares and lewd comments that came from the men. Maybe she would've been safer going out the window, but it was too late for regrets. Besides, heights made her dizzy. She squared her shoulders and kept walking.

Until someone stuck a foot out in the aisle and stopped her.

Layne stared at the man. He reminded her of a ferret. Small frame, black mustache, beady eyes. When he smiled, his teeth looked like a car grille.

What next? she thought wearily. It was turning out to be one of the worst days of her life.

Layne stared him down. "I suggest you move your foot," she ordered.

He looked her over and his smile widened. "Or what, *chica?*"

Lowering her voice, she leaned in closer. "Or you'll be the first one to be hauled into that paddy wagon waiting outside."

The others were so busy cheering they didn't hear her, but it got his attention and his eyes narrowed into thoughtful slits.

He called her bluff. "Who's gonna do the hauling? You?" he sneered.

"No. Him." She gestured over her shoulder. Her bravado slipped a notch when she realized Brant lagged behind. But he watched her and his eyes smoldered in anger. He'd probably dawdled on purpose, she thought, just to teach her a lesson. She watched his tall frame make its way toward her with that catlike grace so uncommon in a man his size.

When he reached her, he elbowed her aside. Murmurs passed through the crowd.

"Got a problem?" Brant directed his question to the man. He kept his voice low and steady as he leaned over slightly. The action caused his jacket to open just wide enough for the man to catch a quick glimpse of metal.

The stranger's eyes widened as he looked into Brant's unflinching ones. Losing his nerve, he moved his foot out of the way and held up his hands. "Hey, man, no problem. Just having some fun."

The crowd, thinking they had been about to see a fight, lost interest and resumed their drunken chatter.

Layne noticed one of the barmaids—the one someone had called Rosita—staring at Brant. The woman's eyes flashed with anger and something else. Hate? Could the man who'd just backed down from Brant be her boyfriend? Layne didn't have time to dwell on the matter because Brant grabbed her on his way to the door.

She held her breath until they were both outside, then let it out slowly.

"Well, that was fun," she said, grateful to be where she could breathe clean air. Her heart thumped with relief.

Brant scowled. "Lady, you're dangerous, you know that?"

She managed a tremulous smile. "We got out, didn't we?"

A few moments ago, when she'd stood up to that creep, Brant had felt a grudging respect for her. He admired courage in a woman. Now, he was just damn angry.

"You could've gotten us killed."

She shrugged a delicate shoulder. "We could've been killed climbing down that rickety fire escape, too," she reasoned smoothly. "Besides, you don't think I'd stand up to that man without knowing *some* form of self-defense, do you?"

He rolled his eyes heavenward. "I don't know you, period. Come on," he said, taking hold of her arm roughly and leading her toward the parking lot. "I want to ask you some questions."

Layne dug in her heels. "It won't do you any good. I'm not going to answer any questions."

Glowering at her he slipped off his jacket, tossed it over one shoulder and held it with his forefinger. "Look, lady, I've got a good mind to run you in, so don't tempt me."

Layne matched him glower-for-glower as she stretched to her full five-foot-six-inch frame. "Oh? On what charges?"

The smile didn't quite reach his eyes.

"How does aiding and abetting, striking a law officer and obstructing justice sound for starters?"

Hostile seconds raced by. She opened her mouth to protest, then closed it again. The badge on his shirt winked at her in the moonlight, silently mocking her with its brilliance. She had a healthy respect for the law and she knew him well enough by now to know he didn't make idle threats. And she was too weary to argue.

"In that case," she said between clenched teeth, "we'd better leave now, before you add resisting arrest to my growing list of offenses."

"Now you're being sensible," he said and turned to lead the way.

She had trouble keeping up with his long strides, so he slowed his steps to accommodate her. Except for the loud hoots of laughter coming from Juan's, the night was otherwise quiet. The silence between them stretched uncomfortably. Layne's stomach growled and she remembered once again that she hadn't eaten anything since noon. Hunger always put her in a bad mood.

She made a concentrated effort to think about something else, like how she'd already decided to humor Brant Wade. Best to get everything over tonight so she could think of a way to help Dan out of this mess. There was no way anyone would ever convince her that her brother had murdered someone. She quickened her step into a determined gait.

As they reached Layne's car a man stepped out of the shadows. Layne's sharp cry pierced the air as she jumped back in alarm.

In a reflex action, Brant pushed her behind him. His jacket lay discarded on the ground.

"Hey, hombre, what kept you?" The man's voice was low, raspy.

"Dammit, Garcia, you know better than that. It's a good thing I was keeping an eye out for you." He straightened to his full height. "Besides, no self-respecting thief would wear a white shirt during a full moon."

"Why do you think I wore it?" Garcia gave a deep chuckle as he walked over to where they stood. He picked up Brant's jacket off the ground and handed it to him.

Layne peered from behind Brant, vaguely aware that her hands clung tightly to his waist. They stood so close their shadows blended together. Tiny shivers raced down her spine as she felt the thin material of her blouse touch his firm muscled back.

Annoyed, she moved back a respectable distance. Now that she realized the man was someone Brant knew, she breathed easier.

"I hope that whatever detained you wasn't too inconvenient," Garcia said in slightly-accented English. His dark eyes were appraising as they rested on Layne.

She moved forward. The man looked familiar and Layne tried to remember where she'd seen him. It suddenly dawned on her that he'd been sitting next to Brant at the bar tonight. Layne looked from one to the other in confusion.

"Miss Tyler, I believe you and Lieutenant Paul Garcia have already met." Brant held out his hand, motioning for her to move closer.

At the moment Layne found it difficult to believe this man was a police officer, let alone Lieutenant Garcia, whom she'd met before on a professional basis. His clothes looked as though they'd been slept in, there was several days' growth of beard on his face and he had twenty pounds on the Garcia she'd met.

Unflinchingly she met Garcia's glance. "If this man is Lieutenant Garcia, then I'm Mary Poppins."

"She wants proof, Paul, so you'd better show her some. Miss Tyler can be quite stubborn when she wants to be."

He was goading her again. She took a deep breath, then watched in amazement as Garcia began to shed his disguise. First the sombrero came off. Next, he unbuttoned several buttons on his shirt and out came the wad of fabric which had made him look portly.

Garcia took one look at Layne and smiled. "Ah, I see you recognize me. I'm flattered that you were taken in by my costume and I apologize, but I had no choice." He shrugged. "I couldn't take the chance that you would recognize me."

"It wouldn't have mattered," she replied. "I wouldn't have known why you were here."

"Come now, Miss Tyler, do you honestly think I'd be spending my time in this place—" he motioned toward Juan's "—if I didn't have some reason?"

"It wouldn't be impossible. You see, I haven't the slightest idea what police lieutenants do on their own time. I spend *my* after-hours working."

"You're angry at me."

"Should I be, lieutenant?"

"Call me Paul, please."

"What questions did you want to ask me, *lieutenant?*"

"In due time," he replied.

Layne's glance took in both men. It was obvious Garcia had come here with Brant in order to arrest her brother.

Garcia switched his attention to Brant. "I waited downstairs like we planned. I made sure no one else went up there. What happened?"

"I ran into a little problem." Brant threw Layne a meaningful glare.

"He got away?"

Brant shrugged. "These things happen."

"Yeah, but not to you, amigo."

Brant shifted uncomfortably.

Garcia smiled, amused at Brant's discomfort.

Layne noted that Garcia hadn't so much as flickered an eyelash on learning that Dan had managed to get away. Had he set a trap somewhere else for Dan? She frowned. They were discussing her brother as though she weren't there.

"Excuse me," she said, "it's late. Do you plan to take me to police headquarters?" She glanced up at Brant. The moon was partially hidden behind a dark cloud, causing erratic shadows to cross his features. She watched him lean casually against her car, his arms folded across his chest. His tall, lean body blocked the driver's side.

"No, we just want to ask you a few questions," he replied. "It won't take long. There's a small restaurant about thirty minutes from here—it's on the way back to Brownsville. We can talk over a cup of coffee."

Layne hesitated.

Lieutenant Garcia spoke up. "Don't worry. Brant can be trusted."

She wondered whether to take his mildly voiced statement at full worth. "All right," she said, resigned to spending another hour in his company. At least they weren't going to take her to police headquarters. Thank God. She needed time—needed to hurry home where she could think and plan her next move. Dan would call her. If not tonight, then tomorrow. She dug in her purse for her keys. "I'll follow you—"

"That won't be necessary. I'll drive your car and Paul can follow in mine."

She shook her head. "I'd rather not," she said, noting his broad chest, the wide, muscled shoulders.

"Don't worry, rush hour is over," he teased. "I promise you, you can trust me with your car."

Layne stared toward the road practically deserted from the late hour. He was asking her to trust him again. Why did that bother her so much?

Garcia chuckled. "I remember a few times when his driving wasn't too great."

"Oh, yeah? Well, if *I* remember correctly, we were kids— and as I recall on several occasions yours wasn't too great, either."

Garcia shrugged. "Well, as you say, we were just kids."

"Not when *you* drove, amigo. This was only a few months ago."

There was a familiarity, a bantering tone between them that comes only from knowing someone well. These two were obviously good friends.

"Brant, you're embarrassing me in front of a beautiful lady. Come, Miss Tyler, we'll ask you only a few questions, then you can go home. I'm sorry for the inconvenience, but it's something that has to be done, you understand?"

"Yes, I understand," Layne answered. He was being kind, even considerate of her feelings. But she wasn't fooled. By either of them. They were priming her for her interrogation, lowering her defenses, just waiting for something to slip. She had done it herself on occasion. Oh, yes, she understood.

Brant walked around to the passenger side and opened the car door for her. "In you go... Mary Poppins."

Layne pretended not to hear him as she slid into the front seat. Minutes later they were on their way with Garcia close behind in Brant's cream-colored Ford.

Across the street, a black sedan slowly eased out onto the road, following at a discreet distance.

Chapter 2

It was just after ten when they entered the small restaurant. Brant's discerning glance swept over every inch of the room with the practiced ease of a bloodhound sniffing the air—a habit that was as natural to him as breathing.

Four booths lined one wall and scattered throughout the room were tables covered with red-checkered vinyl tablecloths. On the opposite wall four large windows were encased in red-checkered curtains that had seen too many sunny days and were now faded to an anemic pink.

As Brant guided Layne over to a booth he studied the three occupants in the room: an elderly man who sat at a corner table reading a newspaper and a young man and woman in their early twenties who were seated at a booth, intent only on each other.

He wondered what Layne thought of the place.

Layne was thinking it wasn't the greatest place she'd ever been in, nor was it the worst. Juan's held that honor. It didn't matter, she thought, because she didn't plan to stay long anyway. In the time it would take Brant Wade to read her her rights in that lazy drawl of his, she planned to make short shrift of their little meeting.

Layne eyed the pale green vinyl of the booth with a critical eye. Someone had attempted to patch up the tears with black electrician's tape. Raising an eyebrow, she glanced at Brant and wondered where he took his dates. Or his wife. She peered down at his left hand. No ring.

"Nice place," she muttered.

"It's private." His eyes mocked her. "And the coffee's not half bad. But order anything else and you're on your own." His eyes squinted with amusement. Layne couldn't help noticing the dark, hawkish features, the high cheekbones that hinted of an Indian heritage. His lower lip was fuller than his top one, making his mouth look more sensual, as if it would be capable of passion and laughter.

"I'm not hungry," she lied, sliding onto the seat.

Garcia sat facing her. Layne had expected both men to sit across the table from her, so she was surprised when Brant slid in beside her, forcing her to move over. His large frame made her feel small and very feminine. She was acutely aware their thighs were pressed together and a sensual quiver ran through her body. She scooted closer to the wall, holding her body in the ramrod posture of a British brigadier. A moment later her back began to hurt from the effort and she forced herself to relax. If he didn't mind their close confinement, then neither would she.

Too bad her quivering senses didn't agree with her mind. Every move he made, every gesture, reminded her he was far too close. She could feel his body heat seeping into hers and she felt oddly warm. Steam practically rose from her body. Did he know? Could he guess what kind of effect he had on her? She glanced up and found those magnificent turquoise-colored eyes studying her intently.

She looked away, pretending interest in the young couple across the room. The girl said something to her companion and they began a heated discussion in Spanish. So much for Latin lovers, Layne thought. These two were definitely not the epitome of a young couple in love. But then what did *she* know about love? She wasn't exactly an expert in that department.

Once, when she'd been in the middle of facing the worst tragedy of her life—the death of her parents and older brother—Layne had regretted the fact that she had no husband or lover to offer a strong shoulder for her to lean on. A man with caring arms who could ease her grief a little. There had been no one. Only Dan, who'd been twelve that summer. And the only strong shoulder had been hers, ready to help Dan get through it all.

Layne had no illusions. She was passably pretty, she supposed, but nowhere near to making men follow her with their tongues hanging out. Which was just fine with her. Being single gave her the right to do anything she wanted, without asking anyone's permission.

She stifled a yawn.

Brant studied Layne's face just inches from his. She intrigued him. One minute she was a fiery tigress staring down a room full of drunks, while another, like now when she'd caught him studying her, she could blush so sweetly.

He took in the scent of her and wondered what she'd say if she knew he was finding it difficult to concentrate with her sitting so close. It had been a bad idea on his part, but he always sat facing the door. Yet the truth of the matter was he felt a strong attraction to her and that wasn't a good idea under the circumstances. Attraction led to other things. Things he wasn't ready for and probably never would be. He was getting too old and set in his ways to believe in everlasting love and the pursuit of happiness. And just because she was smarter and classier than other women he'd known it still didn't mean a hill of beans to him, other than he'd have to stay a step ahead of her. He'd have to keep reminding himself that business was business and pleasure with her would be out of the question. She probably wouldn't even speak to him after tonight. But he was certain of one thing though—Layne Tyler was attracted to him, too.

Leaning back, he stretched his long legs as far as they would go and his thigh brushed against hers.

Layne sighed in relief as the waitress approached their table. The woman's hair was bleached to a coarse wheat color and as she strutted toward them she popped her gum in time with every swivel of her hips.

"Hi, what can I getcha?" she asked, smiling broadly. The interested gleam in her eyes was directed at Brant. Layne wondered if he always received this kind of reception from the opposite sex. She stole a glance at Garcia. He shrugged as if he were used to it.

"I'll have black coffee," she said.

Brant and Garcia ordered the same.

"Is that gonna be all?"

Layne could well imagine the wealth of meaning behind that question. "That's all for me."

Brant nodded. So did Garcia, although his dark eyes twinkled even brighter.

"Okay, be back in a jiff." She placed her order pad in the pocket of her apron, stuck her pencil in her hair and shimmied off.

Brant turned his attention to Layne. "So tell us about yourself."

She wanted to wipe the smile off both their faces. "I would, but I don't think that's what you want to hear."

Brant and Garcia exchanged glances.

"All right, then," Brant said, "tell us about Dan."

Her nerves took a giant leap. "What do you want to know?"

"When was the last time you saw him—besides tonight?"

"About a month and a half ago. August twenty-fifth, to be exact."

"You sure about the date?"

"Positive. It was my birthday." How could she forget? She'd turned thirty and all she had to show for it were new crow's-feet and five extra pounds—mostly around her hips.

"Do you have any idea where he's been since then?"

From the long, measured look he gave her, Layne sensed those eyes didn't miss much. "I really have no idea," she said. Out of the corner of her eye, she noticed Garcia jotting something down on a pad.

"And he hasn't gotten in touch with you since then? That is, not until tonight?"

His tone was a bit too casual, yet she sensed an implication of doubt in those words.

"That's right."

"Why do you think that is?" he persisted.

"Pardon?"

"Well, he came by to pay you a visit on your birthday and you were the one he called for help. You two are obviously close, so why has he waited so long to see you again?"

In spite of herself the edge showed in her voice. "My brother is an adult, Mr. Wade. He doesn't have to check in with me every night."

Garcia joined in. "Miss Tyler, we have no wish to make you angry. We need to know where your brother was on the night a man was murdered. We understand your concern for him, so if you'll cooperate with us we can wrap this up and you can go home and rest."

"I understand what you're saying, lieutenant, but the fact is I don't have much to tell you. My brother visits me whenever he can. Several months ago, he moved into a new apartment close to the university and signed up for some classes there. I haven't seen much of him since then."

The waitress arrived with their coffee. Layne raised the cup to her mouth and took a sip, then set the cup down. "Just who is my brother suspected of killing?"

Brant set his own cup down and looked at her. "Michael Salinas."

The words rolled off his tongue like the syncopated movement of a conductor's wand.

Layne's body went rigid. It was no surprise to her that Salinas was dead; the district attorney's office was waiting for a police report before deciding on a course of action. But to think that Dan was suspected of killing Salinas was ludicrous. Salinas was big-time. Where would her brother have met him?

"Did you know him?" Brant asked.

"Didn't everyone?" she replied. "He was one of the wealthiest men in Brownsville. He owns—or rather owned—Brownsville Shipping, not to mention the Brownsville Towers building." Her eyes blazed. "Tell me, lieutenant, what makes you think Dan killed him? Michael Salinas must have known a lot of people—probably had quite a few enemies among them."

Garcia leaned forward. "Your brother was spotted at the scene the night Salinas was killed. At the time of death, to be exact."

Layne stared coldly across the table. "He was spotted there, lieutenant? Dan is twenty-one years old, medium frame, medium height, brown hair and green eyes. That description fits any number of males in this town who are between twenty and thirty. Do you have any actual proof that he killed the man?''

"No," Garcia replied.

There was a faint tone of disapproval in her voice. "In that case, I suggest you start looking elsewhere for the real killer, because Dan didn't do it."

"You have a lot of faith in your brother, Miss Tyler—an admirable trait."

She kept her voice steady. "I know my brother. He could never kill anyone. Besides, what motive could he possibly have had?"

"'That, Miss Tyler, is what we're trying to establish."

Layne gave Brant a sidelong glance. "Why have *you* been called in on this case?"

Before he could answer, Garcia cut in. "It's not unusual, in a case of this magnitude, to call in a Texas Ranger. As you yourself know, one of their main functions is to assist local enforcement agencies when called upon. They have the full facilities of an excellent crime lab—"

"And *he* can cross the border into Mexico and transport prisoners back into *your* jurisdiction, isn't that right, lieutenant?" Layne interrupted bluntly. "Michael Salinas rates the best, doesn't he? God forbid that one of us average peons should be murdered and not given that same consideration."

"Really, Miss Tyler, aren't you being a bit melodramatic?" Garcia said, with just a hint of impatience.

"I don't think so," she said, pushing her cup away. She was weary of the questions and they knew it.

Brant drank his coffee and watched her. He admired her spunk. Even with her hair mussed and her clothes wrinkled and torn, she exuded a tense dignity. She was a single-minded woman when it came to her brother. Her loyalty intrigued him, too. Except for his mother and sister, Maggie, Brant had never experienced loyalty from any other woman. In fact, it had been just the opposite.

He set his cup down. "Layne, this isn't anything personal. We're just trying to do our job."

"I understand," she replied, "but I've told you all I know."

"All right, but if you happen to think of any place where he might've gone, will you let me know?" He took a small card from his shirt pocket and handed it to her.

"Yes. Of course."

Brant gauged her sincerity. With a casual gesture, he rested his arm along the back of the seat. "If he's innocent, he has nothing to worry about."

"He's innocent."

"Then why is he running?" He caught the momentary flash of pain in her eyes just before it was replaced by one of anger—or resentment. Whether it was directed at him, herself or at Dan, he couldn't tell.

She shifted her body sideways in order to turn and look at him and her knee bumped against his thigh, but she didn't care. "I don't know," she replied, "but I plan to find out. I've been in court for the last couple of days. Tomorrow, I'll look into the Salinas case. When can I expect a police report from you?"

Brant caught the defiance in her tone, as well as the challenge. But it was Garcia who answered. "Your office will have it soon," was all he would commit to.

"I'll be in your office tomorrow, then. Is there anything else you'd like to ask me before I leave?" Her question was directed at Brant.

She was turning the tables on them. There was a flicker of admiration in his eyes as he rose to his feet. "No, not right now."

She slid out of the booth and stood up. "In that case, my keys, please." She held out her hand.

"Come on, I'll walk you to your car," Brant said, handing her the keys.

Garcia motioned for the bill. "You two go ahead. I have a call to make."

Brant nodded, but his concentration was centered on the enticing sway of Layne's hips as she walked in front of him.

A full moon lit an endless sky. Their footsteps crunched across the graveled parking lot as they walked toward Layne's car. Across the street several weather-beaten clapboard houses lined the block. In one of the homes a distant lighted window gleamed with the blurry image from a television set. To their left a narrow road separated the restaurant from the vacant lot next door. The air was filled with the scent of cedar.

Down the street a dog barked. Further down another answered. A slight chill in the air caused Layne to pause long enough to slip her jacket on.

Before she could take another step, Brant's hand reached out and snaked around her arm. "There's something I want to say before you go."

Layne glanced down at his hand. "You know, you have a bad habit of doing that. My arm, please."

He let go of her. "Look," he said, jamming his fists in his pockets, "you can make it a lot easier on Dan if you tell him to give himself up."

She waved a hand in the air angrily. "What makes you so sure I'll even hear from him? Why, he could be clear across the border into Mexico!" Alarm swept through her at the thought.

"That would be unfortunate."

Her eyes flared. "For him or for you?"

"For both of us."

She looked away. "I said I'd let you know if I heard from him. Now, excuse me—"

He gave her a disarming smile. "Why do I get the feeling you're trying to get rid of me?"

She frowned. "I thought you were through asking questions."

"I am. Just one more thing—"

"What now?" she groaned.

"I'd appreciate it if you didn't leave town."

"That's wasted advice. I'm well aware of the rules. I wouldn't dream of leaving town while my brother is in trouble. And don't bother to walk me to my car, I can manage just fine by myself." She brushed past him.

There was nothing else he could say to detain her and the fact that he wanted to do just that surprised him. He wanted to see her again. *Forget it,* he told himself. If there was one lesson he'd learned the hard way, it was never to take anything at face value. He was a simple man and he liked the simple things in life—Tex-Mex food, country music and rooting for the Houston Oilers. What he didn't like was hypocrisy in other people, injustice and getting taken for a ride. And Layne Tyler looked like the kind of woman who could mix him all up. It was just as well she was off limits.

"Suit yourself." He shrugged. "Just don't forget to call me if you hear anything." His voice trailed after her.

He had taken a few steps toward the restaurant when he heard the sound. He stopped dead still to listen. Slowing down his breathing, he waited, listening—every sense alert. Off to his left, the sound carried over the soft breeze. It began as a low muffled rumble, increasing to a higher pitch. Laughter.

Brant turned and walked closer to the road. About a block or so away, several teenagers leaned against a dark-colored late-model car. Their laughter sounded unnaturally loud in the stillness of the night.

Brant relaxed his muscles. Teenagers—most likely bored and out cruising. He turned to walk away, but his muscles tensed again and his skin crawled with the sensation of being watched.

He made a quick sweep of the area, then glanced back toward the boys. One by one, they filed into the car. A moment later, the engine roared to life and tires squealed in protest as the car tore down the road and headed toward them.

Brant still couldn't shake the eerie sensation that someone watched them. Like his Indian forebears, he'd learned to trust his instincts. They had saved his life on several occasions.

Right now the only noise he heard was the roar of the powerful engine as the car picked up speed. It swerved over onto the wrong side of the road. Brant couldn't be sure if the boys posed any threat, but he sure as hell wasn't taking any chances. Forgetting the invisible threat for the moment, he turned to make sure Layne had reached her car.

"Sonofabitch," he muttered under his breath as he attempted to close the distance between them.

Layne, too, had stopped to listen. From the corner of her eye she saw Brant running toward her, shouting something. She turned in time to see blinding headlights racing toward her. A cold knot formed in her stomach and she willed herself to move, but her feet wouldn't obey.

Just as the car veered off the road Brant threw himself at her, tackling her to the ground. They rolled over twice and Brant came up on one knee, his 9 mm semiautomatic already clutched in his hand. There was an unmistakable click of a hammer being cocked as he aimed it at the car and waited to see if it would turn around and come back. Brant watched the taillights disappear along the shadowy road.

"Stay down," he ordered.

Layne sprawled behind him. Tears pooled at the back of her eyes. Grateful to be alive, she tried not to think about the abuse her body had suffered today. She heard a noise behind her and turned to see Garcia running toward them.

"You two all right?" He had his .38 drawn.

"Some boys have a weird sense of humor," Brant muttered wryly as he rose and dusted himself off. He bent over to help Layne to her feet, then walked over and picked up his hat where it had fallen.

When Layne had been tackled, the wind had been slammed out of her. Now she trembled so hard her teeth were knocking together like castanets. "Those idiots!" she cried. "They could've killed me! And *you!*" she shouted at Brant. "For crying out loud, this is the second time tonight you've knocked me down. I appreciate your help, really I do, but *you* could've killed me." She knew she was babbling, not making any sense, but she couldn't help it. She hurt all over and her skin burned in places where the gravel had dug into her body when she'd fallen.

Both men were looking at her oddly. Layne ignored them. She felt a searing pain and reached up to rub the bruise on her arm. Her hand came away wet and sticky and she stared at it in horror. Swaying slightly she closed her eyes, suddenly feeling nauseous.

"I . . . I've been shot," she moaned, staring down at the blood on her hand, then at the hole in her flesh which was now bleeding steadily.

Both men's eyes widened in surprise. Brant felt his own blood slide through his veins like cold needles—*he hadn't heard any shot.*

His arms went around her to keep her from falling, and picking her up gently, he carried her the short distance to her car. Garcia hurried to open the back door, then turned and ran toward Brant's car to radio for an ambulance.

Brant eased her onto the seat, his mind whirling in a hundred different directions.

"Oh, I'm bleeding all over your jacket," she whispered inanely.

"Don't worry about it." He took a handkerchief out of his back pocket and bound it tightly around her arm. "Just hold on, okay? You're going to be all right."

Layne's breathing was coming in short gasps. Brant placed one arm around her and held her. With the other, he reached down and tucked an auburn strand of hair behind her ear, then slowly his fingers moved to her cheek, touching it gently. For a moment, he stared down at her, his throat tight and hot from the rage he felt toward the bastard who'd done this. His arms went around her and he cradled her closer, wanting to keep her warm.

In the distance they heard sirens screaming through the night air.

Chapter 3

"You think it could've been one of the kids?" Garcia asked.

"Maybe, but I doubt it," Brant replied, glancing across the street.

This morning, the incessant stream of sunlight painted another landscape. Everything appeared different in broad daylight—the road seemed wider, the restaurant larger and the houses across the street all stood in line looking like belligerent old fogies. Brant's attention was drawn to one of them and he judged the distance.

Paul came to stand beside him. "You think the hit came from across the street?"

"It's possible. We didn't hear a shot, so whoever it was must've used a silencer. She's lucky it's just a flesh wound . . . a neat, clean hole."

"What about the kids? I don't believe in coincidence." Garcia squatted down on his heels and peered at something on the ground. The glare from the sun reflected off the object and he picked it up. "Think they were in on it?" It was a set of keys.

Brant shrugged. "Who knows? Could be they were paid to cause a distraction so the sniper could get a clear shot. Or maybe he just wanted to throw us off by making us think one of the boys did it."

"A good thing his aim was off." Garcia stood up and handed Brant the keys. "Here. I have a feeling these belong to Layne."

"Unless he didn't intend to kill her."

"You know something I don't?"

"Call it a hunch." Brant replied, shoving the keys in his pocket.

"You're saying he may have wanted to scare her?"

"Could be."

"Why?" Reaching into his inside coat pocket, Garcia pulled out a notepad and scribbled something down.

"Beats me. Either he's a bad shot who missed or a pro who shot her exactly where he intended to. What did the waitress say?"

"Not much." Garcia tapped his pen against the notepad. "She's only been working here a week. I'll question the owner later." He closed the notebook and pushed it back into his pocket.

Brant nodded. "I'm going across the street to see if anyone heard or saw something last night." He ambled off talking over his shoulder. "After I'm through here there's something I have to take care of. I'll meet you back at your office."

"Okay," Garcia said and smiled. "Tell her I said hi."

"I will." Brant started to walk off.

"Hey, amigo."

Brant stopped and turned around.

Garcia gave him a long, level look. "I know it's none of my business, but I remember another time you got pretty involved in a case similar to this one."

Something flickered in Brant's eyes, but he stared steadily back. "Don't worry, I intend to keep this one strictly business."

Garcia shrugged. "It's just that I saw the way you looked at her last night."

Brant scanned the vacant lot next to the restaurant before returning his attention to Garcia. "What can I say, buddy? I'm a man." Brant attempted to keep his tone light, but he knew he wasn't fooling his friend. Garcia knew him too well—had known what that other time had cost him.

Garcia looked away. "Like I said. It's none of my business."

Layne woke slowly. Moving carefully, she winced as a stab of pain shot through her arm. God, she felt terrible! She lay facing the wall and as she rolled over on her back she found herself staring at a broad chest covered by a light blue shirt. Her glance traveled upward until she was staring into turquoise-colored eyes. He blocked out most of the overhead light.

"Hello, Layne Tyler." His drawl was low and lazy and his eyes took on a new sparkle.

"Hello," she answered, wondering if his smile melted all women's hearts within a hundred-mile radius or just hers.

"How are you feeling?"

"Like I was run over by a Mack truck."

His laugh was deep, husky. "It's a good thing you're hard as nails."

"Oh, yeah? Someone forgot to mention that to me."

The doctor chose that moment to come in. Nodding to Brant, he walked over to the foot of Layne's bed, picked up a chart and read it. "Good morning, young lady. How are you today?"

"I've been better," Layne replied. She'd always felt uncomfortable around doctors. She couldn't even remember this one's name.

"I'll step outside." Brant turned to leave.

"No, no, it's all right, you can stay." The doctor moved to the side of the bed and checked her arm. "You're lucky the bullet went straight through, otherwise we'd have had to dig it out. But let's keep you overnight, just in case."

"Just in case what?" Layne asked, suddenly wary.

"You've been running a slight fever. I want to make sure there's no infection and that you don't have any kind of negative reaction to the medication." He peered at her through horn-rimmed glasses, smiled and attempted to put her at ease. "Don't worry. By tomorrow you'll feel better, then we can kick you out and give this bed to someone who really needs it." He gave her a fatherly pat on her hand. "Try to get some rest. I'll check back later."

"Doctor, is that really necessary? I mean, can't you give me some pills or something and send me home?"

"Is there anyone at home who can take care of you?"

She shook her head. "No, but I can take care of myself."

"Any children who need baby-sitting?"

Again, she shook her head.

"Any pets?"

"Not even a goldfish," she replied with a rueful smile.

Brant, who had been staring out the window, turned to regard her speculatively.

"Well, then," the doctor said, "just think of this as a little vacation."

With another fatherly pat on her good shoulder, he left the room.

Brant returned to stand beside her bed. "Looks like you're grounded for the night."

"Yes, it appears so, doesn't it?" Her eyes were big and solemn.

"You ought to take advantage of it and get some rest."

"I suppose."

"Well, I guess I ought to let you rest up, then."

Layne liked his drawl.

"Brant?"

"Yes?" He stared, remembering how soft and vulnerable she'd felt in his arms last night.

"Thank you . . . for saving my life. I know you put yours on the line and I'm grateful." For a heart-stopping moment, they gazed into each other's eyes. His eyes looked as if they were capable of seeing straight into her soul. Layne wondered why she always reacted so strongly when she was around this particular man.

"You're welcome." He smiled again. "I guess I'm just a sucker for a pretty lady." He felt the same pull of attraction between them that he'd felt last night.

Then he remembered why he was here.

"I've got something for you." He fished the keys out of his jeans and gave them to her.

"My keys!"

"You dropped them when you fell."

"You mean when you tackled me, don't you?" she said with a half-amused grin.

He looked uncomfortable. "Sorry about that. I didn't mean to be so rough."

"There's nothing to be sorry about. You did a brave thing. If you hadn't, I wouldn't be here talking to you right now. A few more inches and—" She shuddered.

He stared at her face so drawn and pale, her eyes deeply shadowed. Somehow it became important for him not to upset her. He couldn't form the words to ask the questions he'd come to ask. Just this once, he would make an exception. He wouldn't question her about Dan.

Brant shifted his weight from one foot to the other.

Layne shifted in bed.

They studied each other with the same wary speculation—like two people who were attracted to each other but couldn't do a damn thing about it.

"Get some rest," he ordered. "I'll be back later." He got as far as the door and turned. "By the way, Paul sends you his love." There was a mischievous twinkle in his eyes.

"I'll just bet," she said smiling.

Layne watched him walk away. Why hadn't he questioned her about Dan? Was it professional courtesy? Or something else? She had read concern in his gaze. It startled her to realize she had hoped for more. Brant was a dangerously attractive man—a brave one, too. If only he weren't after her brother... She forced the thought away. Her first concern had to be for Dan, his safety, his future.

She stared at the empty doorway for a long time before turning her head away to survey the empty room. It was decorated in pure gloom and the silence loomed like a heavy mist.

She tried to relax, but it became more difficult by the minute as she struggled with uncertainty. Her life had revolved around her work and her work had kept her busy. But here she had too much time to think. What if she'd been killed? What would people have remembered about her?

She searched her soul. Would they have praised her professional accomplishments and contributions? Probably. But would they remember how much she loved frozen yogurt, walking in a soft spring rain or watching *Casablanca* over and over?

No, they wouldn't, because she'd never let anyone get that close to her. Getting close meant opening your heart to pain. Losing her family had taught her that.

Her glance strayed to a potted plant on the night table, a gift from a co-worker she barely knew. Right now the plant looked beautiful, but once she got it home... She sniffed. She couldn't even manage to keep her plants alive. They all died sooner or later.

Her thoughts returned to Brant. For a while she had forgotten that he planned to arrest her brother. He'd acted like an old friend—had actually appeared to be concerned about her. They were two people who had shared a harrowing experience—who now shared a tangible bond between them. She owed him her life. She sighed. *Fool*, she thought, *he's just buttering you up to make you more amenable—to use you to get to Dan—using the old "get her to trust me" trick. He thinks you know where Dan is.* She shifted irritably in bed.

Another thought nagged at her. Who had shot her? And why? It was rumored that Salinas had gotten wealthy on mob money. If that were true, then where did Dan fit into all this? Had someone meant to kill her? Then again, wasn't it possible that Brant could have been the target? After all, she'd been shot when he had tackled her, so maybe whoever shot her had really been aiming at Brant. In his line of work, he was certain to make some enemies.

She recalled the doctor's words. He had asked her if there was anyone at home who would be waiting for her. No, she thought dejectedly. No one. Oh, she'd had Dan—for a while—and it had taken all her energy and patience to raise a teenager after the death of her parents. And when they died the pain had been more than she could bear, but she'd had to go on for Dan's sake.

What in the world was wrong with her? Why did she feel such blind, unreasonable melancholy? It wasn't like her to feel sorry for herself. Good God, she was acting like a crotchety old woman. She half smiled, then sighed, feeling silly. And scared. It must be the painkiller the nurse had given her. Her eyes burned. Damn it, she wouldn't cry.

But it was already too late.

Shortly before noon Layne received several visitors from work who wished her a speedy recovery. They all wanted her to hurry back to the office because—they added jokingly—they didn't want to take on any more extra cases.

When the office receptionist marched through the door, Layne knew she was in trouble. Marge Bern loved to talk. A tall, willowy woman in her late forties, Marge was heavily into astrology. And from the look on her face, Layne knew she was about to hear a lecture.

"What a terrible tragedy, Layne. How are you feeling?" she asked, plopping herself down on the chair next to the bed.

Like I've been shot. "Better, thank you, Marge." Layne steeled herself for what was coming.

"Well, I wish you'd listened to me. Mark my word, you're heading for some troubled times."

Great! That was all she needed to hear today.

Marge leaned back in her chair, settling in like a cozy old blanket. "Now, let's see—" she said and reached up with a forefinger to push her glasses higher up on the bridge of her nose "—you're a Virgo, right?"

Layne nodded.

For the next hour Marge treated Layne to a brief astrology lesson as she explained how the movement of each planet through each sign coincided with a specific kind of event here on earth. Furthermore, she added, last night there had been a lunar eclipse, which always brought about ominous occurrences. In short, Marge said, expect the unexpected.

Layne yawned. Marge ignored the hint and continued to talk for another thirty minutes.

By the time Marge left, Layne wanted to hide under the covers, just in case someone else showed up. She reached for the remote control on the night table, aimed it at the TV and settled deeper under the bed covers.

The screen lit up with a shampoo commercial. She switched to another channel.

And froze.

The station flashed a photograph of Dan across the screen. An instant later a photo of Layne zapped in beside Dan's. The camera zoomed in for a close-up. Then a reporter came on to talk about the shooting, saying that Layne was in the hospital, listed in critical condition. *Critical condition!* But how? When had the press found out about the incident? And why in the world had that reporter said she was in critical condition? He added that Layne had been shot after meeting with her brother, whom police believed to be linked with the murder of Michael Salinas. He went on to enumerate Salinas's charitable contributions to the community.

Her hands clenched in anger. That miserable cop and that...that...cowboy had done this! They had given a statement to the press. She sat up—too quickly—and clenched her teeth while she waited for the throbbing in her arm to subside.

Damn him! She should have known.

The press was having a field day.

Layne was still fuming an hour later when her boss, Russell Maxwell, stormed through the door. At six feet, he had the thick frame of a football linebacker and distinguished salt-and-pepper hair.

He frowned. "What the hell happened?"

Layne recounted the incident as Russell paced slowly back and forth at the foot of her bed. It was a compulsive habit he had when he wanted to think. When she finished talking he stopped and looked at her through dark, hypnotic eyes and asked her the same question Brant had asked Garcia only a few hours before. "You think it was one of the kids?"

"I don't know," she replied. "But I wish I knew why that reporter lied. Half the world probably thinks I'm dying. If Dan has seen that newscast he's going to be worried half out of his mind. And when I get my hands on that reporter I'm going to wring his scrawny neck!"

"Easy, Layne. You're gonna hurt that arm. Just lean back and relax."

She fell back against the pillow and stared anxiously at the ceiling. "My, God, that's all I've *been* doing! I want to get out of here—now!"

"You can't. So simmer down."

"Russ, what do you know about the Salinas murder?"

He ran his hand through his hair. "We're waiting on a police report, but those damn people are taking their sweet time about it. I'll send one of my men over there on Monday."

"Send *me*. I want to go," she pleaded.

He waved her request away. "You know I can't do that, Layne. Your brother's a suspect. As far as you're concerned everything related to the investigation is a conflict of interest."

Layne's expression was grim. "I have to find him. Last night Dan ran away from a Texas Ranger. You know people are going to assume he's guilty."

"Maybe. But the best thing you can do right now is to get better and you can't do that by worrying yourself to death. Are you eating?"

"Yes." She didn't want to talk about food.

"That's good, 'cause you're already too thin. Get some rest, Layne. We'll discuss this later." He turned to go.

"Russ?"

He paused halfway to the door and turned around.

"My brother didn't kill that man."

He stared at her for a moment, his eyes intent and solemn. "I hope not, sweetheart. For your sake, I hope not."

When Brant walked in her room that evening, Layne didn't even try to disguise her annoyance.

She faced him accusingly. "It didn't take you long to sing to the press, did it?"

He gave her a long, level stare. Gone was the concern in his eyes, the gentleness he'd shown her earlier. He now looked like a man with a purpose. "I didn't give out any information to the press."

Layne wasn't convinced. "Then who did? My God, we were out in the middle of nowhere! Who else could've known?"

Brant shrugged. "I don't know." He stood beside the bed.

Color surged to her cheeks. "What do you mean, you don't know? It had to be someone at police headquarters. Someone you told."

"Not necessarily," Brant replied. "When you were brought to the hospital I made sure you were taken care of right away. The waiting room was filled with the usual Friday night derelicts. Maybe someone recognized you. Hell, it's possible you even prosecuted one or two of them at some time."

She frowned. "Maybe. But if you didn't give out any information, then who did? It had to have been someone who knew I was meeting Dan last night. How else could that reporter have known?"

"They have their ways," Brant answered. "The creep who shot you could've called him. Maybe the guy followed us from Juan's and got his jollies by shooting you, then wanted to read about himself in the newspaper. Who knows? It's happened before."

"But not to me," she almost shouted. "And everything at this point is purely conjecture. I deal in facts and I want answers!"

He could see the rise and fall of her breasts under the covers. "So do I and I'd like to start with a few questions of my own. Can you think of anyone who'd want to shoot you?"

She thought a moment. "No, no one."

"Are you sure? How about a jealous lover?"

"Yes, I'm sure and, no, there's no jealous lover."

"Then how about a boyfriend?" he prompted.

There was a starched stiffness in her manner. "I do date someone, but he'd hardly get angry enough to kill me." She thought of Travis. They had dated off and on for about six months. Even though he'd wanted more out of the relationship, Layne had shied away from any lasting commitment.

"That's what other victims have said before, but it happens." Brant's mouth twisted in wry humor.

"I think I'm a pretty good judge of character." Her shrewd eyes pinned him. "Besides, Travis is out of town right now. We're good friends and we enjoy each other's company. Why, we've never even had an argument!"

Brant raised an eyebrow at that. "Sounds boring. How about someone you've prosecuted? Someone who would like to get even with you—if not the man himself, then maybe one of his relatives?''

She took a deep breath and let it out slowly. "I don't know. It's possible, I suppose, but no one has threatened me or anything."

"What about someone who knows your brother and who might be angry enough at him to try and get even by hurting you?"

"I haven't met too many of Dan's friends since he enrolled in college. I stay quite busy with work." She felt a stab of guilt. Hearing herself say she'd been too busy to talk to Dan or his friends made her sound somehow cold, uncaring. She swallowed painfully. "Why would someone Dan knows want to shoot me?"

His face was thoughtful. "A number of reasons. Your brother could be mixed up in narcotics or gambling debts."

"But why me? Why not go after Dan?"

"It's simple. He's not available and you are. You happen to be a closer target at the moment. It could be someone's way of getting the message across to Dan."

"Do you think one of the boys in that car shot me?"

He shrugged. "Hard to say. It was too dark to get a close look. I don't have enough information to go on right now. All I have is the color and make of the car. I checked to see if any vehicle with that description had been reported stolen, but had no luck there. It's possible someone else shot you and the boys just happened to get in the way."

"Why are you so sure it was me they were after?" she argued. "After all, since you're a law-enforcement officer, I bet you have an enemy or two hanging around somewhere." Her arm began to throb painfully. She reached up and carefully moved her arm in the sling, trying to make it more comfortable.

"If the sniper had been out to get me instead, he could've done it any other time and under better conditions." He shook his head. "No, I think *you're* the target. That's why I'm posting a guard outside your door tonight."

She raised her head and looked into his eyes. "Is the guard supposed to keep me safely in or keep an eye out for my brother?"

"Both," he admitted. "I'm not taking the chance that some creep is going to finish what he started. I want you safe."

Her brows drew together in a frown. "You don't really expect Dan to show up here, do you? This place is too public."

"You don't expect him to stay away once he finds out you've been shot, do you?"

She looked away from his probing gaze.

"I didn't think so," he said.

"And that's what you're counting on, isn't it?" Her voice was barely a whisper.

His eyes were as impersonal as an undertaker's. "If he's in the area, I'll find him."

She clenched her fist under the covers. Her glance traveled to the badge pinned to his shirt, then lifted to stare into his eyes. "With all due respect, Brant, go to hell!"

"I've been there, Layne." He tipped his hat. "See you tomorrow."

She sat up straighter. "I won't be here. I'm leaving the hospital."

"I know. I'm taking you home."

"There's no need," she answered quickly. "My car's here."

He stopped at the doorway and smiled. "No, it isn't. I dropped it off at your house just before I brought the keys over."

''Someone else can take me home.''

It was too late. He'd already walked out the door and she didn't want to shout.

Smug bastard. She'd show him! She wouldn't be here when he showed up tomorrow. He could search for her all over the hospital, but it would be in vain. By that time she'd be happily perched on her couch at home.

She leaned back and closed her eyes. Only then did she remember what he'd said, about already having been to hell.

She wondered what he meant.

Brant's boots clicked down the corridor as he made his way to the elevator. A priest passed him going in the opposite direction and Brant nodded in respect.

He pushed the elevator button and thought about what he'd said to Layne. He'd been to hell all right. Twice. When his Dad had been killed, and much later, when he'd been on a case similar to this one. With the first tragedy, he'd been consumed by guilt; with the second, betrayal.

He and Layne weren't so different after all. She'd had the early responsibility of raising her brother, while he had been left with the care of his mother and younger sister, Maggie. He couldn't blame Layne for trying to help her brother, but he also couldn't let his personal feelings get in the way of arresting Dan. And he didn't want to be attracted to her any more than he already was.

He had to wrap up this case fast—before Thanksgiving.

Brant felt the holiday season hovering over him like a black cloud, wrapping him up in memories and regrets. And guilt.

His Dad had been killed the day before Thanksgiving. Brant sighed, dreading the thought of going home this year, but no matter how hard he tried to stay away the pull of his family was too strong.

He thought of Layne again. Why couldn't life be simple? He could just go up to her and say, *Hey, I like you and I think you like me, so why don't we get together?* But things were never that simple. After this case was over, he'd never see her again.

The elevator door opened and he stepped in.

At least she's tucked in safely for the night, he thought.

Layne lay in the hospital bed vowing that when she left tomorrow her first priority would be to find Dan and prove his innocence. With that goal fixed firmly in her mind, she reached over and picked up a paperback book from the nightstand. One of the female attorneys had left it earlier. Layne glanced at the cover of the romance novel. A man and woman embraced each other while they stared seductively into each other's eyes. Layne studied the hero—tall, dark and handsome. Just like Brant.

Settling herself more comfortably under the covers, she began to read. A few minutes later she was so absorbed in the story she didn't hear the door open.

Nor did she see the visitor until he stood beside her bed.

Startled, she jerked her head up and found herself staring at a priest. He was of medium height, with gray hair tapering neatly to his collar. He had a pleasant face half-hidden behind thick, round glasses. The black clerical suit he wore outlined a medium frame.

As though it were an everyday occurrence, the priest leaned over and kissed Layne on her cheek. When he straightened, he looked down at her and smiled.

Chapter 4

Clutching the sheet tighter to her chest, Layne forced an expression of mild curiosity to her features as she watched the priest remove his thick glasses.

Suddenly her heart skipped a hopeful beat.

She was peering into eyes the same shade of green as her own.

"Dan?" Her voice shook.

"Laynie," he whispered. "Are you all right?"

"My God, it *is* you." Her breath came out in a sigh of relief. "Oh, Dan, I've been so worried. Where have you been? What on earth—"

"Shh, not so loud, sis." Glancing toward the door he placed a warning finger to his mouth, then sat down on the bed and wrapped his arms around her, taking care not to hurt her injured arm.

Layne choked back tears and squeezed him affectionately, not wanting to let him go. She closed her eyes, recalling the day their parents and older brother had died. She and Dan had held each other, crying through the night. Afterward they had pledged an oath to love and protect each other forever. For so long after that she'd felt totally responsible for Dan. So much so that she was now suddenly, desperately afraid something would happen to him. And she couldn't bear it if she lost him.

Dan leaned back to look at her. A shadow of alarm touched his face. "What happened to you, Laynie? When I saw you on TV and that reporter said you'd been shot— God, I didn't know what to think."

"I'm still not sure. One minute I was walking to my car, the next, I'd been shot. But I'm all right, really, Dan. I'd rather talk about you."

He stood up and looked down at her. "I'm sorry, Laynie."

"For worrying me to death? You should be," she chastised, blinking back tears.

"For running out on you when you needed me."

"Why did you? I've been half out of my mind with worry."

"I knew you would be. That's why I had to see you, to make sure you're okay." His eyes looked pained. "Look, I don't have much time, but you have to believe me—I didn't kill him."

Her heart went out to him. "I never thought you did." He pulled a chair up to the bed and sat down. Facing the doorway, he spoke in hushed tones. "I saw Salinas the night he died, but I went to see him so I could tell him I wanted out of a deal."

"What kind of a deal?" Her head began to throb.

"I owed him money. He held my marker for a gambling debt. When I asked him to give me more time, he told me there was another way I could pay off the debt."

"Oh, Dan. Why didn't you come to *me?* I would've helped you."

His jaw set in a hard line. "I got into this mess on my own, sis. I made up my mind to get out of it the same way. Besides, I didn't want you to know I'd been gambling again."

Tears shimmered in her eyes and she fought to hold them back. "Just how did he propose you pay off the debt?"

"He said all I had to do was deliver something for him from time to time."

She frowned. "Deliver what?"

He shook his head. "I don't know exactly—a small suitcase, but I don't know what was in it. I delivered it to a private airstrip. The one out by the old Danvers farm. But I swear, I only did it once. That's why I went to see him that night. I was going to tell him I didn't feel right about the whole thing and I wasn't going to do it any more."

"What did he say?" Her expression was grim.

"That's just it, I never had a chance to tell him. When I got there he was on the floor, already dead. Then someone shouted and I got scared and ran."

"Who did you deliver the suitcase to? What did he look like?" she prompted.

"Salinas didn't give me a name, but the man was thin and bald and when he took the suitcase from me he jotted something down in a small notebook."

Layne nodded, making a mental note. "All right, we'll check it out. I'll call Russell and—"

"No. You can't," he said quickly. "I didn't come here to give myself up. I just wanted to make sure you were okay. As soon as I'm settled somewhere I'll call you. I promise."

Anguish tore at her heart. She was frightened for him. "Dan, you're in a lot of trouble. You have to give yourself up. I'll help you—you know that, don't you?"

There was a slight hesitation in his eyes before it was gone and he shook his head ruefully. "Yeah, I know. But think, Laynie, I owed him money I couldn't pay back and someone, a servant I think, saw me there that night. Do you honestly think anyone's going to believe I'm innocent?" He stood up abruptly, crossed over to the window and peered four stories down into the street.

"I believe you." Layne closed her eyes, feeling utterly miserable.

"Thanks. You're probably the only one who does." There was bitterness in his tone as he stared out the window. Several seconds ticked by, then he asked, "Is the Ranger giving you a hard time?"

"Nothing I can't handle," she lied.

"I've really screwed things up royally this time, haven't I?"

"We'll get through this, Dan—together." She waited, hoping he would agree.

He opened the blinds wider for a better view of the street below. "Remember when we used to go into that church across the street, Laynie? I could never sit still for long. I'd fidget so much until finally I'd get into trouble with Mom. But you always stuck up for me." Dan swallowed, his voice pained.

"I remember." Layne fought to hold back tears. Maternal pride swelled within her. "Give yourself up, Dan. If you keep running you're only going to make things worse."

He turned to face her. "The situation is already worse. You don't understand."

"You're right, I don't." Pleading hadn't worked, so she resorted to gentle bullying. "All I know is that what you're doing is wrong and dangerous. Why are you being so stubborn? I can't believe that you'd turn tail and run. If you're innocent—and I know you are—then we'll prove it. But I'm not going to let you run.'' Her eyes met his squarely. ''You know all I have to do is call out to that guard outside this door and—''

''There's more.''

Anxiety squeezed Layne's heart. ''What do you mean, there's more?''

''I think I'm being set up.''

Layne's shoulders tensed and blood rushed to her face. ''A setup?''

Dan ran his hand through his hair distractedly. ''For one thing, I happen to show up right after Salinas is killed. Then right away, someone pegs me as his killer.''

''That hasn't been proven. Who else besides Salinas knew you were going to be at his home that night?''

''No one that I know of. And *I* didn't tell anyone. That night I called him from a pay phone, so it had to be someone from his end who knew I was coming over.'' Dan clenched his teeth. ''You know something, Laynie? I'm scared, really scared. But I'm more angry than anything else. Someone's using me. I can feel it.''

Layne's spine tingled. ''Why would someone want to frame you?''

''I don't know.'' He glanced at his watch. ''But I've been here too long already. Are you going to turn me in, Laynie?''

The answer in her eyes was obvious even before she shook her head, too miserable to say anything.

''I'd better go.'' He reached down, squeezed her hand affectionately, then picked up the phone on the night table and dialed a number. When he was through speaking, he replaced the receiver and turned to look out the window again. On the sidewalk a man's unmistakable tall figure stood under a dim streetlight. The Texas Ranger. A second later Dan focused on what he'd been waiting to see—Father Joseph hurrying across the street.

Dan studied the Ranger a while longer. Finally he reached for the cord and closed the blinds.

Layne's fear for Dan deepened as she saw the hopelessness in his eyes. She could feel his anxiety as if it were her own. She wanted to rise and push up through the layers of her frustration, to go with him and prove to the world that he could never do such a thing as take another man's life.

After leaving Layne's room Brant had positioned himself outside, close to the hospital entrance. At the moment he watched several people enter the church across the street. Others came out and headed in his direction. He moved to one side. Switching his gaze to the parking lot, he squinted through the oncoming darkness. A light ground fog was already beginning to swirl around him.

But he was in no hurry to leave. Brant knew it was just a matter of time—as soon as Dan found out his sister had been shot he wouldn't be able to stay away. The question was, would he make his move tonight? Would his concern for Layne make him careless enough to show up now? Or would he wait until she had left the hospital tomorrow? The policeman guarding Layne's door had been given strict orders to stop anyone who attempted to enter her room. Brant knew that any doctor other than her own would be asked to prove his or her identity. He was taking no chances.

He watched several more pedestrians leave the hospital. Some walked to their cars, others hurried to enter the church across the street. With the exception of a priest who hurried across the street toward the hospital, everything looked normal.

Watching that priest reminded Brant of many a Sunday morning when he and Paul had sat on simple wooden pews and faced an austere altar with a large crucifix on the wall. For a time they'd even been altar boys. Brant hadn't been to church in a long time. Not since his father's death ten years ago. But, then, his line of work didn't leave him much time to do anything.

He'd been raised in the shadow of a lawman's badge. Having been the son and grandson of Texas Rangers, it was only natural he would follow in their footsteps. Hell, he'd probably spent as much time in a jail as some of the men he'd arrested. As a youngster, he had spent many hours with his dad in the jail building.

Being a Ranger restricted your social life. He remembered too many mornings when his dad said he would be home for supper but didn't make it back for days. It had been on one of those occasions that they'd argued. Just before Thanksgiving.

His attention was drawn to a couple who walked by and looked at him curiously. A little girl of about three walked between them, her head capped by a mass of ringlets the same rich, glowing auburn shade as Layne's. She smiled timidly at Brant. He returned her smile and was surprised to feel a stab of longing. He loved kids. He would be thirty-seven in November, and he wondered if he'd ever settle down long enough to sire any.

He mentally shook himself. He didn't intend to stand here and reminisce any longer; he had a decision to make. Should he leave or go back inside the hospital and wait?

Straightening to his full height, he started toward the parking lot. As he stepped onto the sidewalk his eyes were drawn to a corner window located on the fourth floor.

Layne's room.

His body tensed. A shadow stirred behind the blinds just before someone closed them. Frowning, he wondered if it had been Layne.

Did he want to take that chance?

Even as he was deciding, his long, muscular legs were already taking the concrete steps two at a time. By the time he reached Layne's room he was slightly out of breath from his run up four flights of stairs.

As he burst through the door two pairs of eyes looked up in surprise; one guilty, the other clearly startled.

Brant's shuttered blue gaze slid to Layne before focusing on the priest. "I suggest you step away from that bed, padre, and walk over to that wall."

The priest's ascetic features looked puzzled but he complied.

Layne's heart pounded erratically. Her face, however, remained impassive. "Did you forget something, Mr. Wade? Or are you in need of prayer?"

"Hardly," Brant muttered as he walked up to the priest.

"What a shame," she said tonelessly. "I'm sure Father Joseph would be only too happy to hear your confession."

He flinched, then there was a faint chill in his manner. "On the contrary, Layne, I'm here to listen to yours."

Her gaze was clear and steady. "Then I'm afraid you'll be disappointed."

"That's a matter of opinion," he replied, watching the priest closely. "Father Joseph, is it? Are you sure it isn't Father Daniel?" Brant waited for some reaction. He got one, but it wasn't the one he expected. Father Joseph's shaggy white brows drooped down over puzzled blue eyes.

Brant stepped closer to the priest. "Let's see if this is real, shall we?" He reached out and jerked on his beard.

At Father Joseph's yelp of pain and expression of indignant astonishment, Brant drew his hand back. Not since the age of ten, when he'd gotten caught eating all of his mother's brownies just before one of her bridge parties, had he felt so contrite. He amended that to penitent as he stared into Father Joseph's stern features.

Brant held out his hands in a placating gesture. "I'm sorry. I thought you were someone else."

Layne attempted to hide a smile. "Are we discovering a fetish of yours?"

Brant ignored her. "Carlos!" he bellowed.

"Yes, sir?"

Brant whipped around to face the guard. "I left strict orders that no one was to enter this room. How do you explain him?" Brant gestured toward Father Joseph.

Carlos shrugged his stocky shoulders. "He told me that someone had called and asked him to hurry here. I thought the lady was gravely ill."

"I said *no one* was to enter this room."

"Perhaps I can explain," Father Joseph spoke up.

Brant turned to face the priest. "I'm listening."

"I received a call from one of the doctors here. He informed me it was a matter of life-and-death and that I should hurry to this room number. Naturally I assumed it was to give this patient her last rites. What else was I to think?"

"Who called you?"

"Dr. Murdock," Father Joseph answered easily.

Brant's scowl became directed at Carlos. "I don't suppose it occurred to you to ask him for an ID."

Carlos frowned. "No, sir. He looked legit to me."

"Excuse me," Father Joseph interrupted. "I have other people to see. May I leave?" he asked quietly.

"Of course. Just one more question, Father."

"Yes?" Father Joseph appeared relieved.

"How long have you been here?"

There was an uncomfortable silence as three people waited to hear his answer.

Glare from the fluorescent light above reflected off Father Joseph's glasses. "Not long. About five minutes, I suppose."

"It was more like fifteen minutes or so, wasn't it Father?" Carlos innocently corrected.

Father Joseph hesitated. His gaze was kind as it touched Layne for a moment before switching to Brant. "It's possible, I suppose. I'm afraid I'm not very good at keeping track of time."

Brant's face grew pensive. "Thank you, Father. That will be all."

Layne closed her eyes with a mixture of relief and nervousness. When she opened them it was to see Father Joseph gracefully withdraw from the room.

Brant turned to Carlos. "Call security and have them check out the exits."

Carlos nodded and hurried out of the room.

But there was to be no such reprieve for Layne. Brant swung around to confront her accusingly. "Was Dan in this room tonight?"

Her smile was guarded. "And here I thought you came back because you couldn't stay away from me."

"I'm in no mood for humor, Layne. Who else was here tonight?"

She shrugged. "Father Joseph, of course."

His rock-hard expression made her nervous. She feigned an air of indifference, but her heart was beating like a bongo drum. She wondered if he could hear it.

"Look at me, Layne," his husky voice commanded. Like a petulant child she obeyed. "Was anyone else in this room tonight?" he repeated.

Her mind was busy with the potential ramifications of what she was about to do.

She was about to lie.

She shook her head. "No. No one else." She swallowed as the lie settled like deadweight in the pit of her stomach.

Those turquoise-colored eyes now shone like cold shards of blue glass. Layne could almost feel them weighing her response and deciding on her guilt, swift and sure. She forced herself not to squirm under his scrutiny.

Brant stared at her for a long moment, then to her relief he walked over to the window and peered out.

"Did Father Joseph stand by this window?" he asked softly, opening the blinds.

"No." Too late, she remembered. Had Brant seen Dan close those blinds earlier. "No," she repeated, "but *I* did."

"And what did you see down there?" He kept his back to her.

Layne paused for a moment. "A street. People walking. And a church." She waited for his reaction.

There was none. Instead he walked over to the bed and looked down at her. "Does your arm still hurt?"

The gentleness in his eyes surprised her. "A little," she answered, watching him suspiciously.

"Then you'd better get some rest." His eyes studied her mouth, then lit with masculine interest as they lowered to her breasts.

Layne became overwhelmingly aware that the sheet had slipped down to her waist, exposing the thin, sheer gown and her firm, uptilted breasts beneath. The gown had been a gift from two assistant D.A.s. Layne had decided to wear it instead of the uncomfortable, starchy hospital gown. She had worn it with the certainty that no one else would see it hidden beneath the covers.

Suddenly shy under his steady gaze, her first impulse was to yank the sheet up to her chin. But of course she wouldn't. Her pride wouldn't allow her to show any emotion in front of this man. She managed a small tentative smile. "Thanks, I will," she muttered, sliding down into the bed, then pulling the covers up to her neck.

When Carlos returned a moment later Layne could hear him whispering something to Brant. Then they were gone. Brant hadn't said goodbye. Layne closed her eyes. Not only did her arm throb painfully but she felt sick to her stomach as she struggled with uncertainty and guilt. She hated lying to Brant. After all, he had saved her life. She owed him something for that, didn't she?

Loyalty, mixed with desperation, had caused her to lie— an act that, no matter how involuntary it had been, was still wrong. She was now an accessory after the fact. And if Brant Wade discovered the truth she was certain no amount of excuses or tears would sway him from handcuffing her and hauling her carcass off to jail.

She wanted to forget, to drift off to sleep and wake up tomorrow morning to find this whole episode had just been a terrible nightmare.

She lay there, drifting, and in one of those lucid moments she sensed someone standing near her bed. She opened her eyes and saw Brant watching her.

"I came back to say good-night," he said quietly.

"Good night," she whispered and her eyes closed again. Maybe if she kept them closed he would turn off the light and tiptoe out of the room.

She waited.

The tiptoe sound never came. Instead she heard something heavy being scraped against the floor.

Her eyes shot open.

Brant had dragged a small sofa over from the wall, setting it down close to the bed. He'd left only enough room for her to slide off the bed in case she needed to go to the bathroom during the night. He tossed his Stetson on the night table and sat down on the sofa.

She shot up and winced. "What are you doing?"

"What does it look like I'm doing?" There was the faintest trace of mockery in his voice.

Her eyes narrowed. "It looks like you're getting comfortable for the night."

"Congratulations. You have great powers of observation."

"It doesn't take a genius to figure it out. You gave yourself away when you took off your boots." A warning cloud settled over Layne's features as she pressed a button by her bed.

A minute later a nurse walked into the room. "What's going on in here?" She stared at Layne with cold gray eyes.

Layne's mouth curved into a tight smile. She'd have Brant Wade thrown out of her room on his ear in no time. And here was a nurse who looked like she would be capable of doing just that. She was built like a drill sergeant, with a voice to match.

"What are the rules about someone spending the night in my room? A nonmember of my family and almost a complete stranger?" Layne asked in her most professional voice.

The nurse looked over the top of her spectacles at Layne, then swung over to look at Brant, traveling down the length of him and back. "Is he the one you're talking about?" she asked, gesturing toward Brant.

"The very one." Layne waited for the stern-faced nurse to evict Brant from her room, her imagination ensnared not so much in *how* the nurse was going to do it but *how many* people it would take to get the job done.

The nurse drew herself up to her full six feet and planted both hands on her hips. "Honey, my advice to you is to thank your lucky stars he wants to stay. Here, let me check your pulse," she said, picking up Layne's wrist and holding it in a hammerlock.

"Nurse—"

"Call me Agnes, honey." She pointed to the name badge pinned to her white jacket. "Your pulse is sure racing to high heaven."

Layne snatched her hand out of Agnes's meaty grasp. "Look, Agnes, I want this man thrown out. If *you* can't do it, then I want somebody who can." Her rapier glance settled over Brant, taking in his lazy stance.

"Why? Who is he?" Agnes demanded to know.

Brant's lips twitched. "I'm a Texas Ranger, ma'am. My name's Brant Wade and I'm just doing my job." His drawl was slow and lazy and as his eyes crinkled at the corners the grooves on either side of his mouth deepened. He reached out and clasped Agnes's large hand in his.

Agnes, who was almost as tall as Brant, practically swooned when he shook her hand. It was sickening how some women fawned all over tall, dark and handsome men, Layne thought in disgust.

Agnes smiled. "Humph, far be it from me to argue with the law. Are you planning to arrest her?"

Layne could have sworn she detected a hopeful slur in Agnes's voice just before she plopped a thermometer in Layne's mouth and picked up her wrist to feel her pulse again.

Brant looked at Layne thoughtfully. After a slight pause, he replied, "Nope. But she *is* under my protection."

A snort came from the bed, but neither Agnes nor Brant paid any attention.

"Well," Agnes said. "I guess you have your reasons." She slid the thermometer out of Layne's mouth and studied it.

Layne took a deep breath. "I meant what I said. I want him thrown out. Get the doctor in here. Right now!"

Agnes stared at Layne as though she had sprouted horns.

"Well, Agnes?" Brant's stance was relaxed. "What are you going to do?"

Agnes's tight expression settled into a smile. "I'm going to get you a pillow, that's what." To Layne, she muttered, "I'll be back later when your pulse has lowered."

If Layne hadn't been so angry she would have viewed the whole thing as comical. She should get up this very moment, go find a doctor and demand her rights. But it was late and she was bone weary. In just a few more hours it would be daylight and she could go home.

She glanced at Brant. He was attempting to fold his large frame on the small sofa. She almost laughed out loud when he nearly fell on the floor but sobered immediately when Agnes turned off the light, leaving them in total darkness.

"Y'all sleep tight." Agnes chuckled on her way out.

Layne realized with a mixture of embarrassment and anxiety that she and Brant would be alone in this room all night. He lay close enough to touch her. She found the quiet intimacy disturbing. And yet a part of her wanted to admit that she felt safe with him there.

Funny how the dark seemed to magnify everything. No longer did the scent of disinfectant mixed with antiseptic permeate the air. Now the spiciness of Brant's cologne drifted toward her.

Last night the wail of sirens splitting the air as ambulances raced toward the emergency entrance had kept Layne awake most of the night. Now those same sounds dulled as her senses became highly attuned to the rhythmic rise and fall of Brant's chest each time he took a breath.

From the moment she'd seen him at Juan's leaning against that bar, she'd been strongly attracted to him. There was no denying that he was a very sexy-looking man. But she wouldn't think about that. It would only remind her that there could never be anything between them—not even attraction. But here in the dark, next to him, it was easy for her to imagine him being nice to her. She closed her eyes and wondered how it would feel to lie in the safety of his arms, to press her cheek against his shoulder and to hear his husky drawl whisper words of...

"You know Father Joseph, don't you?"

She jumped as Brant's deep voice intruded into her fantasy.

"What?" she croaked.

"You knew Father Joseph before tonight, didn't you?"

The impact of his words made her stiffen and she shifted nervously.

She wasn't willing to compound the sin of a lie with another.

"Yes. I know him. Dan and I are parishioners of his church." She waited for him to say something. When he didn't, she turned her head toward him—wishing she could see his face.

Silence met her.

And because she was mortified that she'd been thinking about him so intimately, while he'd obviously been busy plotting for a way to trick her into confessing, Layne bit out caustically, "It's bad enough I have to endure your company for the night, but do I also have to suffer through a conversation? Don't you have someone to go home to?"

He rolled over on his side toward her. "Nope. I'm all yours for the night." There was a pause before he muttered, "Who knows? You may talk in your sleep."

Chapter 5

The man was on his second helping of *cabrito* when the phone rang. Before it had pealed a second time he picked it up.

"Yes?"

"She just left the hospital."

"Very well. Keep an eye on her."

"She's not alone. The Texas Ranger is with her."

"Then I suggest you use extra caution. She's our ticket to locating her brother. When he's found, find out how much he knows."

The connection was broken and he turned his attention once more to his lunch. Picking up his glass of wine, he stared at the crimson liquid and sighed.

Dan Tyler was an annoyance he couldn't afford.

But, then, he could pay little men to take care of his little problems.

* * *

Layne inserted the key into the lock and turned it. The door opened into a tiled foyer.

"Thanks for bringing me home." She stood there for a moment, wondering whether to invite him in. She had to admit the whole situation was awkward. On the one hand, he had saved her life by putting his own on the line; and on the other, he'd made it abundantly clear he planned to arrest her brother. That alone was a very good reason for not asking him to stay.

Good manners finally forced her to make a decision. "Would you like to come in?"

He stood on the threshold looking down at her and for a second she thought he would say no. Instead, without offering any comment, he walked past her into the foyer.

Really, Layne thought, if this was any indication of his manners, no wonder she didn't feel comfortable around him.

Slipping past him into the small living room, she threw her purse down on the couch and continued on to the kitchen. "Would you like coffee?" she called over her shoulder.

"Sounds great. Thanks."

"Have a seat. It'll only take a minute." She was conscious that he followed close behind.

"Need any help?" he offered.

"No. My shoulder feels a little stiff, but other than that I'm fine," she insisted.

She set to work plugging in the coffeepot, took coffee out of the cupboard and spooned some into the percolator, then filled it with water, all the while sensing that he watched her. The stiffness in her arm made her movements slow and awkward. While she waited for the coffee to brew, Layne turned to look at him. He was leaning against the counter watching her.

"Why did you invite me in?" he asked.

"Why shouldn't I?" she answered smoothly.

He regarded her in amusement. "Maybe it's the feeling I get that you won't be comfortable until you see my backside for the last time."

And what a nice backside it is, Layne thought. She was aware of the tight jeans that cupped his buttocks and clung to his thighs. Again she noticed how big he was. His masculine frame dwarfed her tiny kitchen and looked pitifully out of place against the backdrop of tiny cornflowers set against yellow wallpaper. Something told her she'd better give him his coffee so she could send him on his way.

She cleared her throat. "I must seem ungrateful to you. Thanks for bringing me home...and for saving my life," she muttered with strained cordiality.

There was a negligent shrug of his shoulder. "It's no trouble—and you already thanked me."

There was nothing else of interest she could talk over with him so she turned away. Opening the cabinet door she reached for two cups, but his hand intercepted hers.

"Let me help." His breath fanned her hair as he whispered in her ear.

Layne felt the warmth of his hard, lean body as he leaned over, placing his other hand possessively on the curve of her waist.

"No, really, I can do it," she replied nervously. He had her trapped against the counter. If she backed up her derriere would touch him, and if she turned she would be in his arms.

She clenched the countertop for support and her knees threatened to buckle from under her at the thought of Brant's very male, very sexy body resting so close to hers.

He set the cup down on the counter next to the one she'd just lowered. Slowly she turned to face him.

She stared up at him, mesmerized. A feeling of utter helplessness engulfed her in a way she'd never felt before and she fought for control. She wanted to cry out for him to stop looking at her that way. For a moment she thought he was going to press her back against the counter, halfway hoping he would, then worried about what she'd do if he did. For a tiny instant, as her heart hammered against her chest, Layne tried to blot out every rational reason why she should push him away. She started to lean closer.

"Coffee's ready," he whispered, staring down at her mouth, his voice husky. He'd understood that look of helplessness in her face and he stepped back to allow her to move away.

Relieved to put some distance between them, Layne was caught between gratitude and a keen sense of disappointment as she poured their coffee.

She handed him the cup. "Would you like to sit down?" she asked, looking nowhere in particular.

"Nope. I'd better drink up and run." He raised the cup to his mouth and wondered what it was about this woman that brought him to the brink of anger and desire at the same time. He'd wanted to kiss her just now, but he knew that once he started he wouldn't be able to stop. The best thing for him to do would be to get as far away from her as possible. Yet he couldn't help wishing they'd met under different circumstances.

He drank the rest of his coffee and set the cup on the counter. "Before I leave there's something I want to tell you."

She waited.

"Someone's going to be guarding your home for a few days."

He'd said it so matter-of-factly that it took Layne a moment before she realized his implication. "How long is a few days?"

He shrugged. "We'll see."

Her cheeks turned a dull red as her eyes locked with his. "I don't want anyone near my home."

"It's for your protection."

She scoffed. "Protection, my foot." Anger flashed in her eyes. "I figured you hadn't brought me home out of the kindness of your heart. And last night you stayed at the hospital just in case Dan showed up. You wanted to be there ready to pounce on him the minute he stepped into that room."

His brows drew together in a frown. "My staying in your room last night served a double purpose. You forget I suspected Dan had already been to see you. I don't know why you were shot. Maybe you just got unlucky, but I'm not taking any chances that someone is going to finish what he started."

Her laugh sounded hollow. "Do you really expect me to believe it's because you're worried about *me* that you've gone to all this trouble? Do you honestly think I believe that guard will be there solely for my protection?"

"I don't expect you to believe anything. But think about this." He stood in that arrogant stance, one knee slightly bent, both hands on his hips. "If I were posting a guard out there to watch for Dan, do you think I'd be warning *you* about it?"

Something flickered in her eyes. He stepped closer. "Are you always this suspicious?" he growled softly.

Her chin lifted. "Only when I think I'm being used."

He looked grim. "Lock your door behind me."

He walked away, leaving Layne staring after him.

"Brant?"

He already had his hand on the doorknob and threw her a look over his shoulder. "Yes?"

"Who's going to be my guard? Carlos?"

Her sarcasm was well aimed. His eyes narrowed to twin slits as he regarded her for a long moment. "You know something? I think I liked you better when you were under sedation." He opened the door and walked out.

A faint satisfied smile tugged at the corners of her mouth. For a moment she wondered what it would've been like to have met him under normal circumstances.

Her smile faded. Nothing would have come of it. He was a law-enforcement officer. He put his life on the line every day. And she'd already lost too many people she cared about. She wouldn't add another to the list.

Layne couldn't sleep that night. She paced in front of a large window that took up one wall of her living room and wondered why Dan hadn't called her. She couldn't stand not knowing where he was, what he was doing. A habit of a lifetime couldn't be broken in one night.

By three in the morning, exhausted and drained from worry, she climbed into bed.

Monday was no better. She was afraid to leave the house for fear Dan would phone and she wouldn't be there to take his call.

That night she lay in bed, again suffering in silence and chastising herself. Why hadn't she been more forceful with Dan? Why hadn't she made him give himself up? At least she'd know where he was right now. But what else could she have done? Dan had always been so stubborn. Right now he must be as worried and scared as she was. Torment gnawed at her heart. She couldn't go on like this. She had to do something.

The following morning she made a decision.

She called the D.A.'s office. When Russell Maxwell came on the line, she said, "I need to see you."

He agreed to meet her for lunch.

The hostess led Layne over to a table where Russell already waited. He smiled and stood up to greet her.

Layne's smile was genuine because she liked him. He bent down to give her a peck on the cheek and she became aware that another person sat at the table. When she turned to see who it was her pulse quickened, even as she experienced a mounting sense of betrayal. Damn, what was Brant Wade doing here?

She turned back to Russell. "I hope I'm not intruding. Did you have plans?" Her smile was fixed.

Russell glanced at Brant, then back at Layne. "No, not at all. Brant and I ran into each other a few minutes ago and he, uh, asked us to join him for lunch. I hope you don't mind. You and I can visit afterward." He flashed her another of his famous political smiles.

"I don't mind." Her tone was polite, but inwardly she was seething. Maybe it was because she needed some essential ground on which to stand as a woman. She didn't want any words forced out of her other than those she was willing to part with. Brant Wade had something up his sleeve.

Russell pulled back a chair and she slid into it. The table was round and Layne had no other choice but to sit between the two men. For a moment irritation gnawed at her, as she realized that Brant hadn't stood to greet her. He'd merely nodded.

She picked up the menu and studied it with feigned concentration. She had no appetite. When the waitress came to their table, Layne ordered a salad.

Folding the napkin across her lap, she glanced up and caught Brant studying her intently. His eyes swept over her mockingly.

She wondered why he was here. That bull about running into Russell here accidentally hadn't fooled her for a moment. This restaurant was Russell's favorite and anyone who knew him was aware of that fact. Oh, no, this little gathering had not been accidental.

By the time their food arrived, Layne had run out of places to look. She picked up her fork and began to chew her food slowly. Every now and then her eyes strayed to Brant's face, finding his attention concentrated on her also, and she looked away embarrassed. The food was tasteless. After two more bites she pushed her plate away.

She grew more uncomfortable as she and Russell made polite conversation, discussing a case she'd been working on. She went through the questions and answers mechanically, trying to find a way to make her exit.

This meeting was getting her nowhere.

Her eyes sparkled with anger. Damn it, she hadn't slept well for four nights and she had neither the time nor the inclination to make small talk. She had something important to discuss with Russell and she wasn't leaving until she'd had her say. Brant Wade be damned.

"Russell," she began, leaning forward a little, "I want to work on the investigation. You know which one." She saw him hesitate, probably thinking politics as usual. "Forget everything except how important this case is to me."

Russell sighed. "It's not that easy, Layne. You know why I can't let you handle that investigation."

Her chin came up. "Why not? Other than it being a conflict of interest, I can't think of any other reason why I shouldn't. Besides, I can't stand by and do nothing. I'm going crazy.''

Russell thought a moment. "I know how you feel, Layne. Hell, you're one of the best people I've got, but I just can't let you do it." At her look of appeal, he added, "I know this whole business is hard on you. I'd feel the same way if it was one of my relatives."

Her voice cut sharply across the table. "He's more than a relative. He's my *only* family."

He reached over and placed his hand on top of hers. "I'm aware of that. I want you to know this is nothing personal. I know you wouldn't do anything to jeopardize the case, but the only thing you can do for us now is to call if you hear from Dan. Will you do that?"

"Sure, Russ," she smiled wryly, pulling her hand from his, "but I don't think Mr. Wade here trusts me to do that. I'll tell you what I told him the other day—I know Dan didn't kill Salinas. He's being set up to take the blame for someone else." Her eyes narrowed as they focused on Brant. She reached for her purse.

Brant eyed her speculatively, as if weighing her words. He shrugged. "It's possible, I suppose. But I don't make conjectures. As far as I'm concerned, a man is innocent until proven guilty." He leaned forward so as to put more emphasis on his words. "But even you have to admit that Dan running away doesn't exactly make him look innocent right now."

Layne wasn't ready to back down. "I didn't think you gave a damn either way. Just so you get your man—round him up, bring him in and make it look good on your record, isn't that right?"

"Layne! That's not fair," Russell chastised.

Brant waved him away. "I can speak for myself. Layne and I have gone several rounds on this subject before." His eyes glowed as he stared at Layne. "I told you before, my job isn't to judge. I'm told to do a job and I do it. As to whether a man is guilty or innocent, that's up to a court of law to figure out. I have no personal stake in it."

She clenched her small fists in her lap. "Well, I have. That's why I want . . . need to handle the investigation. No one else is going to do a better job." This she directed to Russell.

Brant crossed his arms across his chest. "If I don't bring him in, somebody else will."

But it will be you, she thought. A pang of regret sliced through her because she felt so drawn to him every time he came near her. She hated the way her pulse jumped every time he looked at her in that heart-stopping way. Like now, when his eyes were so serious as they traveled over her. Why did it have to be her brother who was in trouble?

Brant wasn't through talking. "Russell's right, Layne. I agree that you shouldn't handle the case for the simple reason that once you allow personal feelings to get in the way, it can cloud judgment. That's when you can make mistakes—deadly ones. And in Dan's case your conscience can become an issue. Are you willing to take that chance?"

Layne frowned at him. "Thanks, but I didn't ask for a sermon." She hadn't meant to say that. In her heart she knew he was right. But she couldn't sit around and do nothing. Angry energy coursed through her body.

Expecting a rebuttal, Layne watched as Brant scowled and opened his mouth to speak. Before he could utter a word, their attention was diverted by the man who stopped at their table.

He was clearly Hispanic, of medium height and build, and under the bright ceiling lights his hair gleamed with a

blue-black luster. His stance was ramrod straight, reminding Layne of a bullfighter she'd seen once.

He inclined his head in greeting. "Good afternoon. My
name is Rico Salinas. Michael Salinas was my uncle."

Russell nodded and made introductions.

Rico smiled. "I was having lunch with a friend and I saw
you. But I'm afraid this isn't a social call. I received a call
from a man by the name of Jesse Alphonso." His dark gaze
took in Layne. "He informed me that he saw Dan Tyler kill
my uncle."

There was a deafening silence at the table. Layne froze;
the blood seemed to have drained from every visible inch of
her.

"When did this happen?" Russell asked.

"He called early this morning. Before he hung up he said
he was going to go to the police to sign a statement."

"And why didn't this Alphonso character come forward
sooner?" Layne asked, hiding her fear with anger. "It's
been two weeks since your uncle died."

Rico shrugged an elegant shoulder. "I'm afraid I have no
answer. You'll have to talk to him."

"Didn't it occur to you to ask him that?" Brant inter-
vened and Layne blinked at him in surprise. He sounded as
if he were on her side. She willed her heart to stay calm.

Rico shook his head. "No, I'm sorry. I've had several
pressing things on my mind. Many calls of condolence have
kept me busy and I've had to take over some of my uncle's
business calls, as well. Right now I'm late for an appointment, so if you'll excuse me . . ." To Layne he said, "I'm
sorry we had to meet under these circumstances." With a
polite nod of his head he was gone.

The silence at the table grew, clung and thickened in the
oppressive air. In Layne's heart it struck a heavy note of
dread.

Russell cleared his throat. "I'm sorry you had to hear that, Layne. I'll look into it."

Her temples thumped and as she stood up she could almost hear the low, wrenching sounds of her lunch coming up. "I'm rather tired," she said. "I'm going home." She looked down at Brant and their eyes clashed.

He rose and picked up his hat from the empty chair next to him. "For what it's worth, I'm sorry, too."

That simple statement coming from him surprised her. But she knew it wouldn't stop him from making her life miserable. He had his job to do.

And so did she.

"Thanks . . . and goodbye." She swiftly crossed the restaurant.

Outside she paused on the sidewalk. There was a roar of blood pounding in her ears. She silently repeated Rico's words. "You'll have to ask Alphonso yourself."

She intended to do just that. Before the day was out, she vowed she was going to find out why Jesse Alphonso had lied.

Alphonso's address turned out to be in a middle-lower-class neighborhood. It was an area Layne was familiar with. An apartment building loomed across the street. His address was one of the older frame houses on the block.

Layne noted the overgrown lawn as she made her way up a small flight of rickety wooden steps. She knocked on the door. When there was no immediate answer, she knocked again. Louder this time.

Frowning, Layne wondered if she had the correct address and peered down at the piece of paper she held in her hand, then up again to read the address above the door. She had the right address.

She clutched the doorknob and turned it. It wasn't locked. She pushed the door open and stepped inside.

"Hello! *¡Hola!* Anyone at home?" she called from the small foyer.

No answer. Could he be asleep? She wasn't leaving until she talked with him.

She called out again. When she received no answer she made her way down a short hallway.

The first bedroom was empty. She continued down the hall until she came to a halt just outside a second bedroom. The bed covers were rumpled. Part of a blanket lay on the bed, the other half sprawled on the floor. A dresser stood against the opposite wall. Layne spied several articles lying on top.

She tripped on the way to the dresser. Glancing down at the bed covers on the floor, she realized she'd hit against something that was tangled in with the blanket. She leaned over and tried to move the cover to one side. It wouldn't budge. She yanked harder. Part of the blanket fell to one side and Layne could see a man's face peering up at her, his eyes open, lifeless.

A slam of fear sliced through her chest and she reeled from the shock.

With a gasp, she drew her hand back and scrambled up. The action made the blood rush to her head.

She couldn't scream. Her vocal cords were paralyzed and she tried to bring her galloping heartbeat back to normal.

A thought hit her. *What if the killer is still in the house?*

Clutching her purse tightly to her chest, she backed out of the room.

Right into a solid human wall.

Layne let out a piercing scream.

Chapter 6

Strong fingers wrapped themselves around Layne's arm and turned her around.

"Take it easy," a male voice soothed.

Layne looked up to see cool turquoise-colored eyes regarding her appraisingly.

"You all right?" He took in her distraught features. Her face was a mixture of nausea and wariness. From experience, it was a look Brant knew well.

She shook off his hands. "No, I'm not. You scared the hell out of me." She sucked in a deep breath. "And I wish you'd stop sneaking up on me like that."

It wasn't the first time she'd seen a corpse, but whenever she'd come face-to-face with a body lying in that curiously boneless disarray of the truly and suddenly dead it always affected her the same way. She felt as nervous as a treed cat.

"Sorry," he said unconvincingly. "I didn't have time to dodge out of your way." He glanced down at the floor. "Anyone we know?"

She struggled to keep her voice from quivering. "I haven't the slightest idea, but he's dead."

Brant knelt and peered down at the man. "You're right." Pushing the blanket aside, he patted a search over the man's pockets and eased a wallet out of his jeans. Barely touching the edge, Brant flipped the wallet open, looked at it, then slipped it back into the same pocket.

Layne crossed her arms over her chest in an effort to keep her body from trembling as she stared down at Brant's head. "I never thought I'd be saying this, but I'm glad to see you."

He stood and regarded her quizzically for a moment. "Either my charm is improving or you're about to become hysterical."

The early afternoon sun, filtering in through the venetian blinds at the bedroom window, slanted a zebralike pattern across Brant's handsome features. Layne wished she were anywhere else but here. Lifting her chin, she drew herself up regally. "I never become hysterical." She shrugged and looked away. "It's just that I'm glad it was you and not the killer who surprised me, that's all."

"Yeah, so am I. Just remember that, the next time you plan to do something like this on your own."

"What does his ID say?" she asked, ignoring his barb.

"He's Jesse Alphonso." Brant paused, wondering just how much to tell her. The last thing he should be doing right now was discussing Alphonso with her. For all he knew, she might know where her brother was hiding. If Dan *were* guilty of murder, Layne could even be an accessory.

And that would make them natural enemies.

Then, dammit, why did he care so much what happened to her? He choked down a harsh breath as he saw her face pale at hearing Alphonso's name. "Come on, let's get you out of here," he said, ushering her into the small living room. There he sat her down on the couch, instructing her to take slow, easy breaths. Sitting beside her, he waited until her breathing was normal again. "By the way," he intoned dryly, "what *are* you doing here?"

"I might ask you the same thing," she replied with a humorless smile.

"No fair, I asked you first." His own smile was brief.

She met his eyes squarely. "You know why I'm here."

"Enlighten me."

The way he was looking at her made her feel like a spider caught in its own web. She glanced down at her hands. "I came to ask Alphonso why he was lying about my brother."

"Did you kill him?"

Her head snapped up. Frowning, she stood up and faced him with small fists clenched on her hips. "How did you guess? Why, I kill everyone who doesn't agree with me," she gestured wildly. "Come on, Brant." She eyed him distastefully. "That's a stupid question, even for you. Of course I didn't kill him."

"Just thought I'd ask." His lazy gaze moved over her body and he smiled.

She looked away in frustration. For some reason, Layne had the sneaky suspicion that Brant Wade enjoyed riling her. Especially when he looked at her that way, with a mixture of distrust and masculine interest.

Brant's face sobered and he stood up. "You'd better leave. This place is about to get crowded." Taking a handkerchief out of his back pocket, he walked over to the phone and covered the receiver before lifting it.

"I'm not leaving."

Brant stood holding the phone in midair. At her words, he replaced it and turned around to confront her with a mildly aggravated expression on his face. "You've been at a crime scene before, Layne, so you know what to expect. I've got to make a report. In about fifteen minutes, all hell is going to break loose around here. Garcia and his men will be arriving right along with the medical examiner to make a positive ID. What evidence is found here is going to be passed around like a pretzel tray at a retirement party." His tone sharpened. "Oh, and don't forget all the curious observers who will litter this place as soon as a squad car pulls up out front." His eyes locked with hers. "Then, there's the D.A. He'll be showing up, too, and I don't think he's going to be too happy to see you."

Her firm chin came up in an obstinate gesture, exposing the smooth column of her throat. "I don't care, I'm not leaving."

Brant sighed in exasperation. "Don't go getting stubborn on me. Do you realize the killer could have been here when you walked in? You could've been killed. I told you to let me handle things."

Layne shook her head. "I can't afford to wait. Alphonso lied about my brother. I came here to find out why and I can't leave until I know what's going on."

"Aren't you forgetting something?" he asked. "Like what's your boss going to say when he finds you at the murder scene of a man who was just about to point the finger at your brother for murder?"

She winced, but she didn't back down. "Which, I might add, is now merely heresay," she intoned dryly.

"Exactly. And you're the one who's been caught standing beside the dead witness." His quiet voice vibrated through the room.

She tensed. "I didn't kill him. You arrived only minutes behind me. There wouldn't have been time."

"I don't know anything of the kind." He stood hovering over her with an indolent, pantherish grace.

Raising her chin she assumed all the dignity she could muster. "Does that mean you plan to arrest me?"

"No," he drawled. "It just means that if you stay here you're going to have to answer an awful lot of questions. I just think you could be doing more with your time, that's all." He shrugged.

What was he saying? she wondered. Did he mean to keep her visit here a secret? But why would he do something like that? What did he have to gain?

"Do you think I'm capable of doing something like that?" She didn't know why, but suddenly it was important to know what he thought of her.

He held her gaze until the heat flooded over her face in embarrassment and she looked away.

"No," he answered finally. "I just wanted to press home a point. That if you stay you'd better be prepared for anything. Remember, you're still fresh news for the media."

She nodded. "All right. I get your point. I'll leave." She paused, looking slightly uncomfortable. "But only if you'll let me know what turns up here? I'd find out eventually, but it will help if I know something sooner."

For a moment she thought he wasn't going to answer, then he nodded with a taut jerk of his head. "Yeah, I'll let you know."

Relief softened the lines in her face and she smiled. "Thanks." She turned away.

"Can I ask you something before you go?" His voice was deceptively mild. As she turned around Brant studied her slender silhouette in the doorway. From behind her the sun lit up her auburn hair, turning it into a blaze of fire.

"Of course," she replied uneasily.

He stood with most of his weight on one foot, one thumb looped over his belt. "If you never become hysterical, then it *must* be my charm, right?"

She left without answering.

Like a big, satisfied mountain cat, Brant smiled.

The waiting became excruciating, getting worse by the minute. She'd straightened the living room, thrown clothes in the washer and now passed the time by pacing back and forth in front of the fireplace.

What if Brant didn't call? After all, it was after eight o'clock and she still hadn't heard any word. What if he'd just told her that so she would leave? That would be just like him, she thought.

By nine o'clock she was a bundle of nerves. She should have stayed. At least she'd know something by now. She paced some more.

When the doorbell rang thirty minutes later Layne flew to the door, opening it wide. Brant stood on her doorstep.

She took one look at his face and knew he didn't have good news.

He followed her into the living room, where she motioned for him to sit down. He declined and came straight to the point. "It doesn't look good."

"Tell me." The anxiety in her voice betrayed her.

Brant wondered how much to tell her. Signs of fatigue and worry showed clearly on her face. He fought to subdue his concern for her, forced himself to forget that he was beginning to care a little too much—a dangerous hazard in his line of business and an unfortunate mistake he'd made once before. What he needed to do right now, he thought as he watched Layne's eyes widen in concern, was to get it over with. *It's simple. Just tell her and go. She isn't your concern. Finding Dan is.*

"The knife that killed Alphonso—"

"Yes?" she urged.

"Has Dan's fingerprints on it."

Layne took a step backward. "Oh, no," she moaned, her eyes wide with undisguised horror.

Now you can leave, Brant's mind ordered. *You've delivered your news, so leave.* But his feet refused to move. He stood there staring into Layne's helpless, shocked eyes and he was at a loss as to what to do. He couldn't just walk out and leave her alone. And he couldn't hold her like he was aching to do. Very badly.

He took a step toward her and stopped.

She took another weary step backward. She'd seen the flicker of warring emotions—indecision—cross Brant's features, and she jerked herself erect. Not ever, not even when her parents had died, had she taken to letting anyone feel sorry for her and Dan. She refused to allow it now. Especially Brant Wade of all people.

She tried to recover from the shock. "No," she whispered, shaking her head. Then with more conviction, "No! Dan didn't kill either of them. I don't care what anybody says. He didn't do it."

His response was cool. "There was no sign of forced entry, no sign of a struggle. Alphonso still had his billfold on him, so it wasn't robbery. I'll have to bring Dan in for questioning of both murders."

"You'll be bringing in the wrong man. Dan's being framed."

"I have no other choice."

"I see. And I suppose you expect me to believe that Dan found out Alphonso was a witness to Salinas's murder, then rushed over to kill him. Oh, but wait a minute," she said dramatically, "Dan made sure his fingerprints would be on the knife. Am I reaching you so far?"

He wanted to convince her. "Layne, I have nothing personal against Dan—I've told you that before. If you want to know the truth, I wish to hell your brother wasn't even mixed up in all of this. I'm having a hard enough time keeping—" *my hands off of you,* he almost said "—tabs on you and searching for him."

She kept her voice low. "In that case, you'd better go. I'm keeping you from your duty. But thanks for dropping by."

Brant wondered what was going on in that mind of hers. She appeared calm. Almost too calm. "If you're thinking of continuing with the investigation on your own, Layne, don't. Stay out of it. Look," he said grudgingly, "I'm not saying you're wrong in all of this, but if you know where Dan is you'd better tell me now."

"I don't know where he is," she said softly. "Besides, I'm not so sure I know who to trust these days."

He sighed. "I guess that's that, then." He touched the brim of his hat. "Good night."

"Can't you at least agree that I'm right about those fingerprints?"

This time *he* left without answering. He couldn't—or wouldn't—tell her what she wanted to hear.

A quiver of regret passed through her as she watched him leave. She had no one to talk to, hadn't had *anyone* to confide in for so long.

Only Dan. And he was gone.

For a long moment Layne stood there alone with her thoughts, feeling weary, yet knowing with certainty that another sleepless night loomed before her.

She sank down on the sofa. Leaning her head back against the cushion, she stared at the ceiling. She had just closed her eyes when the phone rang.

She jumped up, answering it on the second ring.

"Hello?"

"Laynie?"

Her heart leaped in relief. "Dan!" She turned her back to the window. What if Brant was still out there watching?

"I was thinking about you," Dan said. "You know, kind of reminiscing. That's all I've had to do lately." He paused. "Laynie?"

"I'm listening, Dan." Her heart ached with affection.

"Remember when I was a kid and you used to take me to that snow-cone stand every summer? It almost became a ritual. I was ten years old."

Layne closed her eyes. "Yes."

"That snow-cone stand was my favorite place to go. Hey, it still is, you know? After all this time, who would believe it would still be there?"

Layne's senses came alert. What was he talking about? That snow-cone stand hadn't been there for at least three years. The last time she'd driven by on her way to work all she'd seen was a vacant lot and a bus stop.

She gripped the phone tighter. "Dan, are you all right?"

"You know, it's been a while since I was ten, but I can still feel it as though it were yesterday," he said, ignoring her question. "Look, I can't talk long, this phone might be bugged."

"Dan, I need to see you."

"I gotta go, Laynie, but I'll be thinking about you."

"Wait!" Layne clutched the phone so tightly her knuckles ached. But he'd already cut off the connection.

What a strange call. Why in the world would Dan call her just to tell her that snow-cone story? And why would he say the stand was still there when he knew better?

She hung up the phone and walked over to sit down on the sofa. Layne figured she was probably being watched. Brant had told her he was placing a guard outside. There might even be two of them out there somewhere. She picked up a magazine from the coffee table and flipped it open, pretending to read, while in her mind she went over their conversation again.

Was Dan trying to tell her something? He'd mentioned a snow-cone stand that was no longer there. He'd also said he'd been ten years old. That wasn't true. He'd been seven when they'd made that daily trek to the stand. There was too much difference in ten and seven for him not to have remembered.

Closing her eyes Layne visualized that corner. An empty lot. A bus stop. And . . .

An old phone booth.

Her eyes flashed open, sudden understanding *A telephone booth!* Still holding the magazine, she deftly flicked her wrist and glanced down at her watch. It was nine-fifteen. Was Dan trying to tell her he would meet her there?

That had to be it! He wanted her to be at that telephone booth at ten tonight. What else could it be?

Not wanting to attract any attention just in case someone was watching, she yawned, pretending to be sleepy. Laying the magazine aside she stood up, stretched and yawned again.

Although she took her time walking into the kitchen, her mind was racing. It was only a five-minute drive to that corner. On foot it would take her at least twenty minutes, fifteen if she ran. She'd have to leave no later than nine-forty.

Layne opened the refrigerator door, took out a sirloin steak from the meat bin and carried it over to a cutting board. She cut the steak into two equal strips, then wrapped each one separately in cellophane.

Thoughtfully she stared out the kitchen window. It faced her backyard. She would have to walk the length of the yard, over into Mrs. Limmer's backyard, in order to reach the other street. In between, lay two obstacles. The first one—a chain-link fence—presented no problem. The second one however, would take a great deal more time.

She'd have to get past Wolf, Mrs. Limmer's massive German shepherd.

Layne swallowed nervously. Wolf was getting old and his eyesight wasn't all that great any more. Would he recognize her in the dark? As if she were holding on to her salvation, Layne clutched the cellophane packages closer to her chest before laying them on the counter.

She wanted to run but forced herself to walk into the bedroom. Quickly she changed into a black sweatshirt and jeans. By the time she found an old knit cap of Dan's and shoved it into her back pocket, her heart was threatening to pound out of control.

There was only one more thing to do. Throwing on her robe, she returned to the living room, where she closed the drapes and turned off the light.

When she entered her bedroom again she looked at her watch. Nine-thirty. A second later she turned off the light, jerked off her robe and threw it on the bed.

The house, covered in darkness, loomed silent now. Layne swallowed nervously as she made her way down the hall. At the back door she put on the cap, stuffing her hair up under it with trembling hands.

Shifting to one side of the window she peered out toward the night, studying every shadow, every tree and anything that moved. She clutched the doorknob, turned it, pushed the door open—then remembered the meat. Layne grabbed the packages from the counter and walked out into the night.

Nothing was going to keep her from getting to that phone booth by ten o'clock.

Cautiously she crept through the backyard, passing trees and shrubs. Sweat broke out on her upper lip. The knit cap was hot and it made her head itch. It had been threatening to rain all day. Now a light drizzle fell softly against her face. Good, she thought. The leaves would be soaked enough so they wouldn't crackle when she stepped on them.

Reaching Mrs. Limmer's fence, Layne crouched in the dark for a moment.

"Wolf. Here, boy," she called out softly.

She didn't have long to wait. A dark shape streaked through the night. Wolf came with such perceptive softness, Layne would have never heard him if she hadn't been prepared. Wolf growled low in his throat, then paused for a moment before continuing.

"Shhh, Wolf. Put a lid on it. You're going to wake the whole neighborhood."

Wolf gave her an obscene sneer.

"Hey, fella, look what I've got for you," Layne whispered, unwrapping one of the cellophane packages and placing it up to the fence.

Wolf ambled closer, sniffing curiously. As he smelled the meat and her hand through the chain-link fence, Layne reached out and petted his nose. He cocked his head sideways and whined.

"You remember me, don't you, boy?" She gave him another affectionate pat. "Eat hearty," she said, pitching the sirloin over the fence. Wolf trotted over, took another cautious sniff, then lay on his belly, clamping his paws on the tasty morsel, while his massive jaws went to work on it.

Taking advantage of Wolf's avarice, Layne didn't waste time climbing the fence.

"Enjoy the dinner," she whispered, as she crept through the night, keeping close to the hedge. Reaching the front yard, she gritted her teeth as she opened the gate, praying it wouldn't squeak.

She'd done it! But she had to hurry. As her feet hit pavement, Layne broke into a run, keeping to the sidewalk as close to each house as she could.

By the time she reached the phone booth, her sides were heaving from strain and tension. Her shoulders sagged, her side cramped and her tongue felt dry and swollen in her mouth.

She stood there, breathing hard, her legs refusing to go any further.

When the phone rang, she made a grab for it.

"Hello?" she said breathlessly.

"I knew you'd make it, Laynie."

"Dan, I have to see you." She slid the door only halfway so the light in the booth wouldn't come on.

"I can't, Laynie."

"Listen to me, Dan. Things have gotten worse. The police have found the body of a man whose name is Jesse Alphonso and the murder weapon has your prints on it. Tell me you don't know him . . . please."

"I don't know him, Layne. I didn't kill him. I told you someone's setting me up, didn't I? This proves it."

"I have to see you. Turn yourself in. I'll see that you get protection."

"I told you before I'm not turning myself in. Who in the hell is going to protect me from a damned murderer who's killed two people already, tell me that?"

"We have competent men—"

"Sure you do," he interrupted, "but I can't trust anybody. When the real killer is found I'll turn myself in, but not until then."

"Then we're at a stalemate." Layne peered miserably through the half-closed door. She could make out headlights in the distance. As they neared, she stared silently at the depressing drizzle that fell and danced in front of the lights. Just before the car came even with the booth, Layne crouched down instinctively.

"I just wanted you to know I'm all right, so don't worry, okay?" There was a pause. "I may not be calling you again."

She slumped against the wall of the booth. "What are you saying?"

"I'm going to try and leave the country. I may not see you for a while. Maybe never. I'll miss you, Layne. I just wanted you to know that." His voice cracked. "I'm sorry."

"Dan, please listen. I'm working on the investigation. I'll find out who did it. I promise. But we have to keep in touch. I have to see you."

A sigh went through the line. "I can't. I've got to hang up, sis. I . . . I . . . love you."

"Dan, please wait. Please, don't hang up." She heard the unmistakable click as Dan broke the connection. She stood there clutching the phone with trembling fingers, staring into space. Finally she replaced the receiver.

She rested her forehead against the cool pane and watched rain bead its way down the glass. She stood there for a long tormented moment staring at a puddle—a pool of false hope laying like misery on the asphalt. With a shaky breath she opened the door of the booth and stepped outside.

Drizzle came down faster and harder now, mingling with her weeping. As lightning flickered against the sky, Layne raised her face to the rain, wanting to shake her fist at the unfairness of it all.

Do the dead hear you? she wondered. She'd heard somewhere that if you prayed for their souls, their spirits would help you.

Oh, Mom, she whispered. What am I going to do? What if I can't get him out of this one? What if I never see him again?

She felt a shiver run up her spine and something else, too: anxiety. Abandonment.

She'd always fought her own battles. Now she felt so weary, she didn't know where to turn. To Russell? But he had refused her pleas to help with the investigation. It wasn't because he wouldn't. He *couldn't* help her.

Travis? He was still out of town, but even if he weren't, even if he were here with her now, she still wouldn't ask him. She knew he would demand more of their relationship than she was willing to give.

Who else?

Layne believed Dan was being framed. What was she up against? Salinas had been a very powerful man. Who would have killed him? Had it been someone equally as powerful?

Who else could she ask? Her mind raced furiously.

Suddenly she recalled Garcia's words. *You can trust Brant. He's fair and honest.* Twice before Brant had asked Layne to trust him. Could she?

Wouldn't you do anything to see that Dan remains safe? a little voice prodded.

Yes. Anything.

Even ask Brant to help you?

Layne blinked through her tears.

In her job she'd learned what the inside of a jail looked like. A cement tomb. She thought of the open toilets, the lack of privacy and dignity and the stench of sweat, excrement and unrestrained hate.

Yes, she would even ask Brant to help her.

Bracing her shoulders, mustering confidence, she started the run home. She patted her pocket and felt the other portion of meat nestled there. Another incentive for Wolf.

She had to see Brant tonight.

Before she lost her nerve.

Chapter 7

The nightmare caught him unaware. It rushed up from that endless corridor of the past.

Brant's body jerked in shock as he felt the switchblade slice through flesh. A fearful and excruciating pain welled up, causing him to clutch his chest before slumping to the ground.

Gasping for breath, he stifled an instinctive moan and closed his eyes. When he opened them he saw her—Belinda. No remorse registered on her face. She watched him as indifferently as she would have watched a dog lying in the sun.

Her face receded, disappeared from view. He looked up and saw twilight slowly fading under a sky of dying violet. He tried to rise, to call for help.

His eyelids began to flutter as he tried to bring himself out of the nightmare. His body moved convulsively until he jerked himself awake.

He awoke in a sweat, his heart thumping rapidly.

After two years, the dream didn't come as often, but when it did it left him visibly shaken.

He'd fallen asleep in front of the television set again. Heaving a deep sigh, Brant picked up a glass, lifted it to his lips and drained it, then returned his attention to the television set and watched dispassionately as a commercial replaced the late show on the screen.

Thoughts of Layne intruded and Brant winced, recalling the depth of sadness he'd seen in her eyes tonight, a sadness that wrenched his soul. An emotion he did not recognize churned the Scotch he had just poured into his empty stomach. Setting the glass aside, he rose from the large armchair and turned off the TV.

He couldn't help wondering what Layne was doing at this moment. What did she intend to do next? Brant argued silently that his concern over her plight stemmed from a purely male instinct to protect. After all, he wasn't exactly indifferent to other people's feelings.

But how long had it been since he'd been *this* concerned about what happened to a suspect's relative?

The answer came unbidden. *Two years, that's how long.*

And he'd sworn never to do it again.

In a black mood, Brant climbed the stairs two at a time and entered his bedroom. He tore off his shirt and tossed it over a chair, then walked over to the dresser and looked at himself in the mirror. His gaze traveled to the jagged scar, a streak of silver that ran along his chest just below the shoulder.

That scar would always serve to remind him of two things: the emotion of that one night and the sour, humiliating truth that the woman he had loved—or thought he'd loved—had left him to die in an alley full of rats and garbage.

He stood, fists clenched, and closed his eyes. He wanted to forget, yet at the same time forgetting would be the worst thing in the world.

Belinda's husky voice rose up again to haunt him. *Por favor, querido, I need your help.*

A low rumble of thunder brought him back from the past. Brant opened his eyes and his brows furrowed in disgust. *You were a fool!* he mocked himself brutally. He walked over to the bed and lazily stretched his taut body, trying to ease the tired muscles of his back. He reached down to unzip his jeans, but his hands froze in midair.

Someone pounded on his door.

He glanced at the clock on the nightstand and saw it was almost eleven-thirty. The only person who would come by at this hour was Paul, but only in an emergency.

Not bothering to put on his shirt, Brant leaned over, grabbed the revolver from its holster on the night table, and tucked it behind him beneath the waistband of his jeans. The sudden touch of cold metal against warm skin caused him to shiver as he hurried to the door.

Brant flicked on the porch light but kept the foyer dark. He stepped to one side of a window and looked out.

Layne stood on his doorstep, arms resting stiffly by her sides and rain-dampened clothes clinging to her skin.

He opened the door. "Layne! What happened? Are you all right?" Concern rang in his voice as he ushered her inside.

Her glance slid past him. Intrigued, she found herself standing in a room that cast an impression of utter masculinity, from the massive stone fireplace that took up almost one entire wall and reached the two-story-high rustic-beamed ceiling, to the thick, heavy oak furniture which occupied the room. The only softening came from several brightly colored Indian rugs covering the wood-planked floor. The room was so rustic Layne had the distinct impression that any trace of femininity would have looked grossly out of place.

The lion's den.

"You okay?" Brant repeated.

Turning, Layne swallowed a quick intake of breath as she became peripherally aware of a shirtless Brant.

Layne's haste and the dark foyer had kept her from looking at Brant too closely except to make sure it was he who had opened the door.

At his polite inquiry she managed a weak nod, and as her eyes made a critical sweep of his body she couldn't helping thinking that genes or God, or both, had been very kind to Brant Wade.

Like a homing pigeon, her eyes zeroed in on the scar. How could they not? It was the only imperfection on an otherwise perfect body. Her eyes softened and an unaccountable tenderness welled up inside her as she imagined the pain he must have suffered from the wound. She resisted the urge to reach out and stroke his skin.

His was a natural, physical beauty, not one acquired from hours of lifting weights. Strong and powerful looking, his chest showed off well-defined muscles tapering to a slim waist where a soft, dark line of down disappeared beneath his jeans. Women probably closed in on him like a school of starving piranhas.

She averted her eyes.

"Would you like to sit down?" he asked, motioning to the sofa.

"No, thanks." Nervously she bit her lip. She hadn't come here to ogle the man, only to try to get him to listen to reason.

As casually as she could manage, Layne said, "I almost didn't find your place. There aren't many homes out here."

"Yeah, I like it that way."

She wasn't surprised. Brant Wade looked like a man who enjoyed his privacy.

"I realize it's late, but I need to talk to you."

His glance flicked over her damp clothing. "It must be something important for you to have come out here in this weather."

Despite his surface cordiality, Layne couldn't help experiencing a vague disquieting feeling. She saw something in his eyes, something warm, intense, yet wary, and she fought a familiar quivering in her stomach—the same weakness she experienced each time she saw him.

She stood stiffly for a moment. The carefully rehearsed speech she'd gone over and over in her mind on the way over here suddenly evaporated into thin air. Finally she just blurted it out.

"I need your help. I want to go with you when you look for Dan."

For a moment Brant stood there as though he hadn't heard her, then something in his eyes flickered warningly and a muscle clenched along his jaw.

"What did you say?" He asked coldly.

"I said I need your help."

Déjà vu, he thought bitterly, as her words reached him from across a distance, caught between past and present. It was bad enough Layne had arrived just as he'd been recalling Belinda's treachery, but to hear her utter the same sentence almost word for word caused his brain to hum with fury.

He'd be damned if he'd be used a second time.

His long legs closed the distance between them. He reached out and grabbed her by the shoulders, practically lifting her off the floor.

"Don't tell me, let me guess," he sneered. "Now you're going to tell me that once we find him . . . together . . . your brother will listen to you and give himself up, right?"

Layne sucked in a sharp breath. Never had she seen eyes convey such contempt. He stood so close she could smell the liquor on his breath and a flicker of apprehension coursed through her.

"Well?" Brant shook her again.

Layne fought to remain in control. "Now that I know you can read minds, you can let me go," she intoned dryly.

He jerked her closer, lifting her against him. "But we're not through." His voice was as empty of emotion as his expression. "Tell me, Layne, just how far are you willing to go to save your brother?"

Layne was afraid to move for fear of angering him further. She was anxious, but she wasn't crazy.

What if *he* were crazy? She became achingly aware that she stood on his turf, out in the middle of nowhere, and no one would hear her screams. Layne could feel the heat of his body as her heart pounded against his bare chest. She knew now that coming here had been a mistake. She would have never laid herself this open if she hadn't been so frantically desperate to find Dan.

"I said . . . let me go," she whispered.

Brant reached up and caressed her cheek, smiling sadly. "Oh, no, sweetheart." He shook his head. "You said you needed my help. Now tell me what you're willing to do." His voice lowered to a husky pitch. "I bet you haven't learned the art of persuasion yet, have you? Or you'd be kissing me about now." His fingers clamped over her trembling chin. "Never mind, I can't wait," he muttered thickly as his mouth lowered to claim hers.

Layne flinched at the hostility she felt in his touch, in his mouth as it bruised her lips. Gone was the tenderness he'd shown her so far. Now as he crushed her to him, he kissed her with the fierce longing need of someone who'd been denied too long.

She tried to push him away, but she might as well have saved her strength; his body felt like tempered steel.

Layne let herself go limp. A second later she jerked her knee up in order to make contact with his groin, but Brant's hand lashed out and caught it. Strong tanned fingers curled around her leg just above the knee and held it prisoner, his own knee now wedged between her thighs. Caught off balance, Layne clung to his shoulders until he released her and her thigh slid slowly down the side of his own.

His hand continued its ardent journey up her hip, settling over her derriere. His mouth became more insistent.

Anything else she did now would probably anger him more, Layne thought. So she did something unexpected. Something she never would have thought of doing.

She kissed him back.

Her hands slid up his shoulders, then locked around his neck as she met his bold tongue with her own. His skin was warm to the touch and for a moment she felt his body tremble before it relaxed and his lips gentled against her own.

Brant's unexpected warmth drew a response from Layne. As his lips became more gentle and exploring, the queasiness in her stomach suddenly surged with sensations she'd never experienced before. She'd been kissed before, but never like this, with a force, a power so palpable it reached across and touched her soul. Yet her mind fought against the possibility that this man could touch her so deeply.

While to Layne her actions had been completely unexpected, to Brant they were not. He'd been almost certain Layne would react as she had. What else did you expect? he thought.

His moment of triumph was followed by a flash of bitter disappointment.

Why couldn't *she* be different?

With what seemed like an effort Brant released her, thrusting her away from him. Breathing hard, he blinked to clear away the fog in his brain.

His hand went up to rub his eyes, then he looked at her. "Go home, Layne," he rasped harshly. "Get the hell out of my house and let me do my job."

Layne's first instinct was to run away. But she never ran from anything. Yet his words pierced her heart like steel arrows.

Her quiet voice vibrated through the air. "Just for the record, there's no way I'd barter my body to save anyone."

"Not even your brother?" His eyes were fathomless as they looked at her.

He saw her shoulders stiffen, noted the glimmer in her eyes—a mixture of defiance and despair.

"Not even for Dan." She replied, pushing past him to get to the door.

Brant watched her go out into the rain-swept night and closed his eyes, disgusted at what he'd done. His empty stomach rebelled, reminding him he shouldn't have had so much to drink.

You bastard! Why did you have to hurt her like that?

Because, I don't want her to get inside me and mix me all up. I don't ever want to hurt like that again.

He knew the scar on his chest was small compared to the one that didn't show. It was a different kind of wound he carried in his heart and one he found difficult to close. He tried with his mind to draw the edges together, yet fought for fear of its opening wider and deeper.

He couldn't take the chance.

As if agreeing with him several bolts of lightning split the sky in two, and as rain lashed his window he wondered if Layne would make it home safely.

It took him only a second to grab his raincoat and hat.

It wouldn't hurt to follow her and make sure she got home all right. She had a habit of being in the wrong place at the wrong time.

Apparently Michael Salinas had preferred his secretaries very tall, very blond and very voluptuous in the bra department. With spike heels, Shanna Caldwell stood at least six feet tall. She looked long and sleek, like a beautiful jungle cat.

The Amazon was frowning down at Layne. "Someone from the D.A.'s office has already been here."

Layne forced a smile to her lips. "I need more information."

"I'm sorry, but there's nothing else I can tell you."

"Then let me talk to someone who can." Layne gritted her teeth, refusing to be turned away. She was sick to death of people telling her no.

Shanna Caldwell shrugged. "I'll see what I can do."

Layne watched the blonde disappear into an inner office and couldn't help feeling envious. She'd kill for legs that long.

The carpet sank softly beneath Layne's feet as she paced back and forth in front of the desk.

Yesterday she'd gone to *Juan's Cantina* to see Maria Chavez, the barmaid who'd given her Dan's note that night. All Layne had been able to glean from her was that she and Dan had two classes together at the university and when Dan found out Maria worked at Juan's he had asked her for a favor—to hand Layne his note. Maria assured Layne she didn't know where Dan was.

Shanna returned a few minutes later with a slender gray-haired man in tow.

"Miss Tyler, I'm Jim Weston." As Layne took his out-stretched hand, she had the distinct impression he was sizing her up—and down. "I've just talked to someone in the D.A.'s office. I'm sorry, but I've been told not to give you any information."

Shanna peered at Layne with a haughty "I told you so" look.

"I see," Layne said as she disengaged her hand from his. She didn't blame Russell. He was doing what he felt he had to do.

"Perhaps you should call your office and talk to the D.A. himself," Weston suggested.

"Nonsense," a voice said from behind her. Three people turned to see Rico Salinas standing just inside the door. He strode toward them with the graceful ease of a panther. "Since Miss Tyler is already here, we might as well make her comfortable. After all, we have nothing to hide. Come, Miss Tyler." Rico smiled, motioning for her to follow him to his office.

He closed his office door and went over and sat down behind his desk. "Now, what can I do for you?"

From across the desk, Layne sat studying that smooth-shaven angular face, the full lips, the beautiful lines of his dark blue suit and the white silk of the shirt beneath.

"Just answer a few questions."

He tilted his head to the side a little. "All right."

"What will happen now that your uncle is . . . gone? Regarding the business?"

He shrugged. "Business will go on as before."

"I understand you inherited his position in this company."

"That's right." He sighed deeply. "I don't mind telling you it's a very big responsibility. I almost wish he'd left it to someone else."

Layne looked around the room. "Is . . . Was this his office?"

"No. I couldn't bring myself to move in there. My uncle and I were very close. I hope his killer is found soon."

Layne wondered if he made reference to the killer, in general, or her brother, in particular. "I feel the same way, Mr. Salinas. I know my brother is a prime suspect, but I don't happen to believe he did it."

"I understand from Jim Weston that the D.A.'s office doesn't want you on the case."

She nodded. "That's right. In truth, I shouldn't even be here. You have every right to ask me to leave. I appreciate you talking to me. I know it can't be very easy for you under the circumstances."

"Nor can it be for you, Miss Tyler."

"One more question," she said quietly. "Can you think of anyone who would be angry enough to kill your uncle?"

He paused for a moment. "My uncle conducted many business deals. I suppose there are people who didn't like him, but I can't think of anyone who would've wanted to kill him."

"Is Jim Weston your partner?"

He smiled. "Yes. I inherited him as a partner, also."

She stood up, feeling his black coffee eyes traveling quickly over her. "Well, I won't take up any more of your time."

"It's no trouble," he assured her.

"Thank you." Layne said. She didn't like Jim Weston and decided to reserve judgment on Rico.

By the time she reached the elevator Layne wondered what she was going to say to Russell the next time she saw him? Without the D.A.'s office behind her, her course of action was limited. She had only unconnected bits of information that remotely fit together, and no plausible or logical account of the murder.

Everywhere she turned she kept running into dead ends.

In her mind Layne replayed the conversation with Brant again. Two days had passed since the night she'd been to see him. At first he'd been polite, had even appeared to be glad to see her. Then why had he been so angry when she'd asked for his help?

For a moment dull resentment pulsed through her. How like him to banish her last bit of hope.

Layne didn't take defeat lightly.

Besides, there were other ways to get information.

Chapter 8

Leaning back on a chair that balanced on its two back legs, Brant lazily surveyed the woman walking toward him. As she came closer he noticed the determination in her stride and in the set of her chin. Layne Tyler walked like a woman with a purpose.

His gaze took in the neat bun pulled tightly back. A pity. He preferred her hair loose. The navy pin-striped suit she wore did little to disguise her soft curves or a pair of very shapely legs. She was a good-looking woman, no doubt about it.

She stopped and spread both hands on top the clutter of his desk. "You owe me an apology."

"Yep," he replied matter-of-factly.

He stayed seated. Evidently Brant Wade never stood on ceremony of any kind. He crossed his arms over a muscled chest sporting a snug-fitting blue shirt. His booted feet, crossed at the ankle, rested on top of an old mahogany desk that looked as though it had weathered many years. His whole demeanor was one of lazy disregard for convention.

She straightened, stiffening her padded shoulders. "Is that all you have to say?"

"Have you checked your answering machine today?"

"No."

"I called you earlier and apologized."

She threw him a dubious look. "Then I'd better rush home and listen to it, hadn't I?" Her tone was laced with sarcasm.

"It's all on the tape," he repeated, staring down at his boots. He flexed the toe of one boot back and forth.

Layne counted to ten. She looked around the cramped cubicle. It sat toward the back of the building, apart from a larger room where several policemen sat either conversing on phones or shuffling paperwork.

"So, this is where your office is," she said, glancing toward one wall that was nearly obscured by taped-on wanted posters.

"It's where I hang my hat at the moment."

Layne looked down at him. He wore his hat and she wondered if he'd just returned from somewhere or was on his way out. The brim sat low over his forehead shading his upper features, yet she could discern the barest hint of mockery in those eyes.

"I suppose a man in your...profession doesn't stay around too long in one place. I mean, you must travel quite a bit."

"No to your first question and yes to the second, when the occasion warrants it...excuse the pun."

His cool reception made her angry. She wanted to wipe the cynical smile from his sensual mouth. "For a large man you don't expend much energy, do you?" she said, with just a hint of reproval.

His eyes trailed seductively down her body. When they returned to meet her cool, steady gaze, Layne felt as if someone had dropped a bomb in her stomach.

"Oh, I can use up quite a bit of energy when it's needed. Did you have something in mind?" His eyes held hers.

"Nothing I can think of," she replied, recalling how her body had turned to mush at his touch.

His feet came off the desk and the chair thumped down on the floor. He rose and walked over and sat down on the edge of the desk.

Now they were at eye level.

"Let's quit the two-step, Layne. You want to tell me why you're really here? I can't imagine that I'd be on your list of priorities."

"I want to know why you got so angry with me the other night." She was beginning to have second thoughts about coming here.

He reached over, picked up a pencil and began tapping it on the desk. "It's not important any more."

"It is to me. You said some rotten things without hearing me out first. Are you always so narrow-minded?"

He sighed. "Believe me, Layne, I regret the way I treated you. I really mean that. You caught me at a bad time, that's all. Will you accept my apology?" His voice sounded warmly sincere.

She watched the tap, tap, tap of his pencil. "That depends," she replied. "On whether you answer my question or not."

"About being narrow-minded?" At her nod, he shrugged. "No, not always. I just don't . . . trust women."

"All women?"

Brant didn't know why, but suddenly it was important for him to put her at ease.

"No. I trust my granny." He smiled.

His answer surprised her and she gauged his sincerity. Somehow she couldn't imagine Brant having a grandmother.

"Do we have a truce?" he asked.

She met his eyes reluctantly. It was important to her that they be on polite terms. "I . . . I guess so."

He threw the pencil down on the desk. "Now that we have that out of the way, tell me the *real* reason you're here."

It had been a very unsatisfactory week. What else did she have to lose? "Am I so easy to read?"

He smiled.

"Has anyone ever told you that you have a very suspicious mind, Brant?"

"Yeah, my mom. But then, she didn't raise no fool. I can tell when I'm being baited, darlin'. You want something. Admit it."

"May I sit down?"

"Going to take that long, is it?"

"No," she smiled. "My feet are killing me. I ran some errands before I came here. You were the last one on my list."

"I'm crushed." He motioned for her to sit down. When she did, he stared down at her from his great intimidating height.

She glanced at a photo on his desk and picked it up. "Is this your family?"

"Yep."

"Somehow I didn't picture you with a family portrait so near your professional surroundings."

"My mother brought it by one day."

"You could've taken it home."

"Yeah, I could've."

She glanced up at him. His expression was watchful, guarded.

She set the photo back. "Why don't you trust women?" she asked.

There was a lift of a dark brow. "Somehow, I don't believe that's what you want to talk to me about."

She sighed. "You're right. I've done a great deal of thinking and I've made a decision." She glanced at her watch. "As of an hour ago, I no longer work for the D.A.'s office."

"You don't?" He didn't look the least bit surprised.

"I resigned," she said simply. "That's why I'm here. I have a proposition for you."

"Would I be premature if I said I'm flattered?"

"I think you should hear what I have to say before jumping to conclusions . . . again."

"Go ahead. You have the floor." Again, his smile was an attempt to put her at ease. It didn't. She had too much riding on today's outcome.

"All I ask is that you keep an open mind."

"Uh-oh. Sounds ominous. Maybe I should listen to my granny and stay away from beautiful women like you."

"Your granny said that? Not your mother?"

"Oh, no. My mother says if I'm lucky enough to find someone attractive and healthy enough to have a passel of kids, I should grab her and run off to the nearest justice of the peace."

It was the first time he'd ever heard her laugh and he found himself liking the sound. It filled the small room like sunlight. He had a sudden sharp need to reach over and pull each pin from her hair, releasing its silky texture so it could slide through his fingers. He crossed his arms over his chest, as if by keeping them trapped the temptation would go away.

"And what do *you* say?" she asked, joining in the light-hearted mood.

"Who, me?" he mocked. "Between Mother and Granny, I stay confused most of the time." The laugh lines around his eyes crinkled up in amusement.

Layne found she liked him this way. So far, he was a contrast of contradictions. Layne had seen him angry, serious. But not like this—gentle and teasing. Maybe somehow they could agree today. After all, they were adult professionals with common goals. Finding the truth. Maybe he would be willing to listen to her now.

Sure, she thought, and maybe crows would turn white.

She studied him as he sat on the corner of the desk, one booted foot swinging slowly back and forth. Unconsciously her attention was drawn to the taut pull of denim along his thigh. Memory came flooding back of the way he'd molded her to him that night.

She stood up. They were at eye level again and the cramped office afforded her little movement.

She cleared her throat. "The other night I said I needed your help. I still do," she said quietly.

The teasing light in his eyes disappeared. With a sinking feeling in the pit of her stomach, Layne realized he must think all this was just a ploy of hers to win him over.

"Believe me," she hastened to explain, "I wouldn't have come here if I thought there was any other way."

"Desperation has a way of coming back to haunt you, Layne."

"That may be, but right now you're the only one I'm willing to trust." She hated the note of despair she heard in her own voice.

He laughed at the irony of her words. She trusted him, but he sure as hell didn't trust her.

"All I ask is that you hear me out, okay?"

He shrugged. "Fair enough."

Layne set her purse on top of the desk. "I haven't been honest with you and I've regretted that to some extent." She paused. "The night I was in the hospital—I lied to you." She watched him for some sign of resentment and scorn. He stared back at her dispassionately. "At the time I felt I had no other choice." She sighed deeply. "Your suspicions were correct. Dan did come to see me that night."

When she had finished he stood up, walked the short distance to a window and looked out. "Why are you telling me now?"

The room seemed to darken and Layne realized it was because no sunlight came through the window. She remembered the radio had announced rain for that afternoon. "Because I want us to start over. I want desperately to save my brother and if you'll work with me to help prove his innocence I'll tell you everything I know." She tried to relax her shoulders. "That's what I wanted to tell you."

He turned from the window and faced her. "I'm listening."

She wanted him to trust her. "Dan came to see me at the hospital to tell me he was being framed. He owed Salinas some money for a gambling debt and in order to pay it back he agreed to do some delivery work." Layne looked up to see Brant watching her intently. She decided not to mention the airstrip. That would be her ace in the hole.

"Is that all?"

She shook her head. "No. There's more. If I tell you the rest and if I give you my word that I'll let you know the minute Dan gets in touch with me, will you agree to work with me?"

Brant tried to harden his heart against her. They were words he'd heard before. The only difference was that she made them sound more sincere. "Somehow that doesn't sound like the kind of proposition I was hoping to hear from you."

She ignored his statement. "Just think, Brant, if we work together we'll each know what the other is doing. That's better than working against each other, isn't it?"

"No."

Her heart fell. "What do you mean, 'no?'"

He towered over her. "While I sympathize with your problem, Layne, I just don't think it would be a good idea to live out of each other's pockets. My job is to bring Dan in. His innocence is up to a court of law. You're better off to stay out of it."

Layne felt a pang of disappointment. Disappointment because the other Brant, the angry, serious, unapproachable one was back. She could tell by the stern set of his mouth and the tautness of his body.

"For one thing," he added, "you're too involved. It's become a life-or-death struggle for you. For another, you could get hurt, even killed." He shook his head. "Don't go playing cop. You do your job, counselor, and let me do mine."

Her eyes flashed. This whole incident with Dan had ripped her life apart and he was treating it as though it was simply "one of those things." This wasn't just some speeding ticket they were discussing, damn it. It was her life and Dan's.

She faced him squarely. "I can't believe what I'm hearing. Don't you understand what I'm saying? My brother's life may be in danger. To me, there is nothing more important than family. And I'm all he's got."

His voice was low but it carried weight. "The answer is still no. I work alone. I don't need a woman slowing me down."

Good intentions went flying out the window right along with her patience. His arrogance rankled beyond belief. She'd had to put up with prejudice before, but coming from him it was just too much. What in the world had ever possessed her to think she and this man could possibly work together?

So this was to end up in another war of endless futility. Damn his hide.

Her breasts heaved as she closed the gap between them. "If you think that working with a woman will slow you down, then go ahead—work on your own. But think about this while you're doing it. Nothing—" she jabbed her index finger at his chest "—and no one—" another jab "—is going to stop me from finding out who set Dan up, you got that?" She jabbed him again. "So don't even *think* of getting in my way."

She snatched up her purse from the desk and started to walk off but halted abruptly. "One more thing. Didn't your mother or granny ever teach you any manners?" She yanked off his hat and threw it down on top of the desk. "You're supposed to take your hat off in the presence of a lady."

At the door she delivered a parting shot. "You're wrong about me. I don't need a man to hold my hand and I sure as hell don't need male approval. Not all women are alike, Brant, and I dislike you lumping us all together."

Brant's expression was a mixture somewhere between surprise and bemusement, changing rapidly to approval as he watched her progress through the crowded outer office. Several heads turned, first in her direction, then in his. She had reached the main door, but even from this distance he could see her clearly. Brant watched with fascination the way her hips swayed provocatively with each angry step she took. When he'd seen her walking toward him today he'd thought she was beautiful. But an angry Layne walking away was magnificent. She'd been right. Layne Tyler was unlike any woman he'd ever met.

He walked over to the window in time to catch a glimpse of shapely calf as Layne slid into her car.

Even after she'd driven away he continued to stare out the window. How many times would he have to act like an ass before Layne Tyler would have nothing to do with him?

Of course, he could have told her it wasn't because she was a woman that he'd refused her. Hell, he'd worked with women before. The crime lab in Austin had an excellent firearms expert and a serologist—both women. He had the highest respect for them. He could have also said that being near her every day would stir too many emotions in him that were better left buried.

He could've told her all those things but he didn't.

She had brains, guts and determination. A woman like her would always fight to the end for what she believed.

He felt half admiration, half uneasiness.

A woman like that could grow on him.

He rubbed the place on his chest where Layne had jabbed her finger. Where the scar was.

Where his heart was.

He glanced at the photo of his dad, mom and sister, and he swallowed. The clock was ticking. He had to wrap up this case before Thanksgiving, only a month away.

As Layne's car disappeared from view he realized he had never felt lonelier.

Layne entered City Hall at three p.m. She stopped at the motor-vehicle department and asked the clerk to check for automobiles registered to Michael Salinas. Ten minutes later she walked down the hall to the tax assessor's office and asked the clerk for records regarding Salinas's property.

Next she left City Hall and drove to the county courthouse. At the marriage-license section, she asked the clerk for Salinas's application for a marriage license. At the same office, in the birth-certificate section, Layne again asked for information.

For the next several hours Layne continued her paper chase, from the criminal section of the county clerk's office to the courthouse.

By the time she left the courthouse Layne knew a great deal about Michael Salinas.

He had owned his home, three cars and a yacht. His wife, Lena, had driven a Mercedes just before she'd wrapped it around a tree and died. He'd been a Democrat. His wife had voted Republican. Layne knew his birthday, knew he'd been married at nineteen and divorced two years later. He'd married Lena five years ago. She'd been fifteen years his junior. He had owned several businesses and had no criminal charges pending. He had one brother, Leon, who'd been married to Alice Salinas. They had adopted one son, Rico Salinas, Michael's nephew.

Everything she'd learned was public knowledge.

It was his secrets she was after.

Tomorrow she would continue her search until she knew everything there was to know about Michael Salinas.

By the time Layne unlocked her front door she was yawning. On the way to the living room she kicked off her navy suede pumps and limped over to the couch. Groaning, she sank down and rubbed her toes.

Her poor feet and knees ached from hours of standing and walking in heels. She also had back and eye strain from hunching over countless ledgers in poorly lit offices.

Her stomach rumbled.

She wondered which would win out. Her hungry stomach or her tired body. Closing her eyes, she leaned back against the soft cushion. She simply didn't have the energy to walk to the kitchen or her bedroom.

She slumped, discouraged, on the sofa and sighed, then remembered Brant had mentioned he'd left an apology on her answering machine. What had he said, she wondered?

Her imagination ran rampant. *Layne, I made a complete ass of myself and I hope you'll forgive me.*

Or, *I'm terribly sorry. Please let me make this up to you.*

Curiosity tempted her to get up and listen to his message.

"This is Brant," the deep voice said. There was a long pause. "I'm sorry." The dial tone sounded.

She stood there and frowned. That was it? Just *"I'm sorry?"*

The man had his gall.

She settled back on the couch, propped her feet up on the coffee table and closed her eyes. She thought about her visit to the D.A. When she'd handed Russ her resignation he'd looked at it briefly, then set it aside. "I'll handle it whenever I can get around to it. Just don't expect it to be too soon. I'm swamped," he'd roared. God bless him, Layne thought. In his own way, he was letting her know she could have her job back any time she was ready.

She closed her eyes and had started to drift off when the peal of the doorbell made her jump.

It rang a second time. Layne sighed and struggled to lift her tired body from the couch.

When she swung the door open her eyes widened in surprise. She'd recognize that chest anywhere.

Brant stood on her doorstep, looking tall and serious.
"I've changed my mind," he said, pushing past her into the living room.

Chapter 9

"You changed your mind?" Layne stared at Brant's rugged good looks with suspicion.

"Is it so hard to believe?" His dark brows lifted innocently, although Layne could've sworn his eyes were trained on her like a weasel's in a chicken coop.

"Yes, it is," she replied, leading him over to the sofa. With a casual gesture she invited him to sit. He chose a large overstuffed chair. "For someone who's lost his faith in human nature, you made up your mind awfully quick." She sank down on the sofa facing him and leaned back, looking cool and controlled. Gazing at her feet, Layne realized she'd forgotten to put on her shoes.

His glance followed hers. "I gave it a lot of thought before I came here."

She crossed one leg over the other, digging her toes into the carpet. "Let me get this straight. You don't trust me, but you're willing to help me. Why?"

NO RISK, NO OBLIGATION TO BUY...NOW OR EVER!

GUARANTEED

PLAY "ROLL A DOUBLE" AND GET AS MANY AS FIVE GIFTS!

HERE'S HOW TO PLAY:

1. Peel off label from front cover. Place it in space provided at right. With a coin, carefully scratch off the silver dice. This makes you eligible to receive two or more free books, and possibly another gift, depending on what is revealed beneath the scratch-off area.

2. You'll receive brand-new Silhouette Intimate Moments® novels. When you return this card, we'll rush you the books and gift you qualify for ABSOLUTELY FREE!

3. Then, if we don't hear from you, every month we'll send you 6 additional novels to read and enjoy months before they are available in stores. You can return them and owe nothing, but if you decide to keep them, you'll pay only $2.71* each plus 25¢ delivery and applicable sales tax, if any*. That's the complete price, and—compared to cover prices of $3.39 each in stores—quite a bargain!

4. When you subscribe to the Silhouette Reader Service™, you'll also get our newsletter, as well as additional free gifts from time to time.

5. You must be completely satisfied. You may cancel at any time simply by sending us a note or a shipping statement marked "cancel" or by returning any shipment to us at our expense.

This lovely heart-shaped box is richly detailed with cut-glass decorations, perfect for holding a precious memento or keepsake—and it's yours absolutely free when you accept our no-risk offer.

SILHOUETTE "NO RISK" GUARANTEE

- You're not required to buy a single book—ever!
- You must be completely satisfied or you may cancel at any time simply by sending us a note or shipping statement marked "cancel" or by returning any shipment to us at our cost. Either way, you will receive no more books; you'll have no obligation to buy.
- The free books and gift you claimed on this "Roll A Double" offer remain yours to keep no matter what you decide.

DETACH AND MAIL CARD TODAY!

BUSINESS REPLY MAIL

FIRST CLASS MAIL   PERMIT NO. 717   BUFFALO, NY

POSTAGE WILL BE PAID BY ADDRESSEE

SILHOUETTE READER SERVICE
3010 WALDEN AVE
PO BOX 1867
BUFFALO NY 14240-9952

NO POSTAGE
NECESSARY
IF MAILED
IN THE
UNITED STATES

He smiled. "You underestimate your power to persuade."

She studied him for a moment before her mouth curled into a smile touched with irony. "Shame on you, Brant. I'm insulted that you'd even think I'd fall for that answer."

His glance was mocking. "You *were* pretty persuasive today. But to be honest with you, I have other reasons for wanting to help."

"Such as?" She sat there quietly, waiting, as he slouched in the chair and stretched his long legs out, crossing one boot over an ankle. His hands rested lazily on his stomach. Any minute she expected him to pull his hat over his eyes and fall asleep.

He reached over and picked up a photograph from the end table next to his chair and studied it. It was of Layne, her parents and both brothers. He set it back. "I figure if we work together, you'll let me know when Dan gets in touch with you. I want you to try to talk him into turning himself in. I'll do my part by helping you with the investigation." He shrugged. "It would be a mutual arrangement."

She still wasn't convinced. "That's all?"

His gaze traveled down to her bare feet again, then returned to her face. "That about covers it."

"Can't you even admit that there might be some grain of truth to Dan's story that he's being set up?"

He held up his hands. "Don't go reading more into our conversation than there is. I'm not doing this out of some sense of chivalry. While there might be a chance he's innocent, have you thought about what you're going to do if he's not?"

She dug her toes deeper into the carpet. "Dan and I have been so close that somehow I think I'd know if he were guilty." How could she make him see? "I sense that you go a lot by gut instinct, so you should understand."

When he didn't answer, she said, "If he's guilty, then I'll handle the situation as it comes up." She didn't want to tell him that the prospect of facing Dan's guilt was just too much for her to contemplate right now. She had to keep her mind on *how* she was going to prove his innocence. There was no room in her heart for doubt, except maybe where Brant was concerned.

"So we have a deal?" he asked.

"How do I know I can trust you?"

He shrugged. "I'm the only one you trust, remember?"

"That was this morning."

His glance held hers for a second longer. "Think of it this way—you're better off with me than against me."

She sat there frowning, silent, debating with herself, and glanced away for a moment. She wanted to look more closely into his motives, but felt her heart soar somewhere between joy and despair because his offer would double her chances of helping Dan. When she looked back at him her mind was made up. "All right. Where do we start?"

"Wherever you want."

Layne stood up. "I guess we have a deal, then. Should we shake hands or something?"

That drew a smile. "We can do anything you like."

She stretched out her hand and he rose from the chair and took it in his larger one.

"Then it's a deal," she said, releasing his hand.

For an instant she tried to cloak a pang of nagging doubt with a smile, then she reminded herself that for Dan she'd be willing to take a risk. For him, she'd take any risk.

For family, there would always be an exception to the rule.

"Anything else you'd like to discuss?" Brant asked.

"Yes, but would you mind talking in the kitchen? My blood sugar needs a boost." The invitation was issued over her shoulder as she walked into the kitchen.

She flipped on the light switch. "Care for a ham-and-cheese sandwich?"

He shook his head.

"Coffee or tea?"

"Whatever you're having."

She set to work and made herself a sandwich, then took two glasses out of a cabinet, filled them with ice and set them on the table. "Here's what I know, so far," she offered. "Dan delivered the briefcase to a private airstrip. He described the man who made a record of it as short and bald." She walked over and took a pitcher out of the refrigerator, then returned and poured tea in his glass. She filled hers only halfway. "We can start by finding that record."

With an easy motion he pulled a chair out and straddled it. "Do you happen to know which airstrip?"

"The one by the old Danvers farm."

"All right. We'll start there. I'll go—"

"*We'll* go to the airstrip... together," she cut in, sitting down across from him. "As soon as we're through here."

"Whoa. Wait a minute." He held up a hand. "We can't go out there tonight. I need to look the place over, study their routine. Then we'll make our move. Give me a few days."

For a moment, Layne felt disappointed. "You're right, I suppose. It's just that I'm anxious to get this over with."

"I know." His tone was low and gentle.

She drank some of her tea. "I've done a check on Salinas. It's only a paper trail, but it's a start."

He smiled. "I figured you would. We can compare notes later. I want to check out the airstrip first."

"All right." Layne ate her sandwich and drank the rest of her tea.

Brant downed his glass, picked up hers and put the empty glasses in the sink.

Layne watched him, fascinated by the graceful motion of such a large body. Everything about him suggested rugged strength and she felt that strong tug of attraction again. She told herself it was because she wasn't used to a man of Brant's raw maleness. Instinct warned her not to put all her faith in this man. Yet she knew that with Brant on her side she'd have a better chance of proving Dan's innocence.

"You're just planning to check the place out, right? I mean, you won't go out there without me, will you?" Momentary doubt caused the words to rush out before she could stop them, making her feel awkward for sounding like a child who needed assurance.

He was leaning against the sink. Straightening, he walked over and stood looking down at the little pucker between her brows. "I never go back on my word. I'll be back." He studied Layne, his face set, and something hardened in his voice. "One word of warning, counselor. If you're thinking of using me, don't. I don't like surprises."

Layne gave him a wan smile. "Neither do I, Lawman. Neither do I."

Thick grass muffled his footsteps. The airstrip spread across a large part of land that had once been farmland. Brant stood in tall grass surrounded by trees and shrubbery thick and far enough away to hide him. The October sun touched his back, its angle such that it wouldn't reflect off the lens of his binoculars.

Two men worked the premises. He'd been studying their routine for the past two days. One of them fit the description Dan had given Layne. Brant watched as the man gave orders for several crates to be boarded onto a small, private plane before walking over to enter an office. Satisfied, Brant turned and walked the half mile back to his car.

As he drove back to town, he reached over and pressed several numbers on his mobile phone. A second later Layne answered.

He told her simply, "I'll pick you up at midnight. Be ready."

They turned off the interstate onto a graveled road and traveled about a mile before Brant eased the car onto a small incline near a line of trees and stopped. Layne couldn't make out much in the dark and her imagination conjured up snakes lying in wait everywhere.

"We came in from the back. This old road isn't used much any more."

"Why not?" she asked, trying not to think of crawly things in the night.

"About ten years ago the owner leased the land to an oil company. They drilled a well here, but it proved to be a dry hole so they packed up and left." He opened the glove compartment and took out two flashlights. "Wait here," he said, handing her one of them.

She frowned. "Oh, no, you don't. I'm going with you."

Brant sighed in exasperation. "Don't tell me you're going to be stubborn about this. Can't you ever do as you're told?"

"Not when something else will work better," she replied stubbornly. "You promised we'd work together. I'm holding you to that."

He sighed. "All right. Come on. But if we're caught, don't say I didn't warn you."

"Fair enough." She swallowed nervously as she opened the door and got out. In order to blend with the night, she'd worn jeans and the same shapeless black sweatshirt she'd worn the night she'd gone to see Brant.

She walked over and stood beside him. The screech of crickets stopped and Layne's spine prickled with unease as she peered into the dark.

"Don't turn on the flashlight. I don't want to use it until we get to the office."

Oh, great, she thought. She wouldn't even have the benefit of knowing what *kind* of snake had bitten her. It took several minutes for her eyes to adjust to the shadows. A good portion of the moon hid behind dark clouds, casting barely enough glow for them to see where they were walking. Hulking shapes loomed before her in the eerie quiet.

As they crept toward the small building, Layne strained to listen to the night sounds. Grass brushed her ankles and her knees trembled. A second later she stumbled over a dead branch and cried out in alarm.

Brant caught her before she fell. "Shh," he whispered. "It's only a branch."

Layne swallowed nervously. "Did you hear that?"

"What?"

"I think I heard a snake."

"It's just your imagination. Stay close." He kept his voice low.

"Don't worry," she whispered back. "You'll think I'm glue before this night is over."

"What are you going to do if we're caught?"

"Tell them we're just two thieves passing in the night?"

He rolled his eyes heavenward. "Now I've got an ex-D.A. *and* a dangerous comedian on my hands."

"I'm also your backup," she added.

Brant snorted. "Oh, I forgot. You know self-defense, right?"

She glared at him in the dark. "Are you making fun of me?"

He sobered and turned to face her. "No. And I want you to remember something. No matter what happens here tonight, you're to do as I say. If danger comes, you won't have time to think. You'll have to act strictly on instinct. So if I say drop, you'd better drop—and fast, you understand?"

Layne nodded grimly and realized he couldn't see her.

"I understand," she replied.

As they approached the building, Layne noted the airstrip some distance away. The office looked like one of those small buildings someone had moved and set on the land. Stacks of bricks located at each of the four corners held up the structure. Above the door, a sign read *Cargo, Inc.*

Brant picked the lock on the door, then motioned for Layne to stay behind. He entered with caution. Only when he was satisfied did he turn and signal for her to come in.

The beam from his flashlight filtered slowly along the wall from one end of the room to the other. A calendar displayed Miss October in a lively pose. Tacky pictures in cheap plastic frames littered one wall, while several crates stood stacked and lined against another.

They walked over and looked down at scattered invoices and receipts cluttering the top of a metal desk. The unhealthy reek of cigar smoke mingled with that of body odor.

"Why don't you go through those invoices while I check out the crates," Brant said, pointing to several boxes stacked in a corner.

"All right." Setting her flashlight on top of the desk, Layne pulled the chair back and sat down, wincing as it squeaked. She picked up a stack of receipts.

On his way to the crates Brant spied a filing cabinet, stopped and tested a drawer. It was locked. He continued on.

A minute later he jerked his head up when Layne drew a sharp breath. "What's the matter?" he asked.

"Nothing. I just stubbed my toe."

"You all right?"

"Yeah, I'm okay." With a disgruntled sigh, she replaced the receipts in the same spot she'd found them and picked up the invoices.

Five minutes later he asked, "Have you found anything?"

"No. Have you?"

"Nothing." He aimed his flashlight along the baseboard.

Layne replaced the invoices and opened a drawer. "I wonder what was in that briefcase Salinas had Dan deliver here?"

Brant walked over to her. "That's what I'd like to know. Here. Hold this flashlight." He pulled a small camera out of his pocket and took a picture of several invoices. When he was through, he turned to another crate to continue his search.

Layne's muffled curse made Brant look up again.

"What now?" he asked.

"I stubbed my toe again." She stood up and moved the chair to one side. Squatting down on the floor, she reached under the desk and pulled at a box. It was heavy. She eyed the rug beneath it. Grabbing hold of one corner of the rug, she pulled. The rug and box slid out from under the desk. Layne began to rummage through the box.

She paused, then squinted to take a closer look. "Ah—would you come over here for a moment?"

Brant walked over and looked down at the floor. The rug had been covering up a square piece of board—a small trapdoor. He opened it.

Layne kept her voice low. "I knew a client once who had a safe installed beneath the floor in his master bathroom." She looked at him with a superior smirk. "I *knew* I'd find something here."

"So you did." He smiled, gazing down at the safe nestled safely beneath the floor. "Now, how are we going to open it?"

Layne opened her mouth to say something, but she saw Brant stiffen.

Quickly he shut the trapdoor, covered it with the rug and box and pushed the chair back in place. He grabbed both flashlights, turned them off and stuffed them in his back pocket. "Come on," he whispered, grabbing her arm. He led her the short distance to a door and pushed her in.

Layne, facing him, ended up stumbling into the room backward. "What—"

"Shut up," he muttered, following her in and closing the door. "Someone's coming."

Darkness spread around them like black ink. They stood chest to chest in a tiny coat closet. Layne reached behind her to see what was digging into her lower back and felt several wooden crates, one stacked on top of the other. She was trapped between Brant and the crates. Layne stifled a groan and tensed when she heard a key scraping in the lock.

But she had more to worry about than being plastered to Brant in such an intimate manner. If one discounted the rest room, there was nowhere else to hide. This closet would be the first place they'd look if they were suspicious. Her heart, hammering out of control, felt as though it were trying to outrun a treadmill.

After a moment she realized she'd been holding her breath. A thin film of perspiration broke out over her top lip. Exhaling quietly, she tried to relax. They'd been in the closet only a few moments, but already the tiny room felt suffocatingly warm. She found it difficult to breathe in the cramped quarters and Brant's nearness made it almost impossible to keep her mind on whoever had just stepped into the office. She held her breath again, straining to hear what went on outside the door.

The confining space was also taking its toll on Brant. He trembled from the exertion of having to fit himself between the wall and Layne. He breathed in her musky scent. It drove him wild and the enticing thrust of her nipples against his hard chest aroused him to the point of distraction.

He shifted uncomfortably. A mistake. Even hearing the stranger's voice didn't stop the involuntary hardening of his lower body—the movement was about as subtle as a sailor with a six-hour pass.

A light switched on and streamed narrowly across the floor. A man's voice startled Layne, making her jump.

Brant gritted his teeth to keep from groaning.

"This better be good enough to have gotten me out of a warm woman," a raspy male voice complained.

"Don't worry, it is," came the reply. "I've got some more for you." Something plunked down on the desk.

"I'll have to open the safe."

"So what? If you hurry, we can both be out of here in no time."

Layne didn't realize she had a death grip on Brant's shoulders until she felt him stir. She loosened her hold and her breath caught as she felt his body tighten again. Even though she was frightened, the intimacy of the darkness and Brant's obvious arousal didn't leave her unaffected.

They heard the creaking of a chair being pulled away from the desk. Layne imagined the rug being pushed aside. Thank God, she and Brant hadn't touched that safe.

"All right," the raspy voice muttered. "Hand it here." There was a pause. "Fifty grand. That's petty cash."

"It might be to you, but the damn stuff's burning a hole in my pocket. I don't want my old lady to find it. By the way, when can I talk to him?"

"The boss is laying low. We won't be shipping out any more stuff for a while."

"What about the stuff I just gave you?"

"Like I said, he'll probably use it for petty cash."

There was another long pause. A chair creaked as someone scooted it back. "I'll make a note of this, then you can go."

Another pause, another creaking of the chair to indicate the man with the gruff voice had stood up.

"Hey, aren't you gonna put that book back in the safe?"

The raspy voice replied, "Naah. I've already locked it."

A minute later their footsteps drifted away. Brant and Layne heard the door close.

Layne let out a long sigh of relief and waited for Brant to move.

But neither of them made any move to leave. Layne realized she didn't want to. Her heart escalated with an entirely different beat as she felt Brant's hardness against her stomach. Each part of her that pressed against him burned with a curious hunger to know more.

She didn't know why—maybe it was the near brush with getting caught and possibly meeting death, or the heightening of senses caused by the darkness, or knowing that once they left this room they would go back to being strictly professional allies—but just this once she wanted to give up the struggle of being sensible. She burned to give herself up to senses that had nothing to do with logic.

Obeying the impulse, her hands slid gently up his shoulders and she pressed closer.

Just this once, she thought.

"Layne," her name flowed through his lips like a silk caress. "I...can't...move," he groaned. Lowering his head he unerringly found her mouth in the dark. His hands burned a trail upward fitting themselves through her hair as he guided her deeper into the kiss. Their breaths mingled and his tongue stroked hers. Slowly at first. In—out, in—out, the motion resembling physical love.

Layne let out a small moan and strained closer.

His strong hands crept to her waist and lifted her off the floor, then gently sat her on top of the crates. His fingers slid to her hips, raised them and pulled her closer to straddle him. Layne's thighs opened gladly and allowed him to fit himself more comfortably against her.

Never had denim felt so good against denim.

Never had it felt so confining.

"Layne, honey," Brant whispered into her mouth. "You're going to have to stop me...because...I can't," he said, moving against her.

Stop him? Was he mad? Couldn't he tell how much she wanted him? Never had she felt this way about any other man. Here in the dark, in his arms, every move, every fiber, every sense came alive.

He lifted her sweatshirt, his wide palms trailed along her back. She clung to him, savoring the feel of his fingers as they stroked her spine. One hand continued its exploration of her back, while the other caressed its way around to her front. His fingers closed around a soft, full breast. She wasn't wearing a bra. He drew in a shaky breath, deepening the kiss.

His hand moved between them and touched her zipper. "God, I want you," he said desperately. "I want you bad." He stopped and expelled a tormented breath as he put his forehead against hers. "But this place is a little crowded." His body shuddered with regret.

At first Layne's brain refused to shift gears and she pressed herself closer. Then, as what he'd said started to make sense, she broke away gasping. My God, what was she doing? What had she almost done? She'd practically begged him to take her. The fact that he'd offered to help her held little consolation.

She closed her eyes, embarrassed at what she'd almost allowed him to do, what she'd wanted him to do, and miserable with herself because *nothing* would have stopped her had they been somewhere else.

"You're right," she muttered with an effort. "They might come back. We'd better go."

Layne's knees trembled as he helped her down from her perch on the crates. Her lips felt faintly swollen from his kiss. With an awkward movement she fumbled with her shirt, trying to get it straight, thankful the dark hid her face.

In tense silence they walked out of the closet. She didn't want to look at him, but it was hard not to.

Brant held out his hand. "Layne," he whispered. "I shouldn't have done that. I'm..."

She walked past him, cutting him off. "We'd better hurry. Some one else may show up." She knew he'd been about to say he was sorry and she didn't want to hear it. God help her, she had enjoyed every minute. She told herself it was purely physical, that tomorrow it would be forgotten, but she knew better.

She didn't want him to become more important to her than he already was. To say she trusted him said a lot for her, because she didn't trust easily nor did she allow herself to depend on anyone else but herself, ever. She liked to be in control and tonight, just now, she'd felt that control slipping. Shaking herself mentally, she reminded herself she already had one problem. She couldn't deal with two. It was time to prove her brother's innocence. She wanted him home for Thanksgiving.

With an air of resignation, she made her way over to the desk with Brant trailing close behind.

"Where do you think he stashed the book?" she asked.

"It has to be here. I didn't hear him walk anywhere." Brant rifled through several drawers while Layne fumbled frantically through the stack of paperwork on the desk.

"It's not here," Layne stated, a little breathless.

Brant pushed the chair, box and rug aside, then knelt down to get under the desk. He yanked open the trapdoor. There on top of the safe lay a small ledger.

His voice was slightly hoarse. "Hold this, will you?" He handed her his flashlight, then picked up the book and opened it.

Brant saw the light wiggle as her hand trembled and he fought to bring his raging hormones under control. With an effort he focused on a page. There, in bold, masculine script, were names and destinations. Beside each name an amount was legibly written. Brant scanned the three pages that had been filled. The same names kept appearing on each page. His glance zeroed in on two names. Dan Tyler and Jesse Alphonso.

Brant set the ledger down on the desk and picked up his camera to click off a photo of each page. When he had finished he closed the book with a snap and returned it to its spot on top of the safe.

Layne's heart hammering had nothing to do with Brant this time. It was seeing Dan's name under Alphonso's that made her shiver with alarm. She watched Brant close the trapdoor and return the box and rug to its place.

"The fact that Alphonso's name is in that book with Dan's doesn't mean Dan killed him," she said.

"Let's go."

Layne wanted to pursue the matter, but seeing the set of his jaw, she decided it could wait. Side by side they made their way back to the car in silence. They got in and started back along the same gravel road they'd come.

"I'll have the film developed and bring it over tomorrow morning—if that's all right with you."

"Fine." Afraid of what her eyes would reveal, she stared straight ahead.

Brant looked at her for a second before he returned his attention to the highway. He'd been surprised at her response and affected by it. The urge to stop the car and take her out on the grass somewhere became overwhelming, but he nixed the idea. She'd be the kind of woman who would expect satin sheets and her favorite color was probably gold, as in wedding band. Then there was that little matter of Dan. No, he told himself. Better forget about her altogether.

Except how in the hell was he going to do that when they were being thrown together so much?

His fingers clenched the steering wheel tighter. Anger and frustration warred within him. How long would he be able to ignore the passionate green of her eyes and the fiery auburn hair that begged him to remove the pins from its silken tresses? Or the feel of her lips, pliable and warm. He remembered the soft roundness of her breasts. Hot blood flowed through his loins; he wanted to get lost in her. But he wouldn't. Again, Brant reminded himself he would have to keep his mind above his waist. For both their sakes.

"I'm going to Salinas's office tomorrow. Want to come?" he asked.

"I've already been," Layne replied. "Rico was nice enough, but I wasn't greeted too enthusiastically by his secretary. She guards that office as though it held the family jewels."

He smiled. "Don't worry, she won't give you any trouble."

"You know her?"

"I've met her."

Of course he'd know her, Layne thought. She was certain he'd covered as much ground as she had in the investigation. Probably more.

Layne recalled how the tall, well-endowed secretary oozed sex appeal. Shanna Caldwell and Brant would look beautiful together. For a moment, she felt a pang of something very close to jealousy.

Absurd, she thought. She wasn't the jealous type.

They made the rest of the trip in silence.

Chapter 10

Midmorning sun streaked through the kitchen window, spilling across the photograph lying on the table. It had been magnified. Layne's eyes were grim as she stared down at the list of names again.

"As you can see," Brant said, "this name keeps cropping up more than the others." He pointed to one name in particular—H. Cruz. "Looks like he does most of the running. His name is also the last one on the list, so most likely he's the guy we heard talking."

The mere mention of last night's regrettable episode made Layne's pulse beat faster. Her eyes blurred with the memory and she exhaled a soundless sigh. Not by a flicker nor by the slightest inflection did Brant reveal that he remembered anything had happened between them.

Which was just as well, she thought. Nothing like that would ever happen again. She needed no man to dust her life right now, nor to get close enough to cause intimate damage to her heart. She studied his hands as they held the photo, remembering how gentle they had felt as they'd spanned her ribs. And strong, too. Strong enough to lift her—

Layne shook her head trying to clear away the memory. She looked up. His eyes were trained on her face and she realized he'd just said something.

"Pardon?" she muttered, feeling like an idiot for getting caught daydreaming like an adolescent.

Brant's gaze softened before turning cloudy. "I said Alphonso's name is on here several times. And of course Dan's name is on the list once."

Layne studied the list again. There was a number beside each name, followed by two initials. One line read: *J. Alphonso 50 CA*.

"Last night, that man delivered money," she pointed out. "That must be what the number code means beside his name. But what does CA stand for? Some of the amounts are different, but CA is beside every name except for Cruz."

"There's nothing beside his name because he was told the money was only going to petty cash, remember? My guess is that CA is a destination," Brant replied.

"California?"

"I don't think so. Too obvious."

Layne reached into her briefcase and brought out a manila folder. "I ran a check on Salinas and his nephew several days ago and found out quite a bit about them, but nothing that will help Dan, I'm afraid."

"Rico has an alibi, and his servant is backing him up," Brant added.

The doorbell rang.

"You expecting someone?" Brant asked.

"No." She stood up. "I'd better see who it is."

When Layne opened the door, her eyes widened in surprise.

"Travis! When did you get back?"

"This morning. I came as soon as I heard what had happened." Travis walked in and he embraced her. Layne stood motionless, her arms hung limply by her sides. He stepped back, taking both her hands in his, and gazed down at her. "I missed you. Are you all right?"

"I'm fine. How did the trip go?" She asked, disconcerted by his show of attention.

"Great. I've got enough information and evidence to win my case." He beamed proudly, then hugged her again.

Layne opened her mouth to tell him he was suffocating her with his affectionate bear hug, but she felt him stiffen. Glancing up, she saw him staring over her shoulder and followed his line of vision.

Brant leaned a shoulder indolently against the doorway, both arms crossed against his chest. From beneath half-lowered lids, those blue eyes studied her from across the room.

She spoke to Travis, but shot Brant a sideways look. "Travis, this is Brant Wade. He's the Texas Ranger working on the Salinas case. Brant, Travis Adams."

Having gotten over his initial surprise, Travis smiled as he walked over and shook Brant's hand. "Pleased to met you."

Brant straightened, nodded and accepted Travis's hand, but he didn't return the smile. He sized up the other man. Brant's height alone had intimidated many a man and those eyes had a way of pushing deep into a person's soul.

An awkward pause followed, until finally Travis turned back to Layne and put a comforting hand on her shoulder. "I'm sorry about Dan. Any developments?"

She shook her head. "Brant and I are going over some details, but nothing concrete has turned up."

"Well, I'm home now," Travis said quietly. "If you need any help you know I'm here for you."

She didn't doubt his concern. It was there in his tone and expression. Layne experienced an uneasy moment as she shot a brief and distracted smile in Brant's direction. "Thanks," she replied to Travis. Then, for lack of anything else to say, she blurted out, "I guess you've heard I've resigned."

Travis frowned. "Layne, do you think that's wise? I mean, people might think you're doing it because you suspect Dan might be guilty."

He'd hit a nerve. Layne bristled, jumping to Dan's defense. "I believe no such thing. I know Dan is innocent. Resigning is the only way I can work on the investigation, that's all."

"Relax, Layne. I'm just worried about you." He stole an anxious glance at his watch. "My offer still stands. I'll help any way I can."

She suppressed the urge to turn and look at Brant. "Thanks. I appreciate that."

Travis leaned down and kissed her lightly on the lips. "I'd better go. I'll call you tonight. We can have dinner and discuss it."

Layne nodded. "All right."

To Brant, he said, "See you around," and with a polite wave he was gone.

Layne closed the door and turned around.

"So that's Travis."

"Yes."

"He's the man you've been dating."

She shrugged. "We're friends."

"I can see that."

She walked past him. "We'd better hurry, if we're going to make it to Salinas's office before noon."

''Don't worry,'' he offered. ''We'll make it back in time for you and Travis to swap tales of woe over dinner.''

She stopped and turned around. ''Would you mind leaving the list of names here? I'd like to go over them again later.''

''If you like.'' He closed the distance between them and looked down at her. ''Do you have any problem with our plan? We can still call it off, you know.''

His quiet voice vibrated through her body. She looked into his eyes and shook her head. ''Absolutely not. I'll get my purse.''

Shanna Caldwell sat behind her desk when Brant entered the plush office.

Layne remained in the hallway out of sight. She paused to glance in first one direction, then the other. Reaching into her purse, she took out the fake glasses she'd purchased yesterday and put them on. The clear lenses, large and round, practically hid her face. As she leaned over slightly to listen, the glasses slipped halfway down the arch of her nose and she pushed them up again.

She kept her face down, straining to listen.

''Why, Mr. Wade. How nice to see you,'' Shanna cooed.

''Hi. Ms. Caldwell, isn't it?''

''Call me Shanna.''

''All right . . . Shanna.''

''Jim's out of town and Rico's gone to lunch. I was just on my way out. Anything I can do for you?''

''As a matter of fact there is,'' Brant replied. ''I have a few questions to ask you, but I don't want to keep you from your lunch.''

''Oh,'' she sighed. ''I hadn't planned anything special.''

''Lucky for me. Why don't I buy you lunch? We can talk then.''

"Why, how sweet."

"My pleasure."

Layne could just imagine the buxom blonde scurrying to get her purse before Brant changed his mind. She pursed her lips and frowned. Brant had never been that solicitous with *her*. In fact, the night he'd wanted to question her, Brant had made his intentions quite clear. Either she answered his questions or she went to jail.

Shanna Caldwell was getting the royal treatment.

There was a pause and Layne scrambled to get out of the way. She made a beeline for the water fountain a short distance away and leaned over to take a drink.

She heard the door open.

"Here, let me," Brant said. "You push this little button down to lock it, right?"

"Yes, thanks."

Layne pretended to drink water from the spouting fountain until curiosity got the better of her and she sneaked a peek at the couple as they waited for the elevator. Her eyes narrowed. Shanna was taller and more majestic-looking than Layne remembered. In fact, she and Brant made a dazzling couple.

Who cares, she thought, *I'm here to see to business.* Straightening, she pushed the cumbersome glasses back up on the ridge of her nose.

The elevator pinged, its doors swung open.

Layne relaxed slightly, until a sudden move from behind caused her to flinch to attention. She heard a woman call out, "Hold the elevator!"

In a panic, Layne turned and walked toward the woman. A second later, she spotted the ladies' rest room and ducked in.

Turning on the faucet to wash her hands, Layne's brows drew together in a frown as she looked at herself in the mirror. Instead of the severe french knot she usually wore, her auburn hair now fell in soft curls to her shoulders. Gone was the tailored suit. In an effort to blend in and keep from being recognized, Layne wore a comfortable damask dress in a teal-and-brown print. She'd traded her sensible shoes for a pair of sexy brown sling pumps.

She felt conspicuous. After all, she wasn't that well versed in spy tactics. Layne waited another moment before leaving.

When she reached the door Brant had pretended to lock, Layne turned the knob. Cautiously she stepped inside and pushed the button down to lock the door.

She had less than an hour before Brant returned with Shanna.

Layne walked past the secretary's desk to the first office door. The name MICHAEL SALINAS was printed across the door in large bold letters.

She tested the knob. The door was locked.

Hurrying over to Shanna's desk, she opened the top drawer—and smiled. Shanna had been in too much of a hurry to leave; she hadn't locked her desk. Several keys attached to a large key ring rested in the slot of a pencil tray. She picked them up and returned to Salinas's door.

By the time she'd tried the last key and realized none of them fit, perspiration had broken out on her brow. Feeling an anxious fluttering in her stomach, Layne rubbed her clammy hands against her dress. Returning to Shanna's desk she again searched the drawer, groping around the sides and toward the back.

Nothing.

She stared hard at the drawer as if by some miracle, X-ray vision would come to her aid. She thought a moment.

This time she lifted the pencil tray.

A single key lay there. A master key? She snatched it up, replaced the pencil tray and ran back to the door.

Keeping her fingers of one hand crossed, she tried the key with the other.

It fit. Thank God!

Stepping inside the office, Layne drew a sigh of relief and looked around, then walked over to the desk and set the key down on top. She sat down and leaned back in the leather chair.

All right, Layne, she told herself as she set to work, *think of this as a scavenger hunt.* She remembered a private detective had told her once that an hour of good detective work saved one a lifetime of cross-examination. Learn to look at what's left behind, he'd added.

She leaned over and checked the wastepaper basket. Empty. Nothing to raid there.

Opening the top drawer of the desk, she scanned its contents—two ballpoint pens, one pencil, paper clips, and a half-empty roll of breath mints. She slid her hand further into the drawer, toward the back. Nothing.

Her fingers trembled in frustration as she closed the drawer and opened another, until all of them had been opened but one. If only she could find something. Anything. But, then, why should she? Salinas probably wouldn't leave anything around that would be incriminating.

With a deep sigh, she reached down and opened the large drawer on the left. File folders hung neatly in a row. Layne went through them one by one.

A thin film of perspiration popped out on her upper lip and she reached up to swipe at it.

Time was running out. She felt a sharp spurt of anger. While Brant was entertaining Shanna Caldwell and feeding her vanity and voluptuous body, Layne was sitting in this office with her stomach growling and her body burning up with nervous exhaustion. Of course, she had to remember this had been her idea.

She slumped, discouraged, against the chair. She'd gone through almost the entire stack of files when the next one caught her attention. It contained several computer sheets. Layne scanned each page. Her body went taut. This file contained a list of companies Michael Salinas had owned. One in particular stood out.

He had owned Cargo, Inc.

And now, Jim Weston and Rico Salinas owned it. Were they aware, she wondered, that someone had been shipping money out from the cargo company?

Could it be Jim Weston who'd wanted Salinas out of the way? Or Rico?

She jumped up and ran over to the copy machine in the outer office and copied the information. While she was replacing the computer sheets, something fell out of the file. Layne picked it up. It was a cashier's check for one million dollars made out to S & W Corporation. Salinas & Weston Corp.

Layne gasped as she read where the cashier's check had been sent from.

"I got something!" Layne grinned as Brant slid into the car beside her. "By the way," she added, "I've been waiting forever. What took you so long?"

"Shanna's quite a conversationalist," he answered, starting up the engine.

Layne frowned, forgetting her news. "That's nice to hear. I haven't eaten all day."

"We can stop and get you something on the way home," he said, pulling out into the stream of traffic.

"And what did you and Shanna have? A filet mignon or a porterhouse steak?" She knew she was being bitchy, but she couldn't help herself. An empty stomach always put her in a bad mood.

"Neither. She's a vegetarian." He turned a corner.

Layne's mouth flexed with wry distaste. "It's hard to believe that such a . . . tall body got that way eating lettuce and sprouts, isn't it?"

"She also likes pasta," he added. "In fact, she invited me to her apartment tonight to try one of her specialties."

"I'll just bet," Layne mumbled, looking out the window.

"Pardon?" Brant looked at her for an instant before returning his attention to the road.

"I said, just stop at the next McDonald's."

"By the way," he said, "what did you find out?"

Layne turned her head from the window and looked at him. He could be so exasperating. "S & W Corporation owns Cargo, Limited."

His attention perked up.

"And get this," she added, "I also have a copy of a cashier's check made out to S & W for repayment of a loan from a company in the Caymans." She paused to let her words sink in before her voice dropped to a confidential hush. "The Caymans—as in CA."

He gave her a quick look. "The money the men delivered to the cargo office is being shipped to the Caymans?"

"You got it."

"So someone had the money flown to the Caymans, to a company there that has an outstanding loan with S & W. Why?" He turned off the road into a café parking lot. "That's something we'll have to find out. What are you doing?"

He turned off the engine and looked at her, a mocking glint in his eyes. "I thought you were hungry. Come on." He opened the door, got out and walked over to her side.

She opened her door. "This doesn't look like McDonald's," she said, looking up at him.

"No, but the food is good. Are you going to get out or not?"

She smiled sweetly. "How can I possibly pass up an invitation like that." She started to get out of the car, but a loud beep stopped her. It was a second before she realized that it wasn't another car. The beep came from Brant's car phone.

Layne attempted to slide out so Brant could answer from the passenger side. But before she could do so, he had blocked her way and was leaning over to reach for the receiver.

She leaned back against the seat as far as she could, in order to give him more room. It was no use. His left shoulder and arm were molded against her breast and Layne felt the tightening of her nipples as they hardened at his touch. Embarrassed, she closed her eyes.

"I'm sorry. Your lunch is going to have to wait a little longer," Brant's husky voice whispered somewhere in the vicinity of her ear, his breath fanned her hair slightly.

She opened her eyes. Something flickered in the blue depths of his before he straightened. Layne wanted to look anywhere but at Brant. She was almost certain he knew she'd been aroused by a mere touch. For a moment her face flamed.

"I guess you heard that," he said.

"Wh—what?" she asked a bit shaky.

"Someone fitting Dan's description has been spotted in an old abandoned house about ten miles from here. I have to check it out."

"Of course. I'll go with you."

He got in the car and started the engine.

A few minutes later the countryside flew past them as Brant floored the accelerator of the Ford. Layne's heart leaped with hope as she listened to the muffled hum of the engine. She prayed it would be Dan. She needed to see him, to talk to him.

By the time they reached the house Layne was glad she hadn't eaten. Her stomach felt like a clump of tangled knots.

Brant pulled off the two-lane road and parked beside a wooded slope. "We'll have to go on foot from here. The house is up there among those trees."

They got out and edged their way along a thick line of shrubs onto a man-made path that led to the house. As they inched closer they could hear the muted drone of an airplane overhead.

Brant glanced around sharply. "Wait here. I'm going in."

Layne shook her head, refusing to be left behind. "No. If it's Dan you'll stand a much better chance of getting him to give himself up if I'm with you. He'll listen to me. Don't look at me like that. I'm not waiting, Brant," she declared with a stubborn set to her jaw.

"What if it's not him?"

"I don't care. I want to go." It had to be Dan. It just had to. She hadn't seen him in so long. She missed him.

"All right, just calm down," he whispered.

Layne drew up beside him and they continued along the path. Squinting toward the house, she saw someone. His head was bent as if he were deep in thought. She stopped and pressed a hand against her chest as a flicker of hope flared inside her.

He raised his head. For a heart-stopping second, Layne thought he looked straight at her.

She stood there staring at the boy, her heart breaking into a million little pieces.

Brant took a step toward her.

Chapter 11

Layne shook her head in despair. It wasn't Dan. Disappointment welled up so deep within her it threatened to choke her.

"You all right?" Brant asked gently.

"Yes." Her voice was faint.

"Stay here, I'm going to talk to him."

Layne nodded silently, continuing to stare at the boy. He bore a certain resemblance to Dan. It was there in the lean, intelligent features, in the easy way he stood. He was taller, a little heavier, and she realized that he couldn't be more than sixteen or seventeen years old. His jeans were as well worn as his denim jacket. She couldn't tell what color his eyes were from this distance, but she took in the raven-colored hair that touched his shoulders.

There was a sudden rustling of a shrub as Brant left his hiding place. His voice lifted in a shout. "Stay where you are!"

The young boy had been daydreaming. Upon hearing the command he jerked his head toward the voice and froze at the sight of Brant. For an instant he looked as though he wavered between obeying and taking flight.

"Don't try it, son," Brant warned, pointing to his badge.

Layne couldn't bear to stand there any longer. She walked out in the open where they could see her, and as she approached Layne thought she detected relief in the boy's eyes.

Brant risked a quick look at Layne before returning his attention to the boy. "I thought I told you to stay put," he whispered to Layne.

She ignored the curt tone in his voice. "He can't be more than sixteen, Brant. Look at him, he's scared to death."

"What's your name, boy?" Brant asked.

"Dallas. Dallas Smith."

"Smith?" Brant's tone was skeptical.

Dallas Smith straightened to his full height of six feet and squared his shoulders. "That's the truth. I've got some ID."

"Just stand still," Brant ordered.

"My driver's license is in my back pocket. If you don't believe me, take a look for yourself."

"All right, but take it out easy-like, you hear?"

"Yes, sir." Dallas replied. Slowly he pulled out a worn billfold from his pocket and handed it over.

Brant paused to verify the information, noting Dallas would be eighteen years old on December 7. *December 7. His dad's birthday had been on that day.* Brant cleared his throat. "Dallas is your real name?"

"Yes, sir, it's for real." Dallas stuck his hand in his back pocket and put most of his weight on one foot, but the easy stance didn't hide the fact that he was tense.

"You born in Dallas?" Brant asked.

For the first time Dallas smiled faintly. "Everybody thinks that, but no, I got my name when my mom went into labor on Dallas Street in Houston."

"What are you doing here?" Brant asked, returning the wallet.

"I wanted to spend some time alone, that's all."

"Did you run away from home?"

Dallas Smith couldn't hide the truth. He looked away, then back. "Yeah . . . sort of."

"How did you get out here, Dallas? I didn't see any vehicle."

"I thumbed a ride," Dallas replied, gesturing with his thumb.

"Okay," Brant said abruptly. "Let's get moving."

Dallas winced at the words, looking as though someone had just given him castor oil. "Are you taking me to jail? Cause if you are, don't bother to call my mom. She's sick. She won't have the money to bail me out."

"Where's your dad?" Layne broke her silence. Something about Dallas pulled at her maternal strings. Or maybe it was because he reminded her of Dan.

Dallas's gaze shifted to Layne. "He left a month ago. We haven't heard from him since."

"Why did you run away, son?" Brant's gaze softened.

"My mom and I . . . had an argument. I want to quit school to help her out. She said no. We argued." He shrugged. "So I left."

"How long you been missing from home, Dallas?" Brant asked.

"Two days. I spent last night here. I was gonna go back. I wouldn't leave her. It's just that I feel kind of helpless, you know?" His face flushed at having revealed so much and he looked away.

"Yeah, I know." Brant's tone was warm. "Come on, we'll take you home."

Dallas groped for words. "You're not taking me to jail?"

"You're on private property and you spent the night here. That alone would bring a charge of criminal mischief." He paused to let that sink in. "But I'll make an exception this time, only don't let me hear that you did this again."

"Don't worry, I won't." Dallas Smith's eyes glowed with relief. "I didn't break in the house or anything. I slept outside."

As Layne watched Dallas, she made no effort to hide her own relief. Tears pricked at the backs of her eyelids. Her features softened and as their eyes met she smiled.

Brant looked faintly amused. "Say, Dallas. You don't mind if we stop and feed this lady on the way, do you? Especially since you're responsible for her hunger pangs."

Dallas shook his head.

They both looked at her. Their sudden bold smiles made her blush and look away.

By the time the car pulled up into Dallas's driveway, a woman was already standing on the porch. Dallas's mother, judging by her strong resemblance to Dallas.

Layne noticed she looked frail, almost to the point of emaciation.

When Mrs. Smith saw Dallas jump out of the car she started to cry. "Oh, my God," she moaned, "I've been so worried. Oh, sweetheart, I thought something had happened to you."

Dallas stooped over to hug her, being careful not to throw her off balance as she clung to him.

"I'm sorry, Mom." Dallas looked penitent; his eyes appeared glassy from unshed tears.

As Layne watched the happy reunion between mother and son, her heart constricted. She thought of Dan. Would she ever see him again?

Smiling tearfully, Mrs. Smith glanced over at Layne and Brant. Her gaze took in Brant's badge and she frowned.

"Is Dallas in any trouble?" Her voice was soft and weak as though she found speaking an effort.

"No ma'am. He was on his way home. We just gave him a lift." Brant shifted his gaze to Dallas for a moment before returning to smile at his mother.

"Thank you, Mr...."

"Brant Wade. This is Layne Tyler."

Layne smiled and nodded.

"Would you both like to come in and have something to drink? I . . . I have some beer and soda."

"I thought you'd thrown that stuff out." Dallas barked. "You know he's not coming back."

Mrs. Smith flushed. "I was going to. Maybe Mr. Wade would like some—"

"No, thank you, ma'am. We've got to be going."

"All right. But I'm mighty grateful to you for giving my son a ride home."

"Our pleasure." Brant hesitated for an instant, wondering if he should offer her any hope, then decided to plunge in. "Dallas tells me your husband . . . is missing. If it's all right with you, I'll check into it."

Dallas jumped forward. "We don't need him."

"Shush, Dallas. The man is trying to talk."

This time Brant's statement was directed at Dallas. "It's possible something could've happened to him. Maybe that's why he hasn't shown up."

Dallas snorted, clearly not convinced. "If something happened, wouldn't we have been notified?"

"Not if his ID was taken." Brant looked into Mrs. Smith's worried features. "I'll look into it."

"Thank you. For all your help. And Dallas thanks you, too." She threw her a son a reproving look.

"I have something to say to him, too." Brant's stern features turned to Dallas. "I expect you to finish school. If I find out you're not going I'll be back, you understand?" At Dallas's silent nod, he continued. "I know a couple of people around here. I'm sure one of them will give you a part-time job, but only after school—and *only* if you keep your grades up." Brant reached into his shirt pocket, pulled out a card and handed it to Mrs. Smith. "Call me if you need anything."

Mrs. Smith smiled faintly and looked up with tears in her eyes that told him how grateful she was.

Layne had been watching Dallas. Now her attention switched to Brant and she contemplated the gentleness in his eyes with astonishment and pleasure, touched by the way he'd handled the situation. She understood what he was feeling, too. He cared very much that Dallas was caught between feeling anxiety for his mother and anger brought on by the abandonment of his father.

There was a tug at her heart and she blinked, seeing another side of Brant. Under that gruff exterior she detected an underlying tenderness in him, a soft spot for kids. He liked them. She sensed he covered up a vulnerability behind the macho facade. He didn't want anyone to know just how susceptible he really was.

As they waved goodbye to Dallas and his mother, Layne knew without a doubt that Dan would be much safer in Brant's custody.

Maybe there was hope after all.

This was October. With Brant's help, just maybe, she and Dan would be spending Thanksgiving and Christmas together. Right now hope was the only thing that gave her purpose. So much time had gone by and today was one more day that she marked time, praying for some news, something that would clear Dan.

Layne was silent as they drove along the interstate. A sudden jolt brought her out of her musing as the car came to a stop.

Glancing out the window, she realized they'd stopped on a beach. She looked at Brant. "Why have we stopped?"

"I thought you might want to talk." His voice was deep and husky and gentle.

She made a pretense of studying her hands which were folded in her lap. To tell him how she felt would mean giving away a piece of her soul. Was she ready for that? She'd never confided in anyone and for Brant to be the first one told her just how despondent she'd become. She stared out the window again. With a deep sigh she said, "You were right all along."

"About what?"

"Dan will be much safer in your custody. I only wish I could see him to tell him." She turned her head and watched him for some reaction. Brant remained silent and his eyes seemed to understand something.

She looked away. "When I saw Dallas looking so worried and vulnerable, I felt his sorrow. He's so young, and did you notice how frail and ill his mother looks?"

Brant didn't answer and she sighed again, blinking back tears. "Right after our parents died, Dan and I had a similar argument. He was thirteen and he wanted to get a job at the local grocery. I quieted him down long enough to explain that we had Mom and Dad's insurance money and that it would pay off our home and get him through school." She felt a lump in her throat. "I went to law school and got a part-time job at night. Somehow, I thought it would all work out.''

She didn't mention the sadness, the loneliness that came from not spending as much time with Dan or friends her age as she'd hoped. ''And now here I am without a job, without any clue as to what I should do next.''

''Oh, I'm sure we'll think of something.''

''He's all I've got.''

''I know.'' Brant's voice was gentle and his hand, which had been resting across the back of the seat, touched her shoulder. ''Come on, I want to show you something.'' He opened the door and got out.

As Layne slid out of the car an angry breeze ruffled her hair. This time of year in this part of Texas it wasn't winter yet, although it was cooler by the Gulf. She reached down, took off her shoes and left them in the car. Brant slid his hand in hers and led her closer to the water.

They stood there staring out over the surf. ''Ever been here?'' he asked, looking down at her.

''I've driven by, but never stopped. This is Boca Chica, isn't it?''

''Yep. Spanish for 'small mouth.' It's where the mouth of the Rio Grande meets the Gulf. Beautiful, isn't it?''

Layne nodded, staring into the distance where sky met water. A soft wind blew, causing sand to touch her skin, and the salt air made her nostrils flare. Fascinated, she listened to the roar of waves as they crashed, then rolled and churned to shore. Back and forth, back and forth.

She lost count of how many times as their hypnotic rhythm relaxed her to the point of feeling lazy. Her eyes drooped. She opened them just long enough to hear a gull cry out before dipping down to catch some unsuspecting fish. She longed to sit on the sand, but decided against it. They wouldn't be here long.

"Ever been fishing?"

She shook her head. Brant moved to stand behind her, and she leaned back, relaxing against his broad chest. At some point his arms had wrapped around hers which were crossed in front of her and his hands rested easily on top of her own. Funny, she hadn't noticed, not until now, and she felt too lazy to move. She shook her head.

"You'll have to try it some time. It's very relaxing. No worries, no hassles. After my dad died I used to come here a lot." Brant was surprised he'd told her that. What he didn't tell her was that he'd come here to grieve. And to do penance because he was being consumed by guilt. "Look, that's what I wanted you to see," he said, pointing to the sky.

The sunset was turning the sky into hues of orange, yellow and lavender.

Neither of them moved for a long time as they stared, both awed by the beauty of the moment.

He was the first to speak.

"See those trees over there? When a storm comes you'd think they'd be washed away, but they fold and bend in the storm and then they straighten once again. They're never blown off, because they're flexible and ride the storm. Do you understand?"

What a wonderful thing for him to say. Her pulse jumped. It had been such a long time since she'd been able to feel so casual and comfortable with another person. She found she loved the feeling and at that moment wanted nothing more than to tell him how she felt.

For a wild moment she wanted to turn and fall into his arms, to feel the safety, the protection of a man. She longed silently for a time when she wouldn't have to stand alone, when she wouldn't have to be so brave all the time.

When she wouldn't always have to say goodbye to people she loved.

She turned around.

"Yes, I understand. Thank you," she managed to say.

"You're welcome." His face broke into a smile, but it faded when he saw the tears in her eyes. "Layne," he whispered, gazing down at her with a mixture of conflicting emotions. Steadying her hair against the wind, he gently lowered his mouth to hers.

The way he'd said her name affected Layne like a finger stroking her spine. She wanted to reach up and touch his wind-tousled hair. It was the easiest thing in the world for her to raise herself on tiptoe and for him to bend his knees to accommodate their heights.

His mouth moved over her lips, soft and sweet at first, parting them until tongues touched and tasted salt. The kiss was long and slow as they stood beneath the shimmering splendor of sunset and the cooling breezes from the Gulf which forced them to find warmth in each other.

Her breath escaped in a quivering sigh and as she slid her arms behind his neck and arched her body against his Layne felt the frail bridge that existed between them give way.

Welcoming her warm response Brant's arms slid tightly around her, savoring the nearness of her body. His own body craved more than the shattering kiss they were sharing. His mouth eased down her throat, his breath caressed her skin, his fingers traveling along her hips became more demanding.

It felt so right to hold her. Out here there was no one to interrupt them, not the pressing call of Brant's duty nor Layne's guilt. They were two people attracted to each other and they remembered the times they'd come together only to be pulled apart by duty or conscience. Here they were free from restraint by mutual consent from both parties.

But in the end it was those same things that made them pull apart. Brant by duty, Layne by guilt.

With an effort Brant pulled back, reminding himself that when he eventually caught up with Dan he'd have to arrest him.

Layne remembered Brant had a date with a tall, leggy, blonde and she couldn't help wondering whether he was seeing Shanna tonight because he was attracted to her or because he was using the situation to extract information from her. And if that were the case, wouldn't he use Layne if he thought she could lead him to Dan?

The wind had dropped. "It's getting late," she said, "we'd better go."

He studied her features as if committing them to memory. "All right. I guess I forgot about your date with Travis."

Chapter 12

The following morning Brant arrived promptly at nine. The minute Layne opened the door he sniffed the air. "Hmm. Something smells good."

Layne noticed he was wearing his uniform—khaki-colored pants and tan shirt. As always, he wore a cream-colored Stetson. She realized that no matter what he wore Brant always managed to look breath-stoppingly sexy. "I'm fixing some breakfast. Want to join me?" She turned away and headed toward the kitchen.

Closing the door behind him, he followed her. "Thought you'd never ask."

She walked over and stood in front of the stove, her hand poised over the carton of eggs. "There's a fresh pot of coffee on the table. Help yourself. How do you want your eggs?"

"Over easy. Five." At her raised brow, he smiled. "I have a big appetite this morning."

Layne dropped each egg into the hissing skillet. "I would've thought you'd still be full from eating pasta last night."

She could've bitten her tongue. What he did with his nights was no concern of hers.

He watched her lift four slices of bread out of the toaster and plop them onto a plate beside the stove. "As a matter of fact, I had a TV dinner."

Layne's hand stopped in the act of scooping eggs onto a plate beside the bacon she'd fried earlier. "Don't tell me Shanna Caldwell didn't keep her promise and cook you that pasta dinner."

He looked genuinely puzzled for a moment before a light dawned in eyes. "Oh, that," he said.

Layne approached the table with their plates and sat down. She frowned. "You told me she invited you to come over last night for dinner."

Picking up a slice of toast, he shrugged. "Yeah, she did, but I didn't say I'd accepted."

Layne swallowed. "You didn't?"

"Uh-uh. I was pretty tired. Must've been all that salt air."

They locked eyes. Layne was the first to look away. After an awkward pause she stood up. "You'd better eat fast if you want to make it to Rico's by ten."

Her heart soared.

Rico lived in the mansion he'd just inherited from his uncle. Several front bedrooms looked out onto a huge well-manicured lawn and the house and grounds were surrounded by a tall brick wall that ensured privacy. The arched entryway accented the Spanish flavor.

The moment Brant and Layne arrived they were ushered into a dark paneled study where Rico already waited, comfortably ensconced in a wine-colored chair made of Italian leather. As his servant closed the door behind them he stood up and smiled.

"Good morning. Please have a seat," he said, motioning for them to sit in the two chairs placed strategically in front of his desk. "Would you care for something to drink?" His eyes, coffee-black, slipped past Brant and rested on Layne.

Layne and Brant both declined.

"How may I help you?" Rico asked.

Brant took the lead. "We'd like to know if there's anything else you remember about your uncle's death. Something you might've forgotten to tell us."

Rico eyes were thoughtful for a moment. He shook his head. "Nothing other than what I've already told you." He looked across at Layne. "I'm surprised to see you two together."

"I'm not here on behalf of the D.A.'s office, Mr. Salinas. I'm here strictly as an interested party. I have Mr. Wade's permission."

"I see," he responded.

Brant leaned forward. "You mentioned there was a party here the night your uncle died."

Rico nodded. "Yes. A small dinner party." Leaning back, he regarded Brant across the desk.

"Who attended?"

"Jim Weston, his wife, Christina, and their son, Brandon—he's twenty-eight and works for the firm. Saul Moran also attended with his wife, Barbara, and of course I was here."

"Saul Moran?"

"He's president of Brownsville National."

"Then it was a business dinner?"

He shrugged. "Not really. My uncle and Saul have been friends for years."

"Anyone else attend?"

"My uncle's secretary, Shanna Caldwell."

"*Your* secretary now."

"That's right." He smiled.

"Did you and your uncle get along?"

Rico picked up a paperweight from a corner of the desk and regarded it seriously. "Not always. Sometimes we tended to clash over business decisions." He set the paperweight back down. "My uncle was a generous man. Generous with his time. I enjoyed our time together."

"Did your uncle ever confide in you?" Brant asked.

Rico's voice was measured, calm. "If he had any secrets, he took them to his grave. My uncle wasn't a saint, Mr. Wade. There are any number of people who didn't like him. He was a very forceful man. Personally and professionally."

"What about Weston? You think he's capable of killing your uncle?" Layne asked.

"Anything is possible, I suppose. But I don't think so." He regarded Layne thoughtfully. It was the first sign of real interest he'd shown since she'd entered the room. "Forgive me for being candid, but I was under the impression that two witnesses had already testified as to Dan Tyler's guilt."

Brant leaned forward slightly. "One of your servants saw him leaving the premises, but no one actually saw Dan kill your uncle. The other witness is no longer in a position to talk."

"I see. I thought that under such extenuating circumstances it was an ironclad case." He tilted his head to one side, and spoke to Layne. "If your brother is innocent, why hasn't he come forward?"

She looked him squarely in the eye. "I don't know. Maybe he's afraid to. Maybe he knows something and can't come forward. Maybe when Dan showed up that night, your uncle was already dead and my brother saw who did it. As you said, anything is possible. A person is innocent until proven guilty, Mr. Salinas," she said tersely.

Rico sighed resignedly. "You're right, of course. I apologize. It's just that I'd like to have an end to all this." To Brant he inquired politely, "Is there anything else you'd like to know?"

"That's about it." Brant stood up. "Thanks."

Layne nodded her thanks and stood up also.

She glanced around the high-ceilinged room. Against one wall several shelves were lined with books. Among them, were techno-thrillers, horrors and business manuals. A gun collection took up part of another wall.

As they were walking out of the room something caught Layne's attention and she moved over casually to take a closer look. Beside the gun cabinet stood another smaller cabinet. She glanced over at Rico and raised an eyebrow. "These look expensive," she announced, pointing to several knives lying neatly in a row.

"They are," Rico came over to stand beside her. "My uncle began collecting them some years ago."

"Are they always kept locked?"

"No, not always. Sometimes he'd take one out to show friends, then forget to lock the cabinet. I was always after him to do so. The night my uncle was killed he'd been showing Brandon the knife he . . ."

"Was killed with?" she finished for him.

"Yes." For the first time, Rico showed signs of strain.

"I'm sorry. Again, thank you for your time," Layne said quietly.

She was silent all the way to the car, remaining that way until Brant pulled out onto the highway.

"Brant, did any of those knives look familiar to you?"

He shook his head. "No, why?"

"I'm just wondering if the knife that was used to kill Alphonso could have belonged to that collection."

"Could be. Each one of those knives was different in some way. It's possible someone took one and used it to kill Alphonso, but let me remind you you told me Dan went to visit Salinas a couple of times. He could've stolen it."

Why was he so stubborn? "I'll go one better. What if on one of Dan's visits Salinas showed him that knife just like he did Brandon, maybe even handed it to Dan so he could look at it, and that's how Dan's fingerprints got on it? And whoever killed Alphonso knew that and used it to frame Dan."

Brant looked thoughtful. "It's definitely a possibility. I had all the pawn shops check receipts to see if anyone had bought a knife bearing that description during the last couple of months. No one had." He looked at her, assessing her quietly, and there was admiration in his eyes. "There's something I have to do this afternoon, but as soon as I get back I'll take another look at that knife."

"Will you let me know what you find out?"

"Sure."

"I wouldn't discount Weston or Rico as suspects," she said, then added, "or Shanna Caldwell."

He thought a moment. "Weston could be hiding something or could even be covering for his son. Rico, as his nephew, inherited the business, although he already has more money than he knows what to do with. In fact, he could have started his own business. But why Shanna?"

"She could've been Salinas's mistress. Maybe he promised her something. Marriage or money, perhaps."

Brant shook his head. "She could get that from Rico, and he's much younger."

Her jaw clamped shut and she stared out the window for the rest of the trip.

It was eleven-thirty when Brant dropped Layne off at home. She waved goodbye and turned to unlock her door but changed her mind. She was too keyed up to stick around. Brant probably wouldn't call her until this evening anyway and she'd put off running some errands for several days.

Layne slid into her car and drove toward town. Ten minutes later she pulled over and parked.

She walked through the double glass doors into the post office and a few minutes later she'd bought stamps, applied them to her bills and was about to send them on their way when she looked up and saw Dallas Smith.

He stood just inside the door studying the wanted posters on a bulletin board. His jeans looked as though he'd outgrown them and there were holes in them in certain places. Layne remembered she'd laughed when Dan had told her one day that the kids bought them that way.

She walked over and stopped beside him. "Hello, Dallas." She smiled. "How's your mom?"

He looked down at her with a sullen expression and shifted most of his weight to favor one foot. "I just left her. She's in the hospital."

Layne felt a pang of regret. "I'm so sorry. Will she be all right?"

He shrugged. "They're running tests on her. I won't know for a few days." He glanced up at the posters again, then back down at Layne. "I guess I'll see you around," he drawled and turned to go.

"Wait," Layne called out. When he turned to face her, he stood in that arrogant stance that reminded her so much of Brant. His thumbs rested half in, half out of his front jean pockets.

Layne closed the gap between them. Now that he stood so close, Layne noted his long-lashed gray eyes were shot with tiny yellow specks.

She didn't want him to leave. "I was about to eat lunch. Will you join me?" She saw him stiffen and added quickly, "I hate to eat alone. Please?"

He shook his head. "I don't accept charity," he snapped, straightening the proud set of his shoulders.

Her heart filled with sadness, but she was careful not to show it. "So? Who's offering it? Is that the way you speak to a friend?"

He looked uncomfortable for a moment. "Are you my friend?"

"I'd like to be," she said gently. She found that she meant it. Very much.

He looked up at the posters again, then back down at her. For a moment she thought he was going to turn her down.

He shrugged. "I guess so. Can I ask you something?"

"Of course." She smiled.

"Isn't your last name Tyler?" At her nod, he asked, "Do you have a brother named Dan?"

Her eyes widened in surprise. "Why yes. How did you know?"

"Is that him?" he asked and looked up at the wall.

She followed his glance. And gasped.

There on the wall was a wanted poster of her brother.

"I can see you're upset," Dallas said. "I'd better go."

"No. Please." Layne's brain hummed from the shock. "I happen to believe my brother is innocent, but there's nothing I can do about him right now. I still want to treat you to lunch. Will you join me?"

He shrugged. "If you want."

Layne stopped herself from letting out a sigh of relief. "Great. There's a café down the street that serves good food. Just give me a minute to mail these bills."

An hour and a half later Layne let herself into the house and walked straight to her answering machine. A light indicated there was only one message. She turned it on.

It was Travis's voice asking her to call him back. She erased the message and walked on into her bedroom.

Slipping on an old pair of jeans and a sweatshirt she realized with some degree of guilt that she hadn't given Travis much thought lately. Not since she'd met Brant. She argued that the reason she'd been spending so much time with Brant was so she could prove her brother's innocence. And she needed Brant's help.

She hung up her clothes, then sauntered into the kitchen. A minute later she returned to the living room with a cloth and furniture polish. She set them down on the coffee table, grabbed the cloth and began to polish the table.

Nervous energy would keep her busy until she'd heard from Brant.

With a heavy heart she thought of Dan. She remembered the shock of seeing him on that poster. Where was he? Was he eating? Sleeping? She missed him so much. She and Dan had been more than brother and sister. They had been friends. She had to believe he'd be home soon.

Dallas's face swam before her. He was another young man in trouble. Layne had taken one look at his mother and known she was terribly ill. Layne had sensed somehow that Mrs. Smith hid behind a plume of death.

She shivered. What would happen to Dallas? Layne realized she hadn't gotten to know him any better because he'd been careful to keep their conversation impersonal. There were a couple of times when he'd slipped and asked her questions about Brant. Hero worship? Her mouth turned up in a smile. She wondered what Brant would say when she told him.

Her eyes closed for a moment. She recalled feeling a tiny thrill of relief when Brant had announced that he had turned down Shanna's invitation to dinner.

With a tight sigh she ran the cloth around the sides of the table.

She knew that whatever she felt for Brant would never amount to anything more than a professional alliance. If she believed that, why then did she feel such a crushing weight in her chest? Why did she feel frustration knotting up her muscles? She wondered how Brant felt about her. *Never mind,* she thought. *You don't want to know.*

They had only one thing in common. Finding Dan. She had to remind herself that she had to focus all her energy on finding Dan. There was no room for anything or anyone else in her life right now.

It was while she was running the cloth underneath the table that she found it.

It fell to the floor and she picked it up and stared at it.

A flicker, then a flame of comprehension crossed her face. Her eyes registered shock as they locked on the tiny microphone lying in her hand. Like a persistent, intrusive entity the microphone stared back at her, causing her heart to thud wildly. In fact, her heart was hammering so thunderously in her ears, she wondered if the person who had planted the bug could hear it.

But why? My God, how long had it been here? When had someone planted it? A thought struck her and her body began to quiver with apprehension. Had someone come in here while she'd been away? Or had it been while she'd slept, unsuspecting in her bed?

It didn't matter when. What did matter was that someone knew.

Someone knew!

And whoever it was had to know that file was in her possession.

She got up from the floor, almost stumbling, her thoughts shooting in several directions at once. She stood there wondering what to do.

And as she began to think, the more she thought, the more her shock-contorted features changed to a frown of outrage.

How dare someone spy on her!

She stared at the bug in icy silence, then clenched her fist, curling her fingers tightly over the offending thing like a steel trap intent on crushing its prey.

"Go to hell!" she shouted, then regretted her wild impulse. Well, it was too late now. She leaned over and rammed it under a cushion.

Frantically Layne ran to her bedroom. She couldn't take the time to change and there was no time for evasive tactics. Someone had been keeping tabs on her. She had to get that file downtown.

What if Russell weren't in when she got there?

She snatched up the file and her purse and raced out of the house. When she reached her car, she scrambled behind the steering wheel and slammed the door. Layne twisted the ignition key, ground the car into reverse and sped away.

As she raced through intersections thoughts whirled in her head. Who? she asked herself again. Could it be someone whose name was on that list? She glanced over at the briefcase on the seat beside her. The original photograph that Brant had taken was also there. It was *his* file.

Layne knew the killer wanted two things. The file and Dan.

So did Brant.

Yes, but Brant wouldn't bug your home.

Would he?

Layne forced herself to brake for a stop sign, then raced off again. Ten minutes later she was still petrified as she parked her car across the street from the Criminal Courts Building. She grabbed the file and almost jumped out of the car before she'd had a chance to turn off the engine.

Though her heart raced Layne walked steadily to the corner and kept staring straight ahead, ignoring the impulse to look over her shoulder. She reached the corner and in a moment of panic realized she wasn't going to make the green light. She stepped from the curb to make a run for it, but a policeman waved her back.

She returned to the curb. In a matter of seconds a throng of people was standing behind and beside her as they, too, waited for the light to turn green.

Layne felt her hackles rise and she shivered involuntarily. There was a shifting in the crowd behind her, pushing her forward, but she didn't have time to think about it.

The blow jerked her forward, its impact stunning, and she gasped, the wind knocked out of her. As her body pitched forward, she let go of her purse and briefcase and her arms flailed out in front of her in an effort to absorb most of the jolt.

The loud blare of a car horn and the screeching of brakes penetrated Layne's consciousness just before she hit the pavement.

Chapter 13

"Lady?...Lady, can you hear me?"

Layne lay on the pavement, an endless wave of pain slicing through her palms, wrists and knees where they'd taken the brunt of her fall.

"Don't move her," someone warned. Another voice wailed, "Did you see that? It happened so fast—"

"Lady?"

Layne moved slightly. "I'm all right," she managed to say. Her voice was jerky. She sat up slowly and saw a policeman leaning over her, his features impassive, trained to cancel any emotion.

"Take it easy, miss. My partner's already radioed for an ambulance."

She glanced over and saw another officer directing traffic and ushering people across the street. The crowd, curious to see the outcome, lagged behind.

A car honked and a bus roared past, sounding like a plane.

"I'm all right," Layne's voice shook. "Really, I'm just a little bruised, that's all. Will you help me up?"

"Are you sure?" He didn't look convinced.

"Yes . . . please."

He helped her to her feet and over to the sidewalk. Layne bit her lip and stifled an instinctive moan as pain stabbed at her knees. She stood unsteadily and lifted her hands to look at them. A dull blue color was already beginning to show at the junction where wrist and palm met.

"What happened?" he asked, handing Layne her purse.

She clutched the purse to her chest. "Someone pushed me." Her throat felt dry and she realized just how close she'd come to being killed.

"Did you get a look at him? Maybe when he walked up to the curb?" He took out a pad and pen from his back pocket, noted the time and jotted it down.

"No. I was the first one to reach the curb."

"Maybe someone in the crowd got a look at him. Why don't you wait in my car until the ambulance gets here?" he said quietly.

She shook her head. "I don't need an ambulance."

He stared at her impassively. "Then we'll just talk and I can fill out my report."

"All right," she agreed and allowed him to lead her over to his patrol car. Halfway there she halted. "Wait. I was carrying a briefcase."

He looked around. "I don't see anything. Someone must've taken it."

Layne's pulse pounded. The briefcase had been stolen and with it the file she needed to show Russell. She had to get to his office. "Look, officer, the guy who pushed me was probably some weirdo who picked me at random. I can't tell you any more than that. I'm sorry."

"My partner is questioning some of the other witnesses. Maybe one of them will give him an ID on the suspect."

An ambulance pulled up to the curb and a young paramedic opened the door and got out, moving rapidly toward them. "Someone here need help?" he asked.

Layne shook her head, feeling a flush of embarrassment. "I don't need a doctor. I feel—I'm all right. Really."

"Can you walk?"

She frowned. "Of course, I can walk and I don't need to go to a hospital," she said a little more strongly than she'd intended, then felt a spasm of guilt. After all, he was only doing his job. She forced a smile to her lips. "Thanks, anyway," she said by way of concession.

"Maybe we should check you over," he persisted. There was a faint gleam of interest in his eyes, but whether it was professional or personal Layne couldn't tell.

Layne straightened. "There's nothing to check. I'm fine, really, and I'm late for an appointment."

He shrugged. "If you're sure."

"I'm positive." Then a little more softly, "But if I feel bad or anything later, I promise I'll have it checked out."

He shrugged. "Okay. It's your life," the paramedic said, walking away.

She turned to the officer. "I'm with the D.A.'s office and I'm late for an appointment." She took identification out of her purse and flashed it at him. Glancing at it, he scribbled the information on his pad.

Layne attempted a smile. "I realize I'm not exactly dressed for a meeting, but it's a last-minute emergency. Can I call you if I think of anything else?"

His car phone crackled and he walked over to answer it. Layne heard him give their location, then reconstruct what had happened.

When he returned, Layne said, "Look, Officer—" she glanced at his badge "—Lingo. I'm personally acquainted with Lieutenant Paul Garcia. He'll vouch for me. Besides, as you can see, I'm not hurt. I'm sure you have more important things to do than paperwork."

He smiled for the first time and closed his notebook. "I'll tell the lieutenant you said hello."

She returned the smile. "You do that."

When Russell saw her, he informed the person on the other end that he'd call them back and hung up the phone.

"What happened to you?" he said, getting up from his chair.

She limped to a stop. "Someone just tried to kill me."

He blinked in astonishment. "Are you sure?"

"I don't know about you, but I call getting pushed into a street of oncoming cars attempted murder."

His eyes narrowed at her sarcasm. "Sit down, Layne, before you fall down. Over here." He walked around the desk, took her by the elbow and sat her down on the sofa. He sat next to her. "Start at the beginning."

She wondered just how much to tell him. Would he be willing to help her if she disclosed what she'd been doing? "I've been working on the Salinas case."

He sighed in frustration, leaning back against the plush leather. "I knew you wouldn't give up."

She pressed on. "I have reason to believe Dan's been set up."

He raised a slightly gray brow. "What makes you think that?"

Layne rubbed her aching wrists. "He told me."

"You've talked to Dan?"

At her nod he stood up and began to pace slowly back and forth in front of her—a compulsive habit he had when he was thinking. A second later he stopped and looked down at her. "When?"

She raised her head and looked into his eyes. "It doesn't matter when, Russell. The point is, I was on my way to see you with some information we—I uncovered. When I was pushed into the street someone stole the briefcase the file was in. They didn't want me to show it to you."

He continued to glare at her. "How did someone know you had information?"

"My living room was bugged."

He shook his head in disapproval and his tone was sharp. "I have people working on this, Layne. You should've stayed out of it."

Her voice cut across his. "And just how much have *your* people found out?"

He waved her question away. "I'm not going to tell you."

She shrugged and stood up. "Never mind, I'm willing to bet I have more. Still, it would be nice to compare notes, don't you think?" She smiled in a secretive way, tempting him.

He let out a low curse. "I told you to stay out of it. Dammit, you've almost gone and gotten yourself killed— again. Don't forget that sniper who shot you."

"I haven't forgotten." There was a pause. "I won't take up any more of your time." She started to walk away, but his voice stopped her.

"You're a very exasperating woman, you know that?"

"And a good friend and a damn good D.A.," she added.

"There's no doubt about that. Sit down, Layne."

A smug smile lifted the corners of her mouth as she returned to the couch. "By the way, I'm fine, thank you."

He looked contrite. "Oh, I care, sweetheart. I'm damn worried about you and I want you to lay off the case."

"I can't do that."

He sighed. "You're a stubborn woman. That's what makes you such a good D.A. You never give up." He returned to sit behind his desk. "What have you found out?"

She shrugged. "Not much really. I checked out some leads. One of them led to a private airstrip." She recounted what she and Brant had discovered so far. The list of names, the cashier's check and the fact that Salinas had owned the airstrip where the money was being flown to the Caymans.

Russell tapped a pencil lightly on the desk. "You think Salinas was sending money to a bank?"

"Who else would it be? It was his plane."

"Maybe he was sending out a payroll."

"Maybe he was sending out dirty money," she said with conviction. "Someone killed Salinas and wants to make it look like Dan did it. Why, if it isn't to cover up something?"

"I'll check it out."

"What information do you have so far?" She felt a stab of curiosity and desperation.

He shrugged. "You know most of it. Two murder weapons—one killed Salinas, the other was used to kill Jesse Alphonso, who by the way has a police record."

"I'm not surprised," she replied.

"We're checking out several suspects. I have a list of people who knew both Salinas and Alphonso. But you might as well know Dan is still our main suspect."

She stood up. "Salinas had a knife collection. I'm willing to bet there's a knife missing from it. Brant's checking it out—"

"Brant?" Russell's interest perked up.

"He went with me to question Rico."

"I thought you two didn't like each other."

"Strictly professional courtesy." Layne looked away, flustered.

Russell threw down the pencil. "Until I get some kind of proof, Dan is still under suspicion. I need something I can sink my teeth in."

"I'm working on it."

"I miss you around here, sweetheart. When are you coming back?"

"When all this is over, you might not want me back."

"You're too good at what you do. Of course I want you back. Ruth asked about you. Why don't you come over to the house on Sunday? I'll barbecue for you."

"I'll let you know." She stood up and walked to the door.

"Layne."

She stopped and looked over her shoulder.

"We didn't have this conversation today."

"I understand." She opened the door and walked out.

Russell watched her leave. He sat there drumming his fingers on the teak desk. After a moment he picked up the phone, pounded out several digits and waited.

"You idiot," he growled into the phone. "I wanted her watched. She was almost killed." A pause. "I don't want excuses. Don't let it happen again."

Brant had just spent the afternoon following up a lead on another case. Now he'd decided to check up on Dallas. As he drove along the highway something in the distance caught his attention. A familiar figure.

Brant pulled over and waited until Dallas drew up alongside of him. He noticed the boy looked pale and his eyes appeared glassy.

"Want a ride, Dallas?"

Dallas hesitated, then shrugged. "I guess so," he said and walked around to the passenger side and got in.

"Where you heading?"

"Just drive to wherever you're going and drop me off."

Brant threw the boy a brief glance. "You aren't thinking of running off again, are you?"

Dallas stared out the window. "It doesn't matter any more."

Brant saw where he wanted to stop and pulled over. Boca Chica—the same beach he'd brought Layne to a few days ago. He turned off the ignition, glanced at Dallas and noticed him wipe at his eyes. "Want to talk about it?"

There was a brief silence. "My mom's dead. She died while I was having lunch with your friend, Layne."

Brant could hear a world of guilt and torment in that statement. He'd witnessed death and violence, but this boy's plea for help made his gut wrench. He felt a tremor pass through his body, along with an overwhelming need to comfort. But all he was able to say was, "I'm sorry."

"I didn't even get to say goodbye." Dallas spoke quietly, as if he were talking to himself.

"Let's get out, Dallas. I want to talk to you."

They got out of the car and walked over near the surf. Funny, Brant thought, this was his secret place and in the span of a few days he'd brought two people here. Two people who had become important to him. He stared out toward the water and wondered what it was about this boy that tore at him.

"Maybe she wanted it that way," he heard himself saying.

There was a long silence. Brant wanted to look at Dallas, but purposely kept his gaze away. "What will you do now?" he asked finally.

"I'm gonna find my dad."

Brant was surprised until he heard the rest of his sentence.

"And when I do, I'm gonna kill him."

Brant thought he heard one single sob wrench from Dallas's throat but he still wouldn't look at him. "That would be a mistake, son. I don't think your mom would like that, do you?"

"There's nothing else, nowhere for me to go."

Brant wondered why it had been left for him to comfort this boy. Comforting wasn't something he was good at.

Because Brant was doing penance.

"There's something I want to tell you." He didn't question his impulse to confess, only that he had to. "My dad was a Texas Ranger, too, just like his father before him. One night he was called out. It happened to be the day before Thanksgiving. I was angry because it meant that he'd be gone for the holidays. By that time I was old enough to resent the fact that his job took him away for days at a time. This time I was incensed enough to ask him why the hell he'd gotten married to begin with. We had a big argument. He was a big, strong man and I thought he was going to deck me, but he just stood there looking hurt and he said to me, 'When I come back, I want us to talk.' And he left."

Brant heaved a deep sigh, realizing what it was costing him to say these things. He'd thought about it, but he'd never imagined he'd be sharing his own grief with a young boy.

"That night he was killed in the line of duty and I've never been able to forgive myself. I said some ugly words that I never had a chance to take back. I never got to tell him I was sorry or that I loved him. Afterward, I used to come here a lot and think. I still do."

Dallas's head drooped dejectedly and Brant wondered if he was even listening. He knew it was important for him to get through to Dallas.

A sudden thought hit him. He remembered Dallas's birthday was on December 7, the same as Brant's dad. Also, there were certain similarities between Dallas and his father, like the stubborn tilt of his chin and the lazy swagger of his step. Brant had never believed in reincarnation, but now he groped for a way to find, if not total vindication, at least some small relief from his guilt. Maybe by helping Dallas he could ease the ache he'd carried around with him all these years.

"So, Dallas," he said, trying to still the tremble in his words, "I brought you here to my place where the wind and the sky and the earth and water share your grief. I can leave you here for a while to let you say goodbye in your own way, like I did, or—" this time Brant's voice cracked and he swallowed "—or if you like, I can stay and share it with you."

Brant waited, his heart pounding. Still there was no sound from Dallas. Brant understood and started to walk away.

"No. Don't go."

Brant turned and saw Dallas still had his back to him. Dallas's throat made a terrible choking sound and in it was all the pent-up frustration and grief.

Unfamiliar, disturbing emotions dormant for so long welled up in Brant, along with a rage for the father who by abandoning this boy and his mother had absolved himself of all responsibility and guilt. And had given Brant a chance to atone for his.

Brant lifted his hand and placed it on Dallas's shoulder and in that one touch offered him what he hadn't been able to give his own father. Comfort and understanding.

He felt a letting go, as though his soul had been unchained.

Brant didn't hear the news about Layne until after six that evening. Entering his office he headed for his desk, yanking off his hat as he went. Without aiming he pitched the hat toward an old-fashioned coatrack. It landed at a perfect angle on one of the elaborate iron hooks.

Lieutenant Paul Garcia walked in right behind him. If he felt any surprise that a young boy was with him he didn't show it.

"Hey, guess what?" he said. "A report came in about an hour ago. Someone pushed Layne Tyler into oncoming traffic as she waited to cross the street."

Brant's body went taut as a bowstring. Alarm placed its icy finger somewhere in the region of his chest, plunging deeper with every second. "Was she hurt?" he managed to ask.

"She's not in the hospital, if that's what you mean."

"Dammit," Brant hissed brushing past Garcia. *"Dammit,"* he muttered again louder as he hurried to the door. There he turned as if remembering Dallas. He walked back and whispered to Paul. "Would you do me a favor?"

"Sure."

"You know where my key is. Would you take Dallas to my place? Or better yet, do you think your mom would let him bunk over at her place until I get back? I'll explain later."

"Sure, she loves having kids at her place. Just ask my brothers and sisters."

"Thanks."

Paul stood staring after him with a thoughtful frown.

* * *

The ring of the doorbell was followed by a rapid succession of angry pounding. When Layne opened the door her eyes lit up with relief.

Brant closed the door behind him, his glance taking in every inch of her, as if to assure himself she wasn't hurt. For an instant his eyes glinted with anger, his jaw clenched tight. "Are you all right?"

She nodded.

"You're very lucky, you know that?"

There were tears in her eyes, molten, salty. She could only nod.

He hesitated, his heart pounding. He wanted to touch her. He thought he'd explode if he didn't touch her. "You could've been killed. I warned you. I...God, Layne—" Her name came out in a strangled whisper. He reached out and drew her into his arms. She went into them gladly, willingly.

Brant closed his eyes and held her to him in a close embrace, savoring the touch of her, the feel of her skin, the fragrance of her hair. His hands reached up and wove themselves through her auburn hair, tilting her face up. Something painful and yet wonderful ground into Brant's chest as he gazed at her,

Layne's arms hugged his waist tight as she relaxed in the shelter of his arms, his strength like a magnet pulling her closer. "Oh, Brant. I'm so sorry. Someone stole the file. I—"

"The file?" His hold on her loosened for a moment and he looked down at her incredulously. "To hell with the file, Layne. You were almost killed. I can't pretend any longer that you don't matter. You matter—very much. I want you," he muttered hoarsely and lowered his head. "I want you," he repeated, his whisper soft and husky against her mouth a second before his lips connected with hers, smothering any answer she might have given.

But Layne had no intention of stopping him. Her arms slid up his shoulders and locked around his neck.

Brant's head tilted to one side, fusing their mouths together in the most heart-stopping kiss Layne had ever experienced. Her lips parted wider to take in his tongue, its slow, lazy rhythm doing crazy things to her senses.

His hands slid from her hair to her cheeks, down her body, encircling her waist. He stood so close, so tight against her, her heart beat like a muffled drum. She felt his hardness and her body responded instinctively, crying for him to press her harder. Each disciplined thrust of his tongue sent tiny delicious tingles between her thighs in mounting ferocity. She ached to feel that touch everywhere, on her breasts, her stomach, her thighs. She ached to feel him inside her.

Her breath quickened at the thought.

Layne's passionate response to his kisses was driving Brant crazy. He wanted to touch her everywhere. Reluctantly he released his hold on her waist and pulled away slightly to gaze down at her. Her eyes were closed and a pulse beat furiously in the hollow of her slender throat. It matched the pulsating rhythm in his loins.

Sexual desire mingled with an emotion so strong he reeled from the wonder of it, knowing it had never been this potent before.

A small moan escaped her throat.

Brant smiled. "Is that a yes?"

She opened her eyes and he saw the answer in the green depths, heard her breathing grow shallow and quicken as his fingers closed around one breast. He felt it in her body's instant response.

He picked her up and carried her to the bedroom. Light from old-fashioned lamp fixtures mounted on the wall above the bed gave the room a low, soft glow. He lay her gently on top of the bed and peered down into her up-turned face.

"Are you sure?" he asked.

"I'm sure," she whispered and lay very still, suddenly shy.

His mouth found hers and his kiss became eager, hungry. Layne wound her arms around his neck and returned his kiss with an abandon she'd only dreamed about. Again, she felt the same thrill, the same wild pleasure spreading through every pore in her body.

His fingers began to unbutton her blouse. When the last button was undone he sat up, bringing her with him, and slipped the cloth off her shoulders. He drew back and she could feel his gaze on her as his long fingers seared a path along her quivering skin and slid beneath each bra strap easing them down over soft shoulders. His lips followed close behind, to trace along her throat and shoulders.

Her heartbeat escalated. When he reached around to unclasp her bra, his finger pads stroking sensual patterns on her skin, Layne's breasts became a mass of tingling nerves. She reached out and worked the buttons loose on his shirt, pulling it out of his pants.

The breath caught in his throat. "You're beautiful," he whispered, drinking in the swelling fullness of her breasts as they rose sharply in welcoming invitation.

"So are you," she answered, looking at his broad, hairy chest. The strength and width of his shoulders mesmerized her and her breathing quickened.

His hand cupped one taut breast just before the moist tip of his tongue circled a hardened pink-tipped nipple, tasting it, arousing it. Layne moaned with pleasure and arched her back, leaning into his mouth. His breath was hot and heavy on her skin.

His other hand slid along her rib cage, down to the zipper on her jeans. He pulled the snap open and eased the zipper down, then stopped kissing her long enough to pull her jeans and panties off. Layne couldn't peel them off fast enough to suit the eager passion of her body.

He left her to shuck the rest of his clothes, along with boots and socks and as he straightened Layne lay back and took in the sight of his powerful body. He had no tan line anywhere. For a moment she held her breath, taking in his raw, dark beauty. She turned cold and hot and quivery.

When he came to rest beside her again he pulled her close and kissed her passionately, then with more desperate urgency. The moist tip of her tongue crept into his mouth and her breasts trembled against his chest, lavishing him with welcoming warmth. With every breath she breathed into him, she ached to know more of him. She felt his maleness press against her.

His mouth and hands devoured her, touching her everywhere. One hand slid down her body to her thighs, his touch exploring, demanding her surrender. He coaxed open her legs and his fingers stroked and smoothed and fondled.

Layne clutched at him, aroused and throbbing. She didn't want to wait any more. "Brant. Please—"

At her words the burning inside him grew hotter, spreading, rocking him with every breath he took, and as he braced himself over her and parted her thighs with his knees he could feel her female heat pouring off her in waves.

His shaft burned, sought and found, then slowly, slowly slid home. They both moaned with pleasure as he stretched and filled her. He allowed her a second to accept him, then started moving with slow, measured strokes, basking in her dewy sweetness.

His long, slow movements were driving Layne crazy and she whimpered, her nails barely raking across the moving muscles of his damp back. She gloried in the pleasure of her own body. Never, never, had she experienced such mind-shattering joy. Her mouth became more insistent against his own, and she wrapped her legs around him, urging him closer, her loving, curving form nestled closer around him.

Like a power surge, Brant felt her response and with something akin to wonder, he answered all her ardor with his own, driving into her with increasing rhythm, deeper and harder, until she cried out with sudden spasmodic passion. Brant shuddered and his groan mingled with her own as they came together.

Afterward, he reached up and turned off the light, then brushed back stray wisps of hair from her cheek and pulled her close, nestling her in his arms.

She lay sated, feeling his warmth beside her. All the tension of the past few weeks seemed to be floating away in his arms. He'd been everything she had dreamed about and more. She shivered with remembered sensations.

She tried to remember the exact moment she'd fallen in love with Brant. Maybe it had been the day he'd let Dallas go with only a warning. It had been a warm and human moment and his gentleness had reached across and touched her. Or maybe it had been later on the beach, when he'd told her in so many words that he understood her pain. Then he'd kissed her, stripping away her shadow of sadness, infusing her instead with a fresh sense of purpose. That kiss, for her, had sealed the beginning of their friendship.

Yet in a deep part of her heart, the maternal part, palpitated a slight twinge of guilt and she sought to find absolution. After all, she knew Dan was innocent. In time, Brant would discover that fact, too.

Layne reached out and caressed the smooth skin of his chest with her fingertips. "How did you get this?" she asked, tracing the pattern of his scar.

For a moment, she thought he wasn't going to answer, then felt his chest rise in a deep sigh, but whether it was from weariness or a reluctance to talk, she couldn't tell.

"It happened two years ago." He paused. "I'd gone to Mexico to bring back a suspect. We stopped in an alley to talk. My attention was diverted and . . . I was stabbed."

Layne's brows furrowed. Her curiosity was piqued. "Don't you always frisk your suspects?" He'd certainly frisked her, she remembered with clarity.

"It was the one time I didn't."

"Why not?" she persisted.

He shifted in bed, restless. "Someone else was with me that day. A woman. The suspect's lover. Only I thought he was her brother."

There was something in his tone. She felt what he hadn't said. "She was someone you knew?" She raised herself on one elbow and looked down at him, waiting for his answer.

He shifted. Their eyes met in the dark. "I had asked her to marry me."

Layne had been holding her breath. Exhaling, she looked beyond him to the window. Moonlight filtered through the curtains, casting a lonely glow on their naked bodies. She fell back against the pillow. "I'm sorry. I didn't mean to pry. You don't have to say any more."

He was surprised she'd let it go at that. Most women would be asking a lot of questions. His muscles relaxed and he reached out, drawing her closer.

Layne leaned over and gently kissed the scar, her eyes brimming with tears that mingled sorrow and happiness. Sorrow for the pain he'd endured and happiness that he was here with her now.

He was all hers. For now. For however long it would last.

Her slow, hot tears fell as she kissed him, wetting his cheek, his throat, his chest. The hard peaks of her breasts grazed him lightly as her mouth continued its exploration at a heart-stopping pace along the heavy satin of his stomach. Her hand moved insistently, guiding her fingers to wrap themselves around the velvety warmth of his surging arousal. Eager to possess and discover him in turn, her mouth lowered and closed around him, tasting him, wanting him inside her again.

Brant was her fantasy lover come to life. Except that he was no fantasy. He was very real. And very hard.

Eventually they slept.

Chapter 14

Whn Layne woke up the first thing she saw was the sun glaring a path through the mauve-colored curtains. The temperature had dropped during the night and she burrowed deeper under the blanket, pressing against a hard surface. She found herself intrigued by the dark hair that matted a tanned chest, savored the perfection of a body against hers. She smiled to herself and sighed contentedly. In the wee hours of the morning Brant had finally allowed her sleep.

Recalling her joyful cries and his heated whispers in the dark, her cheeks flushed by a dizzying uprush of emotion. She studied his face so relaxed in sleep. She wanted to reach out and run her fingertips over its masculine beauty. No other man had ever looked so appealing. Giving in to the impulse, her fingers threaded themselves through his hair lightly, enjoying the feel of its thick texture. She studied the way his long lashes curled at the end.

He stirred but didn't wake.

Why couldn't they have met some other way? Oddly enough, it had been Dan who had brought them together. Would it be her loyalty to Dan that would pull them apart? She loved them both. She'd been thrown both ends of the rope and a realization floated across her mind, persistent, intrusive, that she might have to make a choice. She glanced at him tenderly, wanting to believe that for her there might be a happily ever after. Hadn't she been alone long enough? How could she bear to lose him after surrendering her heart?

With a sigh she pulled the covers to one side, got up and walked into the bathroom, wincing from the soreness of long unused muscles. As she turned on the shower the memory of being held in Brant's arms, of being kissed senseless, of being made love to, made her body tingle. Stepping under the shower, she closed her eyes. The cool water felt good on her warm skin.

She stepped out and dried herself off. Tucking the towel in front she returned to the bedroom and was in the process of bending over and getting something out of a drawer when his voice startled her and she straightened.

"You left without saying good morning." His voice vibrated through her skin.

He was sitting up looking exceedingly pleased, his back propped against the headboard. The blanket had been pushed aside. Only a sheet covered him from the waist down.

Self-consciously her hand came up to where the towel was tucked in the vee between her breasts. For the space of a second her cool reserve almost slipped, but she rallied. "You looked so peaceful I hated to bother you. And in case you haven't noticed, it's almost noon."

He smiled, but his eyes were on the lacy bit of fluff she held in her hand. "So it is. Why don't you come over here?" He patted a place next to him on the bed.

She tried to sound flippant. "You're insatiable."

His smile was slow and intimate. "That's not all I am."

Her eyes flew down the length of his body clearly silhouetted beneath the sheet and they widened. She hesitated.

He sighed in mock disappointment. "I guess if you're not going to come to me, I'll have to come to you," he drawled and started to pull the sheet aside.

"Wait." Scalding color rose to her cheeks and she moved toward the bed. It wasn't that she was a prude. After all, they'd already seen a great deal of each other. It was just that now, in the light of day, she knew they had to talk. And she couldn't do it without keeping some sort of distance.

She stopped beside the bed and looked down at him. "So how do you want your cereal?"

His gaze was on her legs. "With milk." His palm inched up her thigh.

"No sugar?" There was a tremulous catch in her voice.

He tugged on the hem until she was sitting beside him. His index finger touched her mouth as he looked deeply into her eyes. "I've got all the sugar I need right here," he said in a raw, husky tone. His eyes held hers like a magnet as his finger continued its lazy path down the column of her throat. It came to a stop at the vee of her breast, then curled over the towel, feeling the warm flesh beneath.

She expected him to kiss her. When he didn't she looked puzzled, until she realized he'd taken something out of her hand.

"You know, darlin', for someone who wears Brooks Brothers suits, your... panties are incredibly sexy."

Her panties hung from one finger looking tiny in his large hand. His other hand still rested on the towel at the vee of her breast. "I think it's time we got rid of this, don't you?" he rasped, giving the towel one final tug.

It slid open, crumpling behind her. A soft gasp caught in her throat.

"Brant, we need to talk," she whispered.

"Later. I promise."

As his lips touched hers in a long kiss, Layne began to burn for him again. His fingers trailed seductively over her breast in slow, unhurried strokes, then lowered to her stomach. She pressed her thighs together, feeling a pulsing ache. The sensation was so strong it frightened her and she groaned softly.

They could talk later.

Much later, bathed and dressed comfortably in worn jeans and teal-colored blouse, Layne sat at the breakfast table.

As it turned out, they didn't eat cereal. She'd cooked eggs, pancakes and bacon, and had loved every minute of it.

Brant set down his fork. "Those pancakes were great."

"Would you like more?"

He leaned back, rubbing his stomach. "No, thanks. Six were enough for me."

Layne stood up and began to clear the table. He helped her.

"Where do you want to talk? Here or in the living room?" he asked.

"The living room will be fine. I'll bring the coffee, you bring the cups."

When they were settled on the couch, Layne reached under a cushion and brought out a small canister. She opened the lid.

He glanced inside at the contents, then waited for her to close the canister. After she had done so, Layne got up and left the room. She returned a minute later and sat down. "I set them outside the kitchen door," she said as she poured coffee into two cups. She handed him his, then picked hers up and took a sip.

He looked at her over his cup. "Where did you find them?"

"One was in here under the coffee table. Another in the kitchen and one in my bedroom by the baseboard close to the phone. It was under the carpet. I found them just before you got here last night."

"You think you got them all?"

"I think so. I searched thoroughly, but—"

"I'll send someone over to search some more." He frowned in disgust. "Meanwhile, I'll take these to the lab. A wireless bug is simple to conceal and depending on the strength of the transmitter has an excellent range of a hundred yards to a mile. Then there's a device that's known as a combined telephone tap and room bug. Its range is determined by the distance of the telephone service in use. What's unique about it, is that the telephone number can be dialed from anywhere to pick up the conversation on the phone and in the room as well. Only a physical search can reveal it and it has to be switched on to be able to be detected."

"Don't you see now?" Her mouth was set in a firm line. "I was pushed from that curb so someone could steal my briefcase. Whoever it was wanted that file with all the information we'd gathered."

He nodded. "Tell me exactly what happened when you got to that curb."

She recounted everything she could remember. When she was through, he asked, "He pushed you just as your light turned green?"

"I think so. I know I stood there a long time."

"So the green light for the oncoming cars turned red."

She stared at him. "What are you saying?"

"The night you were shot you were only wounded. Then the information ended up on television. Tell me, what happened after that?"

She thought a moment. "I went into the hospital."

"No, after that," he prompted.

She thought some more—then remembered. "Dan came to see me."

"That's right. I think that bullet was only meant to wound you. And whoever shot you also called the media, hoping Dan would see it on television." He took a drink. "I figure whoever's responsible is using you to draw Dan out of hiding."

Layne's eyes clouded over with concern for Dan. "Then explain why I was almost run over."

He shook his head. "But you weren't, because he *knew* that car was far enough away to be able to stop. He did it so he could steal that file. Whoever bugged your place did it so he could keep tabs on you. And he'd also know if Dan showed up."

The implication hit her. She closed her eyes and said softly. "That has to be it. Now you can't deny that Dan is innocent."

He frowned. "I hope so."

She hastened to explain. "Someone must want to draw Dan out of hiding because he thinks Dan knows something. After all, Dan *was* at the scene. Maybe even while the murder was taking place. He could've seen who killed Salinas." She couldn't control her excitement.

Brant dimmed her hopes with his next words. "Or maybe someone has a vendetta against Dan because they think he killed Salinas. They could want revenge." He leaned forward. "I think you should stay over at my place until this business is over."

"Tell me, Brant, after everything we've found out, do you think Dan is guilty?"

She could see him hesitate as he stared into his empty cup. "It doesn't matter what I think."

"It does to me." She said quietly.

He set his cup down and stood up, then walked over to the window and stared out. "I just want it to be over. I have a lot I want to say to you."

"Why do you have to wait?"

He ran his hand through his hair restlessly. "Layne, I...care for you. But you know I still have to bring him in."

She forced herself to sit there calmly. "I understand that. And you know how *I* feel about you, but are you telling me that your feelings for me hinge on whether Dan is guilty or not?"

They exchanged a look. "I'm saying that I don't know how you're going to feel about me after I arrest him."

"That's funny, I thought we were working together to prove his innocence."

"Tell me, Layne, what would you do if you found out he was guilty? And don't tell me you know he isn't. Granted he might have seen something that night. I'm not ruling out that possibility. But what if he did kill Salinas and the man's family is out to take an eye for an eye? What are you going to do then?"

The room seemed unnaturally still as they stared at each other.

"I don't know," she said finally.

"You see, it's not that simple. I wish it were. I can't form opinions like that. He's your brother. Your loyalty to him clouds your judgment. You also know I have a job to do, but your loyalty doesn't extend to me. I'm caught in the middle."

She trembled and felt the cup of now cold coffee shake in her hand and she set it down. "So am I. I agree with you that Dan needs to be found and brought in. It's better we find him before someone else does."

He was watching her now as if something weighed heavily on his chest. "What would you say if I told you I have a lead on Dan?"

For a moment she looked surprised, then her heart skipped a beat. "I'd say it was wonderful. Let's go find him."

Some kind of emotion shone in his eyes. "I wanted to tell you, but things happened so fast."

"I know. When do we leave?"

"I'm not taking you with me."

They could both hear the clock ticking over the mantel.

She glared at him in exasperation. "Why not?" Then a light dawned in her eyes and she gave him a glance of disapproval. "Oh, I see. You don't trust me." There was no mistaking her anger. She shot up from the couch. "What do you think I'm going to do? Help Dan escape?"

"I don't want to take you because I don't know how long I'm going to be gone. It could be dangerous for you—especially if you're being followed."

She shrugged. "I'll take my chances."

"No, you won't. You're staying here," he said with disappointing finality.

Layne knew it was useless to try and change his mind. She felt an overwhelming sadness. It was as if they'd lost something very special. Something they'd shared together and now he was destroying it little by little.

She felt drained. "I guess that's that." She turned away.

He closed the distance between them and turned her around. "Believe me, Layne, it's better this way."

"So you say." She shook his arms away.

But he refused to let her go. "Please believe that I care too much for you to put you in any danger."

She stepped back. "When will you be leaving?" Her voice was clipped and brusque.

"In the morning. Look," he began awkwardly, "will you stay over at my place until I get back? You'll be safer there. And I have something else to tell you."

"What?"

"Dallas's mother died yesterday." At her look of alarm, he hastened to explain. "I'm going to let him stay at my place until we figure out something."

"I'm so sorry for him."

"Does that mean you'll stay at my place until I get back?"

"I'll think about it. Can I give you my answer tonight?"

"Sure." He sounded disappointed. "I have some business to take care of today, but I'll be back as soon as I can." His gaze softened. "Will you walk me to the door?" It was his way of asking for a truce.

She nodded silently and watched him pick up his hat and the canister of microchips. At the door, he took her in his arms one last time and kissed her goodbye. "Don't open this door to anyone. And promise me you won't go anywhere until I get back, okay?"

Her face closed. "I'll promise to try."

"You're a stubborn woman, you know that?"

"And you're a stubborn man," she retorted.

After he'd gone, she stood there in the silence staring out the window. Finally she turned away. So much for immortal lovers. She'd been right. Already, the situation with Dan had driven a wedge between them.

Simply put, Brant didn't trust her. Why in the world had Layne thought that after a fabulous night of making love he would feel any differently about her? He'd said he cared. It was a far cry from confessing love.

Maybe it was better this way. She should, she knew, be glad that he didn't return her feelings. Remembering the scar among other smaller ones she'd glimpsed, she should thank her lucky stars that she would be spared Brant's violent world, where he might be maimed or killed one day.

And that she couldn't take.

She wondered what to do. Should she follow him when he left? She decided against it. If she stayed at his place, at least she'd know the minute he returned.

She walked into the bedroom, grabbed an overnight bag from the closet and packed a few things. Afterward, she walked to her car and put the bag in the trunk. When Brant returned she would follow him to his home in her car. At least she'd have transportation while she stayed at his place.

She was walking back into the house when she heard the phone ring and hurried to answer it.

"Hello?"

"Miss Tyler?"

"Yes." She didn't recognize the voice.

"This is Maria Chavez. I have to talk to you. It's about Dan."

Layne clutched the telephone tighter. "What's wrong? Has anything happened to him?"

There was an uncomfortable pause. "I know where he is. I'm worried about him. Can you stop by Juan's?"

"I'm on my way."

Quickly she replaced the receiver. Grabbing her purse, she ran out of the house.

Layne spotted Maria the minute she entered Juan's. She stood behind the bar counting receipts. Layne hurried over.

"Where is he?"

Maria stopped in the act of writing something down on a notepad and looked up, her eyes doelike. "I should have told you before."

"Yes, you should have," Layne reproached her. "Tell me now."

Maria stared down at her hands. "He's in Mexico with my aunt and uncle."

Layne slanted her an accusing glance. "You mean you've known where he is all this time?"

"I couldn't tell you. Dan made me promise not to say anything to anyone. Not even you."

"But why? You knew how worried I was about him. Besides, do you realize how much trouble he's in?"

Maria folded her hands to keep them from trembling. "Yes, I know. But...I had promised."

Layne tried to remain calm. "Is he all right?"

Maria shrugged. "As far as I know. I haven't heard from him for several days. Then yesterday these two men came by asking for him. They told me they were detectives. Only something was wrong—I felt it. I think they were lying."

Layne swallowed a knot of fear. "How do I get to your aunt and uncle's place?"

"They have a small farmhouse just outside of Salazar."

"So he's been keeping in touch with you?"

"Only twice. He told me he was going to call me yesterday and he never did. My uncle doesn't have a phone, so Dan has to go into town." Tears clouded her eyes and she looked away for a moment. "That night he asked me to give you the note, he told me what happened. I know Dan. He couldn't have killed that man.''

"I know." Layne squeezed her hand. "Just give me the address, Maria. I have to go. Those men you mentioned, they may be the ones who killed Michael Salinas. I have to get to Dan before they do."

Maria nodded and tore a sheet out of the notepad laying on the bar. She drew a map, then jotted down an address. "The farmhouse is about four hours away. It would be better if you left in the morning."

Brant had planned to leave in the morning also.

Without her.

"I can't wait," she told Maria. "I have to leave to-night."

Maria frowned. "If you leave now, you'll arrive in a lit-tle town called Montania just before dark. You should stop for the night. Believe me, it wouldn't be wise for you to go on. There are bandits in the hills and other dangerous peo-ple. I have a cousin who works at the Arroyo Motel there. You can stop and spend the night. You'll be safe. Tell my cousin I sent you." She turned the sheet of paper over and wrote her cousin's name and the name of the motel on it, then handed it to Layne. "Please believe me, it would be dangerous for you to travel at night."

Layne folded the piece of paper and stuck it in her purse. "All right. I'll spend the night in Montania." She glanced at the phone and thought of Brant.

This was what she'd been waiting for. What they'd *both* been waiting for.

"May I use your phone?" she asked.

"Of course." Maria pushed the phone toward her, then walked away.

Layne picked up the phone and held it for a long mo-ment. By tomorrow she'd be with Dan. Seeing him, talking to him, would be wonderful. This was what she'd labored so frantically for. Her index finger hit the first three digits, then paused over the next number. What if Brant took the address and left without her, anyway? He'd been very determined that she not go. The pressure and the frustration of seeing all her work unraveled made her hesitate.

What should she do? She had to leave now if she planned to make it to Montania by dark.

Brant would be angry.

Slowly she replaced the receiver. Grabbing her purse off the counter, she made her way to the door.

By the time she reached her car and started the engine, her heart was pounding. Her thoughts were raw with misery. She was doing what she thought was best. *Wasn't she?*

She headed south toward the Mexican border.

And Dan.

The woman opened the curtain that hung just behind the bar and watched Layne hurrying to her car.

Her smile resembled a Cheshire cat's. How wonderful, she thought. The golden opportunity she'd been hoping for had landed right in her lap.

Brant Wade had arrested her husband a year ago. Because of the Ranger's testimony, Reuben would be in prison for a long time.

Because of Brant Wade, she was having to work in this dump.

She turned, studied Maria working behind the bar and with a feline grace that had many a man panting at her heels, Rosita made her way to a pay phone near the rest rooms. She wondered if she had time to make two calls before Maria found her. Her mouth curved into a self-satisfied smile as she reached into her pocket and pulled out the card one of the two men who visited yesterday had given her.

Brant grabbed the phone before it had rung a second time.

The voice on the other end coughed, then whispered, "I have information about Layne Tyler. She's on her way to see her brother."

"Who is this?" Brant's voice was curt.

"That's not important. I wanted you to know she's been lying to you."

Brant tensed, his stomach starting to burn. "Do you have proof?"

"You'll have the proof when you see her," came the reply. "She plans to spend tonight in Montania at the Arroyo Motel. Tomorrow morning she'll continue on to Salazar, where her brother is waiting."

"How do you know all this?" The room was silent, except for a distant whisper of emotion which reached his heart.

"Never mind how I know. It's enough for you to be aware that she knew yesterday where her brother is hiding."

Brant's knuckles turned white from gripping the phone so hard. "I don't believe you."

Her next words drove home.

"If you plan to stay and wait for her to return home tonight, you're going to have a very long wait. If you don't believe me, check it out for yourself. I promise you, I'm the *only* one who's telling the truth. Adios."

The line went dead. Brant stood there staring into the distance.

He picked up the phone and called his office.

"Have I had any calls?"

The voice on the other end stated there had only been one call. From a woman, but she had left no message or a number.

He hung up and checked Layne's answering machine. One call. The person had hung up. If Layne had called, wouldn't she have left a message for him?

His throat ached. Was that why she had let him make love to her? So he wouldn't suspect she knew where Dan was hiding? He looked around the room wanting to smash something, so great was his feeling of grief.

He could stand here all night and make assumptions, but they'd be meaningless without proof.

He had to know.

He picked up the phone again and dialed a number. When a voice answered, he snapped, "I want a chopper. Right away."

Layne hung up the phone and returned to her table. She stared out the window of the café. The town practically receded into the darkness. It was composed of a gas pump, a café, a motel and several clapboard houses dotted here and there.

She stared down at the half-eaten hamburger, wondering why she'd ordered it, blanched and pushed the plate aside. Her stomach was so tied up in knots she felt nauseous.

Dropping a tip on the table, she picked up the bill. Leaving the Arroyo's diner, Layne crossed the patio toward her room. Her frazzled nerves and the long drive had tired her out. She doubted she'd get any sleep tonight.

Her room, located toward the back, could barely be seen in the shadowy gloom. A soft ruffle of sound came to her in the dark from behind her and she glanced over her shoulder. She saw no one, but quickened her step anyway.

She shivered, praying daylight would come quickly so she could be on her way. Her heart leaped happily at the prospect of seeing her brother soon.

As she dug the key out of her purse, her thoughts switched to Brant. Last night had been the most beautiful night of her life. What had it meant for Brant? she wondered.

She fitted the key into the lock and pushed open the door, again feeling ill at ease at being in a strange place—in a strange town.

Closing the door behind her, she reached out to flip on the light.

She never made it.

A hand clamped over her mouth.

Chapter 15

The silence in the room became deafening for one heart-stopping moment. Terror clutched at Layne's throat, choking her, and she clawed at the large hand covering her mouth.

"Don't scream, darlin'." His drawl was a low, lazy whisper.

Layne's eyes widened as recognition set in and she ceased her struggling.

"That's better." He let her go and flipped on the light.

She spun around to face him, anger making her breasts heave in indignation. "You bastard! You scared the hell out of me. Why did you do that?" Her voice trembled and she had to sharply control her breathing.

"I didn't know if you'd be up to seeing me," he said simply.

She blinked in confusion. "What?"

"We didn't exactly part on amicable terms this afternoon." But they had parted on intimate ones, he thought
grimly.

"What are you doing here?" she asked.

"I might ask you the same thing," he replied without
emotion.

"I mean, how did you get here so fast?"

"Helicopter." *She's hedging,* he thought.

She looked genuinely surprised. "I can't believe it. I
only called you about twenty minutes ago—you couldn't
have—"

"You called me?" He tensed.

"Yes, but you couldn't possibly have gotten my message that fast. How did you know I was here?"

"It's not important. I'm here now."

"I'm glad you're here." Her voice warmed consider-
ably. She flung her arms around his neck and kissed him.

"But how did you know which room I was in?"

Trying not to show his anger took a great deal of effort.
"That was the easy part. After I flashed my badge, the
clerk was only too happy to tell me what I wanted to
know."

His muscles went taut and he flinched. He couldn't believe it. He'd actually caught her on her way to meet Dan
and she still managed to look so damn innocent. He didn'
know what he had expected, but it certainly wasn't to see
her so happy to see him. He blanched. So the woman who'
called him had been telling the truth. The realization fueled
his anger to the point of boiling. He wanted to shake Layn
until her teeth rattled. Instead he stood there letting her kiss
him.

At last she stepped back and smiled. "I've been trying t
call you. Oh, Brant, I don't care how or why you're here
I'm so happy to see you."

He saw she was caught up in the excitement of the moment and that she'd failed to notice his lack of enthusiasm. Or maybe she pretended not to, he thought.

"I . . . know where Dan is," she blurted out.

His face remained blank, but something in his eyes flickered. Then, as if making a decision about something, his mouth tightened in a smile. "So you found him."

"Yes. Now that you're here we can leave tonight, if you want," she said.

He shook his head. "I think we'd better spend the night." He didn't add that he feared having a knife stuck in his back while he stood in the dark. He wouldn't be that foolish twice. Last night he'd been so sure she cared about him. The need to take care of her had become a physical ache. He'd believed her.

He had begun to trust her.

And for that she would pay.

"I suppose you're right," she said. "We'll leave early in the morning." She picked up her overnight bag and headed for the bathroom.

Brant walked over to the bed and unbuttoned his shirt. He heard the sound of the shower as he undressed and slid into bed.

When she came out he watched her turn off the light. A second later he felt the bed sag as she slipped into bed beside him.

Neither of them moved. Finally she leaned over him. "I love you." Her whisper was low and throaty. "And I'm happy you're here so I can tell you." Her voice echoed softly in the gloom and he thought he detected pain laced with desperation. Or had it been guilt?

Her arms went around him and he felt a shiver pass through him at her touch. "Are you?" he replied. In the dark his eyes bore into hers for a moment longer. "Show me, Layne. Show me just how much you missed me."

She did, pressing closer to him, her lips warm and soft on his own. He thought this would be the last night he would ever make love to her and wondered if, without her, he would ever have any peace, any comfort again. He knew that what he felt for Layne was unquestionably love. For a moment his heart pounded with indecision, with the pain of choice. He could simply turn away. Or he could love her one last time.

He slipped off her nightgown. His arms closed around her, causing her breasts to flatten against his chest; and he felt her response to the angry thrust of his tongue. His hands moved from her waist to her derriere and pulled her more firmly against his body. His erection nudged her thigh and he shifted slightly until it nestled in the soft tuft of hair between her thighs.

His hands moved lightly over her breasts, then he replaced them with his mouth as he took first one pink-tipped nipple into his mouth, then the other, kissing and suckling until they were hard. He tasted her clean skin, so soft and pliable, and wanted to bury himself in her right then, until she ached and writhed beneath him. His hands moved along her body, stroking its sweetness as his mouth lowered, savoring all of her until she was shuddering with pleasure.

Layne arched her back and groaned, clutching him close. "I don't want to wait. Please, Brant. I want you now." Her voice was husky with passion and like the satin fold of a petal she opened wide for him.

He took her hand and placed it over his throbbing sex. "In that case, darlin', let's not waste time." His tongue sank into her mouth again.

Layne's fingers touched the smoothness of his groin. Cupping her hand gently around him, she guided him to her, arching up at the same time to meet him. The tip was barely in, but her moan of pleasure sent tremors of wild pleasure along Brant's skin. He responded by settling himself deeper, then pulling out slowly, keeping to a long, slow rhythm. Their mouths and bodies meshed. His heart beat a hard rhythm against her own. Hot and wet, they lost themselves in each other.

He felt her tightening around him just before her shattering climax and he quickened his pace until with a long, deep groan he, too, released himself inside her.

Later he lay beside her in silence, waiting for her to go to sleep. When he heard her deep, rhythmic breathing, he turned his head and studied her face, so innocent in sleep.

He wanted to hate her.

Instead he reached out and drew the covers over her.

Layne came slowly awake. She moved to clasp Brant close to her, but found an empty pillow instead. Frowning, she blinked in an effort to see more clearly. Turning her head, she saw him.

Beside the bed he straddled a chair, his arms rested across the back. He was staring at her intently.

Suddenly embarrassed, Layne clutched the sheet to her chest and sat up. "What's the matter?"

When he didn't answer she lowered her feet to the floor, still holding on to the sheet. "Why didn't you wake me?"

Something shifted in his eyes as they raked over her. He shrugged. "You looked comfortable." He stood up, walked over to the window and stared out.

Confused, she struggled to understand his unexpected brusqueness. "Brant? Is something wrong?"

He didn't turn around. "Why do you ask?"

Something was wrong. She knew it. She'd sensed it last night when he'd made love to her and again just now.

She stood up and took a few steps, the sheet trailing behind her. "I don't know. I suppose I'm just a bit jittery. I'll feel much better after we pick up Dan." She started toward the bathroom.

He whirled around, frightening her. "Shut up, Layne. I don't want to hear any more."

She frowned. "What did I say?"

"It's what you haven't said." He clenched his fists.

Her shoulders stiffened. She held on to her patience and the sheet at her chest. "I don't understand."

His glance raced over her body, but not with desire. This time there was white hot anger behind the turquoise depths. "You've known where Dan's been for several days." It wasn't a question.

She threw him a blank look. "No. I only found out yesterday afternoon. How can you say that? You and I spent last night together. I would have told you."

"I got a call from someone who swore you'd known for several days. She told me where to find you. How do you explain that?"

Layne shook her head. "I don't know, but I swear I only found out yesterday afternoon. Maria Chavez called and asked me to come by. She knew where Dan was hiding. She gave me the address."

"So why didn't you let me know?"

She raised her hand in an appeal for him to understand. "I did—I mean, I was going to call you when I first found out, but then I changed my mind. I thought that if I told you you still wouldn't let me come with you. Last night at the café I decided to call you." She was stumbling over the words like a blabbering idiot, but she couldn't help it; he was making her feel like a criminal. And she found it difficult to stand here and argue with him when she was acutely aware of her nakedness under the sheet.

"Then why didn't I get a message from you on your answering machine? You knew I would return."

Her head was beginning to pound. "I couldn't take the chance. In case the machine was bugged."

"I called my office. There was no message that you'd called," he accused.

Her voice was edged with irritation. "That's because I didn't leave one—earlier, that is. By the time I decided to leave a message you must've already been on your way here." She closed her eyes and whispered, "For God's sake, Brant don't stare at me like that." When she opened her eyes again, she glared at him defensively. "I know this looks bad, but I've always understood that you have your job to do. If you recall, I'm the one who told you I wanted you to find Dan. And I did call you, dammit."

She was losing him. She could see that with every word he was retreating farther and farther away. She knew he'd been hurt before. But she refused to pay for what another woman had done to him.

"That all sounds well and good, Layne. Do you have any proof to back it up?"

Her head came up. "What are you trying to say, Brant? That I used you? That I purposely kept you occupied until I could meet Dan later, so we could disappear into the sunset together?" She gave him a bitter laugh. "Don't answer. I can see it in your face."

He wanted to believe her, but trust was all too new for him. "Let's just say I've had a sober reassessment."

Her head snapped up. His words slashed through her heart like a probing knife. So her shining knight had developed a crack in his armor. Love was a myth, she thought sadly. A myth that existed only in the silken cocoon of her dreams where it was destined to stay. She sighed. "I know you don't believe me and I can't force you to."

"You've lied to me before." His voice echoed softly in the gloom.

She nodded. "Yes. When you asked me if Dan had been at the hospital. But I haven't lied to you since. If you can't believe that, then I'm sorry." Her chin lifted slightly. "Just remember what I've told you here today, Brant. We'll see which one of us is right." She turned abruptly, not wanting him to see how much his words had hurt her.

"I told you I wouldn't be used," he murmured from behind her.

She turned and blinked her eyes to hold the tears at bay. "If anyone was used, it was me. If you hate me so much, why did you make love to me last night?"

He shrugged, a defensive hardness appeared like a shield in his eyes. "It just happened, that's all." He regretted the words as soon as they were out, but he didn't bother to cover them up. To tell her that he'd wanted her more than anything, still wanted her, would be giving her too much power over him.

"I see," she whispered, clutching the sheet closer. Straightening her shoulders, she disappeared into the bathroom.

He had seen the pain in her eyes. Dammit, *he* was the one in pain. Couldn't she see that? He wanted to believe her, but she'd made it damn hard to. He thought back over the past couple of weeks. How she'd come to him for help, then ended up making love with him. Had she planned it all? Had she and Dan set up this whole thing; the sniper, the second threat, just to save Dan from going to prison? Hadn't she once told him that family was more important to her than anything else? She'd even given up her career. Didn't that prove to what lengths she'd go to save her brother? He wavered for a moment, then mentally shook himself.

In the bathroom Layne gazed at herself in the mirror. Tears gathered, threatening to spill, but she refused to cry. She'd shed too many tears already—for her parents, her brothers—people who'd loved her. She wouldn't give Brant the satisfaction of having him see her cry. She slid the shower curtain aside and turned on the water. She called herself every kind of fool for having wasted her love on him. He could think anything about her he wanted, but after this business was over she'd never let him near her again.

When she was dressed and ready to leave, he held out his hand for her keys. "I'll drive."

"Suit yourself," she said, slapping them in his hand.

A heaviness settled over her heart, threatening to crush her with every step she took.

At the hotel café, they both drank their coffee in silence. Afterward Brant paid the cashier and they left. They were walking toward Layne's car when Brant grabbed her by the arm and ducked behind the building that led to the receptionist's office. He touched his lips in silent warning.

A man walked past and Brant reached out, grabbing him by his shirtfront. The man's brows contorted in alarm and he gasped as he felt his collar tighten.

Brant leaned close. "Why are you following us?"

The stranger sucked in a breath. Brant loosened his hold slightly. "I'm not following you," he managed to whisper.

Brant tightened his grip again. "Like hell you're not. I saw you hanging around here last night. Just now, in the restaurant, you watched us. You'd better talk and you'd better talk fast."

The man flinched. His eyes turned bleak and he shook his head. "Okay—okay, just let me go."

Brant released him and the man took several deep breaths. "I'm supposed to be keeping an eye on Miss Tyler."

A gasp came from the direction where Layne was standing.

"Tell me something I don't already know," Brant snapped. "Like who gave the order to spy on her."

Straightening his necktie, the stranger glanced at Layne. "I'll probably lose my job over this."

"I'm waiting," Brant said.

"My orders came from the D.A.'s office."

Layne's head came up and she stared at the man in confusion. "Who in the D.A.'s office?" she demanded.

The man stared down at his feet. "The D.A. himself."

"Russell?" Layne stammered, shock evident in her voice. "Why would he want me followed?"

"After you were shot he got pretty worried. He guessed whoever was after you was probably after Dan, too. He couldn't come out and be public about wanting to help you, because of a conflict of interest. So he called me in. No one else knows."

"Is that the whole truth?" Brant asked.

"I swear it's the truth. There's one other thing. The day Miss Tyler was pushed from that curb I was supposed to be following her, but halfway from her home I got a flat tire and had to stop. I could've prevented what happened." He held his hands out. "That's it. If you want to know anything else you'll have to ask him."

"I intend to do just that." Layne's voice was curt, but there was an answering warmth in her eyes.

"All right, you can go. But if I find out you're still following us, I'll run you in." Brant stated. "And tell Maxwell I'll talk to him when I get back."

Relieved, the man nodded and walked away.

* * *

They'd been on the road for twenty minutes when Layne turned and threw Brant a cold look. "At least Russell believes I'm innocent."

Brant eased his foot from the accelerator, pulled off the road and turned off the ignition. He sighed. "I think I'm about to have another sober reassessment."

She crossed her arms over her chest. "Well don't let *me* stop you. I'll just sit here quietly and hate you." She sat up straighter. "On second thought, I'll give you privacy," she said and got out of the car.

Brant got out and followed her to the front of the car.

Thousands of acres of land lay before them under beautiful blue skies and the cool breeze of autumn.

She refused to look at him. "If you want to arrest Dan, you'd better hurry."

"If Dan's there, he can wait a little longer."

"I wouldn't want you to think I'm stalling."

He leaned against the hood. "Layne, I've been on my own for a long time. In my job I've seen a lot and some things I can't talk about. I want to tell you something I've never trusted to another human being except Paul."

He straightened and came to stand behind her, just as he'd done that day at the beach.

"When I asked Belinda to marry me, she said yes. One day I received a report that her brother had killed a man. At least I thought he was her brother. She begged me to take her with me. I did. When we found him, she pleaded with me to let him go. I refused."

Layne turned to face him.

"I was putting handcuffs on him when she called my name. I turned and she . . . stabbed me. I was laid up for a while. When I got better I went out and looked for them."

"You found them?" Layne asked softly.

"Yeah. I brought them in. Later I testified."

Layne tried to soften her heart toward him, but found she couldn't. "I'm sorry for what happened to you, but if you'll remember I told you once I disliked you comparing me with other women."

"I didn't mean to hurt you. The things I said—"

"Please, Brant. I don't want to hear anything right now."

"When we bring Dan back I'll do what I can to help him."

She looked up at him, wanting to throw her arms around him but couldn't. Her pain was still too raw. Last night's memory flared, reminding her of his hand on her bare flesh, the heat and the impact of it. Now in the cold light of day she was left with a bitter hopelessness and an ineffable sense of loss, of loneliness.

An eighteen-wheeler whizzed by and honked, reminding her they were out in the middle of nowhere, bringing her to her senses. "We'd better go."

"All right," Brant whispered.

As they drove down the highway Layne stared out the window, her thoughts on Dan. The closer they got to the farmhouse, the more her palms felt clammy, her mouth dry.

Brant turned off the main highway onto a narrow road. He drove for several miles and slowed down. "That should be it over there," he said, pointing to a farmhouse on the right.

Layne squinted toward the house. "Why didn't you pull in?"

"Because I don't know what kind of reception committee is going to greet us."

"As far as I know Maria's aunt and uncle don't know I'm on my way, and I hardly think they'd be expecting you. Besides, there aren't any cars in the driveway."

"Could be the cars are in the garage," he added.

"I don't see Dan's motorcycle, either," Layne said.

He made a U-turn and drove the short distance back to the house. In the drive he turned off the ignition and turned to face her. "I want you to wait here while I check things out."

There was a stubborn tilt to Layne's chin. "No way. I'm going in with you. If Dan's in the house he won't come out unless he sees me."

Layne was about to open the door when he reached over and placed his hand on top of hers. "Not just yet. Let's wait and see if anyone comes out."

She glanced toward the house. "Maybe he doesn't know we're out here. What if he's asleep or something? Or maybe he's not even here." She started to honk the horn, but he stopped her.

Brant stared at her until the growing silence in the car and his black look clearly told her what he thought. She shot him a withering glare. "Don't tell me, let me guess," she said. "You think I want to send some kind of code, don't you?" Seething, she presented him with her loftiest, most superior smile. "Actually, one honk means you're with me. Two honks signals him that I came alone."

For a moment his eyes flashed in anger and he leaned forward. Layne feared she'd gone too far. She could almost read his mind. He was probably thinking that if he choked her to death, no jury in the world would convict him. She instinctively shrank back and her hand traveled to her throat in a defensive gesture.

Burying his hand in her hair, he pulled her to him and ground his mouth to hers in a soul-searching kiss that seemed to shut out the rest of the world. She was still trembling when he let her go.

"Seems to be the only way I can shut you up." He opened the door and unfolded his long body from the car. "Stay here," he ordered.

A trace of annoyance crept into her voice. "Why? What are you going to do?"

He looked down at her. "I want to look around. Just stay here and do as I say." He closed the door carefully.

Layne watched him walk over to a barn, disappearing inside. "I wish he'd make up his mind," she muttered under her breath. "One minute he wants me. The next he's flinging me away." She slid her tongue along her bottom lip and drew in a shaky breath, recalling the feel of his mouth against hers.

A few minutes later she saw him come out and frowned as he walked the perimeter of the house. Panic caused her heart to soar to an alarming speed. She couldn't stand not knowing whether Dan was here or not and she'd never been one to sit back and wait. If Brant had known her well he would have known she'd never take orders so easily. She edged across the seat, opened the door and slipped out, careful not to slam the door.

There was a heavy smell of damp earth in the air as she walked along the grass, nearly losing her balance in her effort to keep Brant in sight. She'd had enough of waiting. She'd rather be with Brant than out here alone.

She started to follow him, but a movement caught her attention and she turned her head to look toward the house. A tiny Hispanic woman had just stepped off the porch and was motioning to her.

"Señorita Tyler?"

Layne turned to stare toward the barn where Brant had disappeared, then toward the woman. When the woman had almost reached her, Layne instinctively backed away.

"Señorita Tyler, my name is Consuelo. I am Maria's cousin. I live here."

She looked harmless enough, but Layne opened her mouth to call Brant.

"Dan is here."

Layne closed her mouth.

"Please, do not be afraid." Consuelo seemed nervous as she glanced toward the house. "I'm so glad you have finally arrived. Dan is very ill and I am afraid for him." She wrung her hands.

Layne's tension mounted. "Ill?"

"Yes, he caught a fever yesterday. Today it is much worse. He has been asking for you. We received word from Maria that you were on your way. I must get back. My husband has gone for the doctor." Obviously distressed, she turned to run back in the house.

Layne's tension mounted. Dan ill? What had he been doing all this time that he hadn't taken care of himself? She shuddered, recalling with horror that her mother, father and older brother hadn't survived long enough for her to tell them how she'd felt.

Forgetting everything but her brother, Layne hurried to join Consuelo.

Brant had just left the barn. He'd seen Dan's motorcycle and wondered where Maria's aunt and uncle were. Why hadn't someone come out? Something was wrong. Things were too calm, and in an area this quiet, noises stood out. He took in the land and house again and caught the red flash of Layne's jacket as she stepped on the porch.

Damn it! The stubborn woman was doing it again. She was blatantly disobeying an order. He should've known. She seemed to take extraordinary delight in getting his hackles up and always chose just the right thing to set him off. His eyes followed her an instant longer and with a disgusted sigh he ran toward her.

Layne followed Consuelo into a small living room. If she had known which bedroom Dan was in, she would have shouldered the small woman aside.

She didn't even get a chance to call his name.

Someone from behind grabbed her, silencing her screams with his burly hand. Her breath caught in her throat as it was cut off by the man's hand over her mouth and nose. She whimpered, deep in her throat. Deep, stark terror wrapped its cold tentacles around her heart so fiercely it made her nauseous. Her arms flailed weakly and she stopped struggling. He was going to smother her to death, she just knew it. *I'm going to die.* Somewhere in the frightened corners of her mind, she thought she heard her name being called and wondered if she had imagined the heavy sound of boots echoing on the wooden porch.

"Good girl," a voice whispered just above her right ear. "There's a gun pointed at your boyfriend, so you'd better keep your mouth shut." The rasp of his voice filled terror in her heart.

He took his hand from her mouth, lowering it to curl around her neck and upper shoulders, and she gulped in a large quantity of air. Tattooed on his forearm was a black cobra whose eyes and fangs embraced the hairy back of his arm. Layne's eyes were glued to the blood red dye which dripped from deadly fangs. She smelled the sweat in his shirt and some kind of cheap after-shave.

Brant cursed from the porch, angry that she'd gone in without him. He moved in after her. He came to a halt just inside the room, his eyes going first to Layne's face, then to the silenced automatic in the man's grip.

He didn't have time to draw, but he took a step toward her, his muscles bunched around his neck and shoulders like a bull about to charge.

"You make any sudden move and she gets it," the man spat, gesturing with the automatic.

"Let her go," Brant ordered.

"I'm afraid we can't do that." Another voice surprised Brant from a doorway on his right. He turned to confront the man. He'd seen that ferret face before.

"Bring the girl in here," the ferret said to his tattooed companion, then gestured for Brant to follow, stopping him long enough to strip his revolver from beneath his jacket.

Panic made bile rise in Layne's throat as she was half dragged and pushed into a dining room. She stumbled, grabbing on to the nearest thing in the room—a dining-room chair. She looked up and her eyes flared with shock.

In front of her Dan sat on a wooden kitchen chair, his hands tied behind him.

And beside him stood Rico Salinas, pointing a gun to his head.

Chapter 16

"Well, well, if it isn't the dynamic duo." Rico's voice was deep and filled with insolent amusement.

Layne's attention was riveted on her brother. The only thing she heard was the rapid thudding of her heart. In the shadowy gloom she could see he had lost weight and his face looked gaunt. She stared helplessly as he struggled against his bonds and made a strangled noise of frustration behind the handkerchief that covered his mouth.

Layne took a few steps toward him, but one of the men barred her way. She clenched her fists. It made her ache to stand so near, yet not be able to talk to Dan.

Her gaze slid to Rico. He lifted the shade, his obscene shadow blotting out the sun.

"So, Layne, we meet again."

Surprise and fear quickly turned to anger. And hate. She hated this man for what he had put her and Dan through.

"I can see why you'd be angry, but our meeting was inevitable." He shrugged a delicate shoulder. "This way I solve several problems at once." His smile remained relaxed, but his eyes lacked any softening humor. "By the way, you remember Freddy, don't you?"

A slam of fear sliced through her chest as she stared at the smaller of the two men. She'd seen him at Juan's. He'd been the ferret who'd refused to let her pass his table.

"Yes, I can see you do." Rico smiled. "He and Turk have done an excellent job."

Layne glanced at Brant. Flanked by the two men, his expression was unreadable.

Her gaze swung to Rico. He stood resting most of his weight on one foot, shoulders straight, his lean body looking very much like that of a matador who'd just made his kill and now gazed at his audience with arrogant dignity.

She wanted to wipe that smile off his face.

"So, it was you all along," she said. "I'm not surprised. I never did like you, you know that?"

His smile faded. "I'm not out to win any popularity contests."

"Where is Consuelo?" Layne asked, suddenly fearful for Maria's relatives.

Rico's eyes snapped with scorn. "I'm pleased that she did such an admirable job of luring you here. But, then, I offered her an incentive. You see her husband is tied up at the moment in another room." He chuckled at his own joke.

"Why Dan?" she said quietly. "Why not someone else?"

"He was ripe for the part. I knew he was coming over that night. He was supposed to be caught near the body, only he arrived a little sooner than I expected."

Layne clenched her fists. "So you waited until just before Dan arrived before killing your uncle."

"Correct." Rico flashed her an amused glance. "My uncle was called into the study to take an urgent phone call. I set that up, too. By the time I was able to get away, time was running out." He sighed. "And timing is so important."

"And your servant?"

"Is on *my* payroll. What can I say?" Spreading his hands, he shrugged.

"Don't you feel any remorse?" Layne's voice cracked in disbelief. "He was your uncle, for God's sake."

"Only by marriage. I'm adopted—as I'm sure you know."

Layne inhaled, fighting to stay calm. "What did you have against him?"

"It was business," Rico said quietly.

"Business?" Layne answered, the word tinged with disgust.

"He and I were part of an organization. A very important one. My uncle got greedy. I had to put a stop to it." Rico said it as if he were merely discussing which color suit he was going to wear.

The color drained from Layne's face. "And in return you inherited everything from your uncle."

"Yes. Along with a high position in the organization."

"I bet he wasn't the only one stealing money."

They all turned at the sound of Brant's voice.

"Go on," Rico urged.

"I'm willing to bet the money flown from that airstrip was money skimmed from the top of your organization."

Rico gave him a genuine smile. "Yes."

"And flown to a bank in the Caymans where it became converted to cashiers' checks." He looked at Layne. "You found one of those checks in his uncle's office, remember? They were brought back to the U.S., most likely deposited to corporate accounts, substantiating the fact that the funds came from an overseas source. My guess is that they were documented with loan agreements and correspondence to make it appear they were legitimate loans. That way, Rico evades the IRS."

"Yes. *Yes!*" Rico nodded his head slyly.

"I doubt the Feds are going to be happy." Brant's voice was bland.

"Who's going to tell them. You?" He began to laugh. It came out an ugly, harsh sound.

Brant's gaze sharpened. "Let her go. She won't say anything as long as you set them both free."

"How can you be so sure?" Rico asked.

"You have me. No one else has to know we've been here. She won't tell." Brant saw Layne tense up.

Rico looked from one to the other and smiled. "Why, it looks like we have a budding romance going on here." He looked down at Dan and patted him on the shoulder. "Danny boy, do you realize you're a matchmaker?" He watched Dan struggle to free himself. Rico laughed as if he'd thought of something funny, then sobered almost as quickly. "Too bad nothing will ever come of it." He looked at his watch and sighed. "I hate to break up the party, but I have another engagement."

Freddy turned to Rico. "Can I be the one to kill him?" he asked gesturing toward Brant. "I have a score to settle with the bastard."

"If you're referring to what happened in Juan's, I still think you're a coward," Brant stated.

Freddy hissed beneath his breath. "You, I plan to kill quickly."

Brant's eyes were cold turquoise chips. "That's a relief. I hate long waits."

Freddy's face flamed with anger.

"Not yet," Rico warned.

Brant glanced at Layne. Her face had gone pale. He could see her visibly trembling. He wanted to help, to go to her, get her out of here.

He made a split-second decision.

Brant slammed his boot against Freddy's legs, causing him to stumble. Spinning around, his fist connected with Turk's ribs. Doubling over, Turk let out a loud whoosh.

He didn't have time to do more. Events seemed to proceed in slow motion. Brant felt something slam against the side of his head. The blow jerked him sideways, its impact stunning on the left side of his skull.

He fell to the ground.

"No!" Layne cried, desperation in her voice. Turk stopped her headlong forward rush. She struggled against his strength, her body trembling with shock as she looked down at Brant, lying so still.

"What do you want us to do with him?" Turk asked, gesturing toward Brant.

"Take him to the barn, then return and escort our friends here to join him." His smile was sinister. "You know what to do. Burn the barn, then the house. I'm going to radio for my helicopter."

Layne turned to Rico. "Will you untie my brother? I want to talk to him. Hug him one more time." Her heart ached with affection.

Rico shook his head. "I'm afraid I can't do that. But I'll let him speak to you," he replied, removing the handkerchief from Dan's mouth.

Layne watched as Dan fought to stand, straining against his bonds.

He stared at Rico in a murderous rage. "You bastard. Let her go. It's me you want."

Rico frowned. "Don't make me regret I took away the handkerchief."

A noise from the door alerted them that Turk and Freddy had returned for them.

With a final piercing look, Rico bade them goodbye.

The stab of pain shooting through his head reminded Brant he was still alive. He felt something wet on his cheek and reached up to touch his temple. His hand came away wet and sticky and he stared at the blood. He could feel more of it sliding down the side of his face.

Holding on to a wall, he struggled to stand. His legs shook so badly they barely held him up. Attempting to focus, he swayed and leaned closer to the wall.

The smell of hay and manure filled his nostrils. What the hell was he doing in a horse stall? Closing his eyes, Brant tried to remember. Something tugged at his memory. Bits and pieces drifted into focus. Then he remembered. *Layne.* She and Dan had been in the house.

A finger of ice trailed down his spine.

He had to find Layne. Brant took a tentative step and faltered. A ringing in his ears subsided long enough for him to make out the sound of voices.

A shaft of sunlight filtered in through the overhead rafters and fell on the four people who stood on the other side of the barn. He shook his head to clear it and pain streaked through him again. The two men, Turk and Freddy, stood with their backs to Brant. Where was Rico?

Brant's eyes focused on the smaller of the group. He saw Layne standing there proud and defiant. The hatred in her eyes was directed at Turk, who was pointing a gun at her.

For an instant, Brant thought she looked in his direction. Her eyes widened, then flicked away.

Brant measured the gap between them. He took one fal-tering step. Then another.

He froze in midstride. Layne's small fists had un-clenched and were sliding up her hips. The gleam of anger in her eyes shifted to one of provocative surrender. She smiled at the men.

And began to unbutton her blouse.

What in the hell was she doing? he wondered.

Layne knew exactly what she was doing.

She wasn't ready to die. Especially not now that she knew Brant was alive. Keeping her eyes focused on Turk, she un-buttoned the top three buttons of her blouse. Layne sighed in satisfaction as Turk's beady leer darted to the opening of her blouse. Lust flickered, then blazed to life behind the ebony eyes.

She had to draw him closer.

"Tell me, Turk. What would it take for you to let me go?" she asked coyly. She had two buttons to go and could almost hear him thinking. He looked toward the door, then back at her again.

"I promise I won't tell anyone," she whispered. "And the Ranger's dead, so you don't have to worry about him. If you let us go, Dan and I will settle somewhere here in Mexico, won't we, Dan?"

She looked over her shoulder at Dan and an unspoken message passed between them.

"What do you say, Turk?" Her voice dropped to a husky whisper. "You could come see me any time you wanted." She wanted to gag in revulsion. Instead, her finger lin-gered on the last button. *Come on, you bastard. Make your move.*

She darted another glance over Turk's shoulder and saw Brant stop and weave for a moment. The right side of his face dripped blood. Layne held her breath and forced herself not to cry at the sight of him.

Turk took a step forward, but Freddy's voice stopped him.

"Hey, man, Rico's gonna wonder why we're taking so long. After he radios for his chopper, he's gonna be in a hurry to leave."

"Don't worry," Turk replied, ogling the creamy skin of Layne's breasts peeking above the black lace of her bra. "We got time. Rico's gonna leave in the chopper and we got our car. Don't sweat it, okay?"

Freddy's face turned into a sullen mask, his gun still pointed at Dan's chest. "He's gonna be pissed."

"Naw, he won't. If he comes in here, just tell him I'm having me a little fun. He won't mind." Turk grinned. "And you can be next, okay?"

Freddy's face brightened at the thought and the bulge in his pants strained in anticipation. "Okay, but hurry," he urged.

"Will you let us go afterward?" Layne asked. She knew what Turk's answer would be. She also knew he would lie.

She wasn't disappointed.

"Sure, baby," he replied. "After we make our exit, I'll be sure and leave the door unlocked so you and Dan can get out."

Layne tensed as Turk closed the gap between them. She forced herself to smile, noting with satisfaction that both men had their attention trained on her. *Good.*

Her heart pounding in fear, Layne's fingers shook slightly as they rested on the last button of her blouse. She recalled bragging to Brant about her knowledge of self-defense. All she knew about that skill was what she'd learned in two Saturdays at the local gym.

Turk came closer. Still holding on to her blouse, Layne kicked out, landing a hard blow to his groin. His knees buckled and his lungs expelled a whoosh of air. Hitting the ground, he doubled over in pain and lay groaning, his gun forgotten at his feet.

Freddy wavered, his eyes widening in surprise. Dan kicked out, hitting Freddy hard just below the ribs forcing him to stagger back, then ran to him, raining blows on him with his feet.

"Bitch!" Turk screamed, throwing Layne off balance and landing on top of her. "I'll kill you," he snarled.

Layne saw the blow coming and tensed her body. Turk slapped her with such force Layne thought surely he'd broken her neck. There was a roar in her head. The taste of blood filled her mouth where he'd split her lip. Layne's eyes filled with tears.

Brant's bellow of rage filled the air as he grabbed Turk from behind and spun him around. Fueled by anger, he delivered several well-aimed blows to Turk's face.

Layne's heart thudded wildly. Standing, she ran and jumped on Turk's back, pulling his hair, his ears, trying to gouge his eyes.

Brant's fist landed another blow and Turk stumbled backwards, taking Layne down with him. Turk quickly shook her off and came up off the ground rushing toward Brant.

Layne desperately looked around for something, anything she could use to stop Turk. A pitchfork! She grabbed it and turned just in time to see Brant land a punch that forced Turk to crash against the door. It flew open, taking him with it.

Brant staggered after him. He squinted in the sunlight and took deep, unsteady breaths. Sheer stubbornness forced him to stay upright.

A far-off drone caught his attention and he looked up. Off to his left the low, rumbling roar of a helicopter swooped closer until it hovered above them. Brant's ears throbbed as he choked on flying dust.

As the chopper landed, Brant saw Rico running toward it. He urged his body to move, attempting to close the distance between them, but he knew he wasn't going to make it.

Just before Rico reached the chopper, he pivoted around to face Brant. Even from this distance Brant could make out the contemptuous smirk. The light in Rico's eyes took on the venomous gleam of a cobra ready to strike.

Reaching into his coat pocket Rico drew out a gun, aimed it and fired.

The noise was deafening and the force of the bullet slammed Brant backward.

Layne screamed as she raced to reach Brant's side. Dan followed close behind. They heard another explosive crack of gunfire, but Layne didn't stop.

Frantically she stumbled to kneel beside Brant. Cradling his head on her lap, she lowered her own head and heard the ragged draw of his breath. Thank God he was still alive, but a red stain spread over the front of his shirt with alarming speed.

"Here," a familiar voice said, handing her a thick towel. "One of my men found this inside the house. It should help stop the flow of blood until we can get him to a hospital."

Her heart leaped in relief. "You!" she exclaimed, staring up at Lieutenant Paul Garcia. She took the towel gratefully and applied it to Brant's wound. "You were in the chopper?"

"Yes." Paul glanced down at Brant and his brows furrowed in concern.

"Where's Rico?" she asked.

"Let's just say he isn't your worry any longer."

Brant groaned and opened his eyes. Focusing on Garcia, he whispered, "Hey, amigo . . . you're . . . on the wrong side of the border."

Paul smiled. "Yeah, buddy, you can thank me later."

"How did you know where I was?"

Paul's glance shifted to Layne before returning to Brant. "Your lady friend here decided it was in Dan's best interest that we find him. Actually, she called for you, but since you weren't there I took the message."

"Layne?" Brant closed his eyes, then opened them again. "*You* called?"

"Yes," Layne replied softly.

She never got to hear what he was going to say next. He lost consciousness again.

Chapter 17

Layne sat next to the bed staring down at Brant's sleeping features. The doctor had assured her he would be fine. The bullet had gone straight through his shoulder, coming out on the other side without damaging any nerves or tendons. The doctor had been more concerned about the wound to his head, assuring her they would monitor him closely in case of concussion.

Brant had woken up one other time. In the chopper. He'd given Layne a weak, disarming smile and whispered, "Hey, darlin', that was some fancy footwork back there. Remind me never to mess with you, okay?"

A mental picture of Layne trying out the same kick on Brant seemed ludicrous and she smiled.

He didn't wake up again.

Much later, as she stared down at him, she thought he looked so sweet, so peaceful lying there. She felt intense, raw longing.

Garcia spoke from the doorway. "He'll be all right, Layne. He's too stubborn to die."

She smiled again. "I know."

"By the way, Dan said he'd see you later." At Layne's worried brow, he added, "He faces a few charges, but under the circumstances I think they'll go easy on him."

Layne nodded, her gaze returning to Brant.

"He was almost married once. Did you know?"

"Yes, he told me." Layne recalled what Brant had told her about Belinda. No wonder he hadn't trusted Layne. Of course, *she* hadn't made things easy for him when she'd left Brownsville in such a hurry without telling him. He thought she'd been using him to let Dan get away. *Oh, Brant. Couldn't you tell how much I loved you?*

"He's a good man," Garcia interrupted her silent musing. "I know you're nothing like she was, Layne. Brant does, too."

The compliment warmed Layne. It was important to her that Garcia approve of her. He and Brant were lifelong friends. She smiled again. "If he'll have me, Paul, I'm going to spend the rest of my life proving it."

"I'm going to hold you to that," Brant whispered from the bed.

"Hey, buddy, it's about time you woke up. It's almost nine o'clock at night," Garcia spouted, looking down at his watch. "That's a hell of a way to get leave, you know. Why don't you try going through regular channels?"

Brant didn't answer. He and Layne were too busy staring at each other.

Garcia coughed. "Well, now that I know you're okay, I have to get back to work."

"Paul?"

"Yes?"

"How is Dallas holding up?" Brant asked.

"A hell of a lot better than you. My mother is clucking over him like a mother hen. He's probably eaten so many enchiladas by now, he's gained ten pounds."

"Did you take care of things for him?"

"Yeah. Don't worry." In the doorway he turned. "By the way, I've posted a guard outside your door." He strode out the door whistling.

Layne looked puzzled. "A guard? Why would you need a guard?"

"Just one of Paul's jokes." His eyes crinkled at the corners.

"I don't understand."

"You will."

Layne opened her mouth to say something, but Brant beat her to it. "I'd like to sit up. Would you mind grinding this thing up for me?"

She leaned over and pushed a button. The bed whirred to a sitting position.

"Is this all right?"

"Yeah, thanks." He lowered the sheet, exposing a wide expanse of muscular chest. His right arm was in a sling and he flexed his fingers.

But Layne wasn't looking at his fingers. Glancing at the down of dark hair on his chest, she experienced a gnawing ache to run her hands all over him. She pushed to her feet and turned her back on him so he couldn't see the desperate love in her eyes.

"How are you feeling?" she asked.

"I'm okay."

"The doctor says you're fine. They're going to keep you another night, though, just to make sure."

He gave her a slow smile. "My head's too hard to have anything hurt it."

"That's good." She stared at the door.

"I'm a stubborn man. Layne, will you turn around so I can see you?"

She turned to find his beautiful turquoise eyes regarding her seriously.

"I don't want you to leave," he muttered thickly.

He suddenly seemed all raw and exposed, his rough exterior melting to show a sensitive, caring man.

"Wild elephants couldn't make me go," she said with the faintest hint of a smile.

"You mean wild horses," he corrected.

"Whatever," she replied.

"In that case turn off the light and come over here." His voice lowered to a husky rumble.

"The room will be too dark." She couldn't look at him without melting.

"Not at all. I'll just turn this one on." He flicked a switch by the bed and a low, soft glow spread over the room.

Layne's fingers shook as she turned off the overhead light. She took slow, deliberate steps to his bedside. How could she tell him that she didn't want to spend the rest of her life without him? That she wanted to have his children. Anxiety almost made her knees buckle.

He reached out and pulled her closer to the bed. His arm encircled her waist, then dipped lower as his fingers trailed a scorching path over her hip, down to her soft derriere. Brant nudged her closer until Layne was half sitting, half lying beside him.

When he kissed her, any doubts Layne might have harbored as to how he felt about her vanished. She moaned in pleasure as his tongue mated with hers. Her hand flattened against the solid wall of his chest, then slid up to curl around his neck as her fingers twined around the shaggy ends of his dark hair.

An arousing pressure grew in the lower part of her body. She experienced a moment of frustrating urgency because his sheet and her clothes insulated her from closer contact with his long masculine body.

Layne was so absorbed in the kiss she didn't realize what he was doing until she felt his large palm cupping her breast. She exhaled a sigh of pure delight until it dawned on her which hand he was using. He had managed to unbutton her blouse.

She pulled back slightly. "For someone whose arm is in a sling, you're doing surprisingly well."

He dragged his mouth across her cheek to nuzzle her ear. "As you can see, the sling is just at the right height. All I have to do is aim my fingers . . ."

And he did. Then his mouth took over.

She reveled in every satisfying, intimate moment of it.

A second later Layne whispered, "You'll hurt yourself."

"Sweetheart," he groaned, "I'll hurt if I *don't* touch you." His head dipped down as his mouth took possession of one pink nub.

Layne was practically on top of him. Closing her eyes, she strained against his mouth. Then her eyes opened again. "Oh, Brant, I wish you were well and home and—"

"I told you I'm fine. I've had a lot worse happen to me."

"Brant. The nurse."

"What about her?" he muttered thickly, resuming his intimate inspection of her body.

"She might come in."

"No, she won't."

"What about Paul?" she persisted.

"He won't come in, either."

"How can you be so sure?" Why did men always think they were right?

"Why do you think he posted a guard outside the door?" His head lifted, but only to trail kisses down the sensitive cord of her neck.

"Oh!" was all she had time to say before he parted her lips again to tease her tongue.

God, how she wanted him. She opened her mouth to tell him. "Brant, I—"

"Layne!" he said sternly, pulling away from her. "Are you going to be quiet so we can make up?"

Her eyes narrowed, but the longing in them still burned intensely. "Not until you turn out that light."

With a deep chuckle, Brant reached over and turned off the light. This time when he kissed her, Layne went crazy with desire for him. If only they could make love. Being near him would be enough for now.

Brant shifted in bed. The light came back on.

"What are you doing?" Layne managed to choke out.

"There's something I want to tell you first. Something I've been wanting to say for a long time."

"Really, sweetheart, it can wait."

"No, it can't. Every time I get close to you, I can't think straight, so be still and let me say what I want to."

"All right." She sounded disappointed. She didn't want to talk anymore. She just wanted him to kiss her.

"Ever since that first night we made love, I've wanted to tell you how I felt, but something held me back. I even tried to deny it to myself. When I thought you were using me to help Dan escape, I was so angry, I told myself I was lucky to be rid of you. I thought in my head that I could let you walk away, but in my heart . . . there was no way I was going to let you go. I love you. Can you ever forgive me for doubting you?"

Tears welled in her eyes as they moved over his face, feature by feature. She had never thought she would hear those words from him.

"There's nothing to forgive. You had every right to think what you did. If only I had called you sooner." Her hand reached up and caressed his cheek. "I'm so lucky," she whispered. "I think I fell in love with you the night we were trapped in that silly closet."

"God, don't remind me," he said. "I couldn't sleep that night nor the next for thinking about you and wishing you were lying beside me, all warm and soft." He turned his head slightly and kissed her palm.

"Oh, Brant, I'm so glad you weren't killed."

"Layne, sweetheart, I have a proposition for you."

"Oh? What do you have in mind?" she purred, running eager fingers through the dark mat of hair on his chest.

"Protective custody. For life." He pulled her closer.

Layne pretended to mull it over. "How soon would you make it official?"

"As soon as I can get out of this damn sling," he groaned.

"That long?"

"I heal very quickly."

"In that case, I agree." She smiled. "I also applaud your very wise decision." Her green eyes turned stormy with passion. "But there's one other thing," she whispered seductively, sliding her hand under the sheet.

Brant groaned with pleasure. "Yes, darlin'?" he managed to say.

"Please turn off the light so we can finish making up."

He gave her a wicked grin. "Yes, ma'am. Anything to please a lady."

Epilogue

Five years had gone by much too fast, thought Layne as she added the finishing touches to her makeup. She and Brant had been married shortly after he'd gotten out of the hospital. Their second child had just turned six weeks old.

"You almost ready, darlin'?" He bent down and placed a lingering kiss on the sensitive pulse of her neck.

She closed her eyes and groaned. "Mmmm. Yes."

"Are you sure you wouldn't rather stay here a little longer?"

Layne opened her eyes and sighed. "As much as I'd like to, we can't. Dan and Maria will be here soon."

"Paul and Dallas can entertain them."

Their eyes met in the mirror and held. Layne stood up and Brant enfolded her in his arms. "Do you think your sister will make it?" she asked, kissing his chest where his shirt was still unbuttoned.

"Who knows. Maggie shows up when she shows up."

"But it's Christmas Eve. I really like her and—"

His mouth cut off her words.

When he lifted his head, he held her for a long time, then together, they walked into the adjoining room. Both of them stared down at their three-year-old daughter and six-week-old son.

"I'm so lucky to have all of you," he whispered.

"I'm the lucky one," she replied, her heart swelling with pride.

They stood there enjoying the moment, realizing how lucky they both were. Layne felt an enormous tide of emotions. In a few hours, she would have her family all together.

She thought of the last five years. Brant had been promoted to captain. Dallas attended college and was majoring in criminal justice. He planned to be in law enforcement and Layne smiled knowingly, because she knew he wanted to follow in Brant's footsteps. At twenty-three, he was almost as handsome as Brant. A strapping six feet two inches, he still wore his raven-colored hair long, and she'd seen how those intelligent gray eyes could pierce even the strongest woman's heart.

From downstairs, came the peal of the doorbell and they broke apart.

"That's probably Dan and Maria," Layne said.

Downstairs, Lieutenant Paul Garcia was busy checking the homemade rolls he'd just made for their dinner. Dallas sat at the kitchen table reading the sports page of the local newspaper.

Hearing the doorbell, Paul eyed Dallas. When Dallas didn't make a move to get up, he said wryly, "Don't strain yourself. I'll get it."

When he opened the door, Dan and Maria stood there with an armful of presents.

"I hope one of those is for me," Paul said with a smile.

They smiled back and brushed past him. He started to close the door but a latecomer stuck a scarlet cowboy boot against it to keep him from closing it.

Paul glanced up and his face registered surprise. A tall, beautiful woman of about thirty glided past him. Thick hair the color of ranch mink flowed down her back. Her eyes were the color of turquoise.

"Hello, Maggie," Paul said quietly. "I thought you were still out of the country."

"I wouldn't miss my nephew's christening for anything in the world." She eyed him distastefully. "You've gotten more domestic since the last time I saw you, Paul. That apron goes well with your badge."

He gave her left hand a brief glance. "And I see you're still an old maid."

They glared and circled each other like sparring partners.

That's the way Brant and Layne found them when they reached the bottom stair.

That night, as Layne joined Brant in bed, she confided to him that Paul and Maggie had looked as though they'd been performing some pagan mating dance.

"Ridiculous," Brant replied. "Those two hate each other."

A small indulgent smile played along Layne's mouth as she switched off the lamp.

*   *   *   *   *

COMING NEXT MONTH

#487 COLD, COLD HEART—Ann Williams

Rescuing kidnapped children no longer interested rugged
American Hero Jake Frost, but to save her daughter,
Rachel Dryden was determined to change his mind. Could
Rachel warm his heart to her cause . . . and herself?

#488 OBSESSED!—Amanda Stevens

Both shy cartoonist Laura Valentine and undercover FBI agent
Richard Gentry were pretending to be something they weren't. But
complications *really* arose when they realized their passion wasn't
a fake. . . .

#489 TWO AGAINST THE WORLD—Many Anne Wilson

All Alicia Sullivan wanted was a little peace—and *maybe* a nice,
normal, sane man. Instead, she found herself stranded with
secretive Steven Rider, whose mysterious nature was far from safe.

#490 SHERIFF'S LADY—Dani Criss

Fleeing cross-country from a powerful criminal, C. J. Dillon
couldn't afford to trust anyone. But when Sheriff Chris Riker
offered his assistance, C.J. longed to confide in the virile lawman.

#491 STILL MARRIED—Diana Whitney

Desperately worried about her missing sister-in-law, Kelsey Manning
sought out her estranged husband, Luke Sontag. But as they
joined forces on the search, could they find the strength to save
their marriage?

#492 MAN OF THE HOUR—Maura Seger

Years ago, fast cars, cold beer and easy women had been bad boy
Mark Fletcher's style. But he'd changed. Now his only trouble
came in the form of single mother Lisa Morley.

Take 4 bestselling love stories FREE
Plus get a FREE surprise gift!

INTIMATE MOMENTS®

10TH
Anniversary

Celebrate our anniversary with a fabulous collection of firsts....

The first Intimate Moments titles written by three of your favorite authors:

NIGHT MOVES	Heather Graham Pozzessere
LADY OF THE NIGHT	Emilie Richards
A STRANGER'S SMILE	Kathleen Korbel

Silhouette Intimate Moments is proud to present a FREE hardbound collection of our authors' firsts—titles that you will treasure in the years to come from some of the line's founding members.

This collection will not be sold in retail stores and is available only through this exclusive offer. Look for details in Silhouette Intimate Moments titles available in retail stores in May, June and July.

SIMANN

SAVE 30¢
ON THE PURCHASE OF ANY
SILHOUETTE SHADOWS™ TITLE

TO THE DEALER: Harlequin/Silhouette Books will pay 30¢ plus 8¢ handling upon presentation of this coupon by your customer toward the purchase of any Silhouette Shadows book. Any other use constitutes fraud. Proof of sufficient stock (in the previous 90 days) to cover coupon redemption must be presented upon request. Coupon is nonassignable, void if taxed, prohibited or restricted by law. Consumer must pay any governmental taxes. Coupons submitted become the property of Harlequin/Silhouette Books. Reimbursement made only to retail distributor who redeems coupon. Coupon valid in the United States and Canada. Reimbursement paid only in country where product purchased. LIMIT ONE COUPON PER PURCHASE. VALID ONLY ON SILHOUETTE SHADOWS BOOKS IN THE U.S.A. AND CANADA.

IN U.S.A., MAIL TO:

SILHOUETTE SHADOWS
P.O. Box 880478
El Paso, TX 88588-0478

Coupon redeemable at retail outlets only.
OFFER EXPIRES AUGUST 31, 1993.

SHIU

65373 100695